D1189892

THE
KREMLIN
CONTRACT

THE
KREMLIN
CONTRACT

James Barwick

G. P. PUTNAM'S SONS, NEW YORK

G. P. Putnam's Sons
Publishers Since 1838
200 Madison Avenue
New York, NY 10016

Library of Congress Cataloging-in-Publication Data

Barwick, James.
    The Kremlin contract.

    1. Stalin, Joseph, 1879–1953—Fiction.   I. Title.
PR6060.A453K7   1987   823'.914   86-25476
ISBN 0-399-13238-4

Designed by Helen Granger/Levavi & Levavi
Typeset by Fisher Composition, Inc.

Printed in the United States of America
1   2   3   4   5   6   7   8   9   10

The Gopak *is the massively energetic, classic Ukrainian-Russian dance performed by both men and women. Following World War II, it was also the Soviet code name of the battle plan for the attack on Western Europe. The plan was abandoned by the new leadership on the night of Joseph Stalin's death, 5 March 1953.*

I never met a man more honest, gentle and kind.

—H. G. WELLS

(on first meeting Joseph Stalin)

PROLOGUE

Georgia, Russia, 1920

A low mist clung like a veil to the flat, becalmed sea. The sun was still hidden beneath the eastern horizon, but the cloudless sky was already bright with the predawn radiance. At a steady twelve knots, the U.S. heavy cruiser cleaved through the dull gray skin of the water, the bow wave foaming and hissing back along the eight-inch-thick armor-plated sides of the dreadnought, parting the mist, swirling it up to wave and eddy around the massive gun turrets and superstructure of the great ship. High on the open bridge, the officer of the watch turned to look astern at the mist folding in behind them, closing up the bubbling wake. The flotilla of destroyers was back there somewhere, fanned out in defensive formation.

At an upstairs window of the U.S. consulate, Charles Trenton stood looking out across the bay to the mist-laden sea beyond the Georgian town of Batumi. A tall young man, barely out of his twenties, with the confidence of old money, Groton and Harvard, Charles Trenton's extraordinary gift for Slavic languages had taken him first to a U.S. consular post in the St. Petersburg of the tsars and now to his position as consul to the last remnant of the old Russia, struggling in its death throes against the advancing Red Army.

He stood, pulling on his jacket. The consul's residence commanded a spectacular view of the port and small natural harbor. The sun, now rising, began to clear the layer of mist with its pale warmth. There was no sign of the U.S.S. *Polk* and its escorting destroyers, though he knew from the latest dispatches that they must be very close now. Already thick knots of people had gathered down on the quays. Even at a distance, they looked fearful, perhaps angry. Coats or blankets hung from their stooped shoulders; the men moved about, forming small groups, searching for information. Had the navy been delayed? How close were the Reds? Were the Russian nationals to be allowed aboard? There was a rumor that all women and children, regardless of nationality, were to be rescued. But there was no one to tell the men for certain, so they hurried from one huddle to the next, holding anxious, impotent conferences. In contrast, the women seemed resigned to whatever fate awaited them. Installed amidst piles of belongings, they stood motionless, moving only to shepherd a straying toddler or restack the valises into some new pattern.

Trenton turned away from the window. As he came down the wide staircase to the first floor, he could see an agitated throng of people packed into the small entrance hall below. Many he recognized, Americans, English and French primarily, people who had put their capital and faith into Georgian wine, grain and tobacco. Now their voices were raised. "The Reds are advancing down the coast road," one of them shouted.

"They're less than fifty miles away," another yelled desperately.

A Frenchman reached out and took Trenton by the lapel. "We want a place on the ship. You understand me?"

Trenton twisted himself free and pushed his way into the office. Simpson, his aide, slammed the door closed behind him and locked it. Outside, they could still hear the shouting men. From time to time someone banged on the door with his fist.

In the large, high-ceilinged office, with its lavish decoration of intricate plaster, servants were packing the contents of the filing cabinets into tea chests.

"A word with you, Simpson?" Charles Trenton led Simpson over to a large desk in the far corner of the room. "It's my wife. She and the boy are not yet back from the summer house."

"When did you expect them, sir?"

"I sent a messenger to say they must return here immediately. That was yesterday evening."

"Perhaps," Simpson said carefully, "Mrs. Trenton was not happy to travel through the night. If she and young Alexander had left at dawn this morning, they'd be here in half an hour or so."

"The possibility remains that the car has broken down somewhere."

"I'll organize a search party immediately," Simpson said.

"No." The consul shook his head. "I have no right to put consular personnel at risk for private reasons. We'll wait."

"But the evacuation is to be completed by 1800 hours, sir."

"I know that, Simpson," Trenton snapped, then stopped, shocked by his own lack of equilibrium.

"Let me send out a search party," Simpson said. "If Mrs. Trenton's car has broken down somewhere between the summer house and here, we'll find them."

"Do we know exactly how far the Red forces have advanced?" Trenton inquired, as if the answer had no special significance.

Simpson looked at him, pitying the consul's inability to show his feelings. His wife and son might well have been engulfed by the Reds: a normal man would be racked by anxiety. "No, sir," Simpson said. "Last night's reports showed them over fifty miles away."

"It's the *Polk*!" one of the servants shouted in excitement. Simpson and Trenton turned to look out of the window. Moving in toward the harbor, through the last shreds of mist, was the unmistakable mass of the U.S.S. *Polk*. Down on the waterfront, the people saw it moments later. A shout went up and they rushed forward, jostling for a place at the very edge of the quay. The great ship inched to a halt a hundred yards from quayside and, with a sudden explosion of sound, the anchor was released. Then the mighty propellers bubbled the water, and the warship swung around in a slow-motion quarter turn until it lay parallel to the shoreline. The crowd was silent now, mystified. A klaxon was wailing a series of short, urgent blasts, and they could see sailors running along the massive deck.

Now the main gun turrets were swinging around in practiced unison, until the long barrels pointed directly over the town. The consular officials with their faces pressed against a small side window gave a spontaneous cheer and shouts of encouragement.

"The captain's taking no chances, sir," Simpson said.

Trenton nodded in agreement. He knew that the reason for the cruiser's repositioning of its guns might be that the Reds were much closer than he had thought.

"I could be back in three or four hours, sir," Simpson said. "Sooner, if she's had a breakdown between the summer house and here."

Trenton nodded. They were all in love with her, of course. All his staff.

Karilvan was in ruins. Sunlight crept over the piles of rubble and heaped rubbish. Even as the morning became a bright, clear-skied day, the streets remained empty.

As the sun climbed higher over the sodden plain, a bearded priest crossed the cobbled main square, stopping from time to time to listen to the gunfire coming from the hills. At the corner of the square, a single cart appeared and pulled around in the direction of the priest. The horse faltered for a moment, skating on the stones. On the bench next to the driver sat a woman and a small boy, swaddled in heavy cloaks. The cart rumbled to a halt in front of the priest. The woman pushed back the folds of her cloak and clamped one arm tightly around the boy beside her. There was an energetic quality to her movements.

"We've come from outside Batumi, priest," Vanessa Trenton said in heavily accented Russian. The high pitch of her voice seemed to demand attention.

The old priest looked up at her. "We have nothing to offer strangers here. Leave before the Reds arrive, your honor." The woman's thick red hair swung loose from the hood as she leaned forward, and she brushed it back to free herself from it. The boy watched her intently.

"I have spent half a day traveling here. I am not fleeing from the Red Army. I am here to welcome them."

*   *   *

The clock on the mantelpiece chimed the half hour. It was 5:30. Trenton had shaved and changed into a dark suit and now stood at the uncurtained window, staring out over the empty quays. Only Americans, British and French had been allowed aboard, and a few Russians with expensive monogrammed luggage. When the others saw the marines' rifles, they had screamed abuse. A volley fired over their heads had driven them down the quay.

All that remained now was the battle cruiser, the light of the falling sun behind it, giving the illusion of a gigantic cardboard cutout on the flat mirror of the sea. All detail was lost. Only the looming silhouette stood sharp and clear, dominating the harbor. A sudden belch of dark smoke erupted from the twin funnels. The *Polk* was getting up steam, preparing to weigh anchor at six o'clock.

Charles Trenton pressed the tips of his fingers together. Simpson had sent a message that Trenton's wife was not at the summer house. That had been almost three hours ago. Since then there had been no further word.

"Anything else in here, sir?"

Trenton turned from the window. It was the navy lieutenant sent ashore with the cutter to supervise the evacuation.

"No, I don't think so."

The office had been cleared, the files and documents packed and taken to the ship or burned. The grate had been found inadequate, and a fire had been started in the rambling garden at the back of the residence. The faint tang of its smoke now seeped through the house.

"It's just the contents of the safe now, sir," the lieutenant said.

"I'll deal with it straightaway."

As the consul walked through the telegraph office to the small anteroom housing the safe, slivers of broken glass crunched beneath his feet.

"Sir." Simpson stood in the open doorway.

Trenton saw immediately from his aide's expression that his wife and son had not been found. He walked through to the safe and began to spin the combination lock. Simpson followed.

"I'm afraid Mrs. Trenton left the summer house early this morning."

"Are you certain?"

"Yes, sir. For some reason she chose not to take the car. She hired a cart and driver. She left at first light."

"Where was she going?" His hand was on the dial of the safe.

Simpson hesitated. "The servants claim she was heading to Karilvan."

"Karilvan! What about Alexander? He was with her?"

"Yes, sir."

Trenton released the lock and pulled the safe open.

It was one of the few times Simpson had felt sympathy for the man. He was married to a woman who was too beautiful, too headstrong, too accustomed to flirting with members of her husband's own staff, or with the new Bolshevik ideas. "What will you do, sir?"

"Do?" Charles Trenton raised his eyebrows. "What is there to do?" he said bitterly. "My wife has made her decision. What can I possibly do about it now?"

The Red Army column approached Karilvan at dusk. Thin drizzle spat over the town. In the church, the old priest roused them without ceremony. The American woman threw off her blanket hurriedly and started to gather up their possessions. The little boy sat up sleepily, still swathed in his cloak. The priest spoke over his shoulder, with bitterness. "Your wait is over. The circus is coming," he said.

The woman turned to the priest. Her hands rested on her hips. When she spoke, her voice was soft but firm, admonitory, as if she were talking to a child. "It has always been a struggle to persuade the Church that the common people have a destiny here on earth."

"A destiny here on earth?"

"To live like free men. Not as chattels of the rich." Her voice was raised a little now.

In the distance, the grumble of the approaching column fragmented into a thousand recognizable human sounds.

"I cannot listen to you, madam. Nor can the thousands who are dying every day throughout Georgia. Tell your fairy tales to the Reds." He spat out the words.

He swung open the heavy door and hurried out. Vanessa Trenton moved toward the young boy and drew him close. "Do you hear it, Alex?"

The boy nodded. The armed columns were beginning to assemble in the square. The noise was growing.

"It is a celebration. A great man has come to share it with us," the woman whispered in the darkness. "He is one of the new heroes of this great nation and the best friend of the people. He has fought many hard battles and won great victories. Are you excited, Alexander?"

"Yes, Mother," he said.

The men of the columns had been slogging through the rain and mud for seven weeks. They were tired, hungry and footsore. It was almost dark as they formed into ranks around three sides of the square. Now a number of carts rumbled over the cobbles. The first was filled with wood and fallen branches gathered in the march. The firewood was thrown down and stacked into a rough pile. A man in a grimy blue coat splashed the pile with oil from a battered can, then ignited it. Men fired their rifles into the air. Others in the ranks responded with shouted slogans. Somewhere a band started to play. An atmosphere of expectancy began to build. The crowd of villagers began to thicken.

A cheer spread from the end of the square. As if by design, the fire took hold and burst into life. The oil-soaked wood quickly became a bright, flaming mass. Some of the men broke from the ranks to light torches and hand them back into the crowd. By the time the leader, standing on the rear of a dray pulled by two horses, came into sight, most of the townspeople found themselves cheering and pressing forward. Someone started a chant. Quickly taken up, it swept through the throng and was driven on by the stamping of feet. "Sta . . . *lin,* Sta . . . *lin,* Sta . . . *lin.*"

The young American woman clutched the boy and yelled the name with a passion that seemed to vibrate through her whole body. "Sta . . . *lin,* Sta . . . *lin,* Sta . . . *lin.*"

1953

CHAPTER
1

Moscow

It could almost have been a scene from the days before the Revolution. In the banqueting hall of the Yusopov Palace, the women paraded around bare shouldered in silk dresses, their necks glittering with jewelry. The men wore black dinner jackets or uniforms of one of many countries. Only careful scrutiny would have revealed that among this glittering international gathering the representatives of the Soviet Union were noticeably more dowdily dressed than their foreign guests.

Near the door, beside a long table loaded ostentatiously with pots of caviar and bottles of Georgian champagne, two men stood together looking out into the main part of the room. The older man, dressed in civilian clothes, was in his fifties, not tall, but powerfully built. His thinning hair revealed a blunt, square head in keeping with the cruel line of his mouth and the uncompromising nature of his chin. General Pavel Semyonovich Petrov was not a military general, but he was nevertheless a force to be reckoned with in Stalin's Moscow. He was a department head of the MGB, the secret police force which had already changed names several times since Lenin's day and would, in the not too distant future, be renowned in its next incarnation as the dreaded KGB.

The younger man standing beside Petrov also wore the

green uniform of the MGB. His red shoulder boards indicated his captain's rank. He appeared to be in his mid thirties, tall and slenderly built, with a combination of dark hair and blue eyes most would associate with the Irish. At international gatherings like this, Western women gave him more than a passing glance, not so much because of his good looks as because of an ease of manner, which was notably absent among Russian officials in Moscow.

The captain, Alexander Trenton, had had his career laid out for him, his steps guided into the State Security Police by General Petrov, who had lived with his mother since early in World War II. For Alex Trenton, it had been a career that had protected him from most of the dangers and humiliations inherent in the Soviet bureaucracy. His command of English, complete with a faint New England accent, had made him a natural choice for the American department, which Petrov controlled. For nearly eight years, he had acted as Petrov's adjutant, privy to all but the most closely guarded secrets.

There had been one false step. In 1945 Petrov's niece, Xenia, had emerged from the war a partisan heroine. The eight years since had added three times that number of pounds to her figure, thanks to her habit of drinking nearly a bottle of vodka a day. Following the war, Alex Trenton had been persuaded by his mother that he was at least half in love with Xenia. General Petrov had said that marrying her would neatly seal a Petrov-Trenton connection that could lead them both to the very top of Soviet government. Alex would be building a dynasty, they had argued. But the cornerstone was already fatally cracked.

The two men moved away from the table and stood against one of the great pillars that formed the entrance to the hall. "The man I'm interested in," Petrov said, "is the one in the far corner." He indicated a man in perhaps his mid forties, tall, in a well-cut blue suit, his face retaining a permanent tan, talking to a plumply attractive Russian woman.

"The American," Alex said.

"I told Natasha to be friendly," Petrov said in explanation, as they watched her smile up at the tall American and touch his arm. "Do you know him?" Petrov asked.

Alex Trenton nodded. "Jones. My group has been watching

him since he joined the embassy. He's very senior for a military attaché. What's he doing here?"

Petrov nodded approval of the question. "He's continuing the work he does in Washington. Counterespionage."

"You have had considerable success in Washington this year," Alex said. "Particularly with the Iron Cross."

"I believe General Jones is here to put an end to my success. I think his mission in Moscow is to discover the identity of Iron Cross."

"Why come here for that?"

"Because he's had no success so far in Washington."

They stood watching the tall American. The young woman from the British embassy had joined him and Natasha. "As you see," Petrov said, "he's a ladies' man. But strong, too, and clever in an instinctive way. An opponent for you, Alex."

"What do you want me to do?"

Petrov hesitated. "I want him out of Moscow. No diplomatic repercussions." Petrov smiled. "Just something between the two of you. As one professional to another."

In the uppermost room of the roofless building, the cold wind blew in through broken windowpanes and the gaping splits in the bomb-shattered walls. In the street below, the driver of a public truck refused to take a drunken passenger; a motorcycle with sidecar laboriously coughed its way up the hill; couples leaving the subway station talked in low tones as they passed on their way home. Inside, the wind rattled the loose window frames and drove the snow around the room. A piece of torn curtain flapped like an injured bird.

Hal Jones leaned his back against the wall, his hands deep in the pockets of his overcoat. His face, half obscured by shadows, was ruggedly handsome, though no longer young. His hair, cut short in a military style, was iron gray. Hearing a footfall on the stairs outside the room, he looked expectantly toward the door.

"Mr. Jones?" a man called from the outside landing.

"I'm here," Jones answered.

A Russian entered the room. "You took care not to be followed?"

"Nobody followed me," the American said.

There was a pause. "Very well. I would like to see your credentials."

Hal Jones took a leather wallet from his pocket and threw it across the gap that separated them.

The Russian took it and held it at arm's length so that the shaft of light from outside fell upon it. "A general."

"A brigadier general—not quite the real thing."

"And your function?"

This time it was the American who paused. "My function," he said at length, "is to deal with people like you. Russians who want to cross over to the West."

The other man came forward into the center of the derelict room, extending the wallet in his hand. Light from the street lamp outside, angled through a hole in the brickwork, touched his shoulder, leaving his face in shadow.

"You claim to be a member of the secret police," Jones said, pocketing the wallet.

"I work for the MGB, the Ministry of State Security, yes," the man said in heavily accented English.

"And you wish to defect."

"I wish to investigate the possibility."

"Why?"

"You're asking me to tell you the story of my whole life. I am what I am because of the past, the present, even because of the fears and hopes I have for the future."

"What's your name?"

"Nozenkov, Vassily Nozenkov."

Something twitched at the American's nerve endings. You always asked them their name. Mostly they ended up telling you. But seldom this fast. "You want to leave the Soviet Union."

"Yes. Isn't that enough?"

"You must have served in the war."

"At Stalingrad."

"I detect a note of pride," the American said.

"Yes," the other man said slowly. "Is that unreasonable? Our two countries were fighting the same enemy, Nazi Germany."

"You were decorated at Stalingrad?" Jones asked.

The Russian paused. "Yes."

The American grunted. Taking out a pack of Lucky Strikes, he handed one to the Russian and, cupping his hands, carefully, snapped his lighter. As the other man inhaled, Jones studied the face in the flicker of yellow light. A very Russian face. The man was about thirty-five years old, short, over-weight, with a heavy mustache and light brown hair. A pleas-ant-looking guy.

"What rank?"

"Captain," the Russian said.

"An MGB captain. Not bad—if that's what you really are."

"It's what I really am."

"Your English is good."

"I work in the Foreign Language Division. American sec-tion."

Shards of glass crunched under the American's feet. "A nice comfortable berth." Hal Jones smiled, a formal movement of the mouth. He felt no sympathy. "So what happened to make you ask for this meeting? Did you suddenly fall out with your colonel? Perhaps you've been fooling around with his wife?"

The Russian was silent.

"You must realize there'll be a price?" Hal Jones said.

"A price?"

"Information."

"I'm asking for political asylum," the Russian said. "I am not here to betray my country."

Hal Jones blew a jet of smoke through the clear, cold air. Most defectors were different. They were braggarts, exalting in their own importance in the Soviet system, or pathetic, frightened men. "How soon would you want to move on this?" he asked.

"Immediately." The Russian swayed forward from the place he had deliberately selected in the darkest corner of the room.

Hal Jones shook his head. "This thing needs preparation, planning."

"I must move quickly," the Russian insisted.

"It's going to take a month to organize the whole package."

"A month?"

"We don't run a travel agency," Hal Jones said brusquely. "And in any case, we have plenty of clients."

The Russian's face moved back into the shadow. "I might have guessed," he said without bitterness. "It's not as easy as I thought."

A surge of irritation passed through the American. Why

should it be easy? It wasn't easy for the millions struggling to
live through another winter in the MGB's labor camps. Why
should it be easy for a fat cat who's put his foot in it by laying
his colonel's wife or whatever?

"Usually," Hal Jones said slowly, "with a guy like you, anxious to leave, we ask for a piece of specific information. Then,
when he's paid his dues, we arrange a journey."

"What sort of information?"

Hal Jones shrugged. "Just this moment," he said, "we have a
leak in Washington. Your colleagues are proving just a little too
informed about matters in general. The code name for your
man in the United States is Iron Cross."

The Russian was silent. "No more than one or two senior
MGB generals know the identity of Iron Cross," he said at
length. "Certainly no junior officer knows."

"The Washington leak has a Moscow outlet. Do you know
who that is?"

"It's not my field, General. I told you—I'm a translator."

"We'd like to get the name of Iron Cross's contact in Moscow."

The other man shook his head. "I realize I have been naive,
Mr. Jones. Liberty, I see, has its price."

Hal Jones shuffled his feet. "Yup," he said. "It'll cost you."

In the shadow, the Russian nodded slowly. "I'll think it
over," he said.

In the street below, a line of three MGB jeeps had drawn up.
Captain Alexander Trenton sat at the wheel of the first. Beside
him, a younger secret-police captain looked through the gaping windows across the street. "They must have had time
enough," Roy Morosov said.

Trenton nodded unhurriedly. "When the American comes
out, remember, you approach him and *salute*."

"If he refuses to come with me?"

"Then use force. Minimum force, Roy," he added wearily.
He pointed to the entrance to the ruin. The American came
out quickly, hunching his shoulders against the wind. "Don't
forget, Roy. Minimum force. I'll inform the United States embassy as soon as we've got him safely at the ministry."

The flickering black-and-white screen showed the corner of
the foreigners' bar in the Hotel Moskva. The crude soundtrack

picked up the clatter of glasses on trays and the voices of three French embassy secretaries who were sitting at a table by the bar. A man and woman entered the room and moved toward a point in front of the fixed camera.

As they walked into focus, it was clear even in the poor light that the American, Hal Jones, and the handsome young woman were arguing.

Over the sound of the French embassy secretaries, the hidden microphone on the bar picked up her voice. "I did not ask you to meet me here," Natasha said firmly. "I had no idea you would be here and I refuse utterly to do what you ask. I am a Soviet citizen."

Hal Jones stuck his hands deep into the side pockets of his jacket. "What is it I'm supposed to be asking you, Natasha?" He turned to face her.

"We are not on such terms that you should call me by my given name."

"At our last meeting, you were asking me to call you Natasha. You insisted. What's changed?"

"I refuse to give you the information you have asked for," she went on, facing the screen. "I will also have to report this conversation to the Security Services."

On the screen, Jones suddenly glanced up. "Where's the camera?" he said, looking along the bar. Then he stepped forward, pointing toward the lens until his index finger filled the screen.

The whirring stopped, and the screen went dark. The group of men in the Foreign Ministry theater remained seated as the houselights came on.

On one side of the aisle, Brigadier General Hal Jones leaned over to face Robert Jackson, the U.S. embassy's Head of Chancery. "It's crude stuff, Bob. They need a bigger peg than that to hang their hat on."

"They also picked you up leaving a rendezvous with a would-be defector. Remember?" Jackson said dourly.

Hal Jones scowled. "The would-be defector is sitting comfortably across the aisle," he said, pointing to where Vassily Nozenkov sat with his fellow MGB officers. "Like the rest of the evidence, the meeting was set up. But why?"

Jackson stood up. "Okay, let's see what they want."

Ten minutes later, in Ministry of Foreign Affairs meeting

room B23, Senior Captain Alexander Trenton waited while the U.S. Head of Chancery and Jones were served tea.

"There's no point in wasting time, gentlemen," Trenton said briskly. "You've seen the material. There is, of course, in addition, a recording of General Jones's meeting with Captain Nozenkov."

Robert Jackson leaned forward, teacup in hand. "Normally, of course, we would be discussing this matter with a member of the Foreign Ministry, not with the MGB."

"My senior officer, General Petrov, believes that by keeping discussions on the present level we might be able to avoid further strain on U.S.-Soviet relations," said Alexander Trenton.

"What is it you want, Captain?" Hal Jones said.

"We want you to leave Moscow immediately. No diplomatic incident. No publicity. We're prepared not to publish the evidence we have against you."

"What have you got against me? Personally, I mean?"

Trenton smiled. "We're both professionals, General. It's no secret that you have been the most active military attaché that your embassy has ever had in Moscow. You're too good, General. We want you out."

Robert Jackson shifted uncomfortably in his chair. "Perhaps, Captain, we should stick to formal channels."

Trenton shrugged. "The result would be the same."

"In diplomatic terms," Jackson said, "I regard your approach as completely cynical."

Jones got up. "When do I leave, Captain?" he said. "There's no point in dragging this out."

Trenton came around the desk. "Would tomorrow morning be convenient?"

"It'd be the first available plane."

Robert Jackson stood stiffly in the middle of the room. "I must warn you, Captain, that I will recommend that the American ambassador take up the matter."

"Of course." Trenton inclined his head. "It's your privilege, Mr. Jackson."

The Head of Chancery walked past Hal and out into the corridor.

Captain Jones and Trenton followed. "Don't you ever hate your work, Captain?" the American said as they walked down the long, polished corridor. He pointed to a large portrait of an avuncular Stalin on the wall. "Your boss can't be the easiest man to work for."

They were walking stride for stride. "No worse than yours," Trenton said.

"You mean that notorious warmonger, Dwight D. Eisenhower?"

Trenton laughed. "As a matter of fact, I have considerable respect for your new president. General, we're both servants of vast and powerful countries. You and I are bound together by the fact that we have to compromise constantly—for good or ill."

Hal Jones shook his head vigorously. "No moral relativism, kiddo," he said, his face set. "Any way you look at it, we're nicer guys than you."

The guard was holding the door as Robert Jackson turned to shake hands with Captain Trenton. Jones stepped past them, out into the bitter night.

On his way home, Alexander Trenton sped through the dark, snow-covered streets, still thinking about the American's words. The jeep he drove was an ancient wartime lend-lease model, and blasts of freezing snow stung his face through the gaps in the snapping canvas top. The brakes, he knew, were badly worn; but in the early hours of the morning, the streets of Moscow were empty. Or so he imagined until he crossed the canal bridge and suddenly had to spin the wheel frantically to counter a sudden violent slide across the frozen roadway. He had seen the dark figure on the bicycle only at the last moment, glimpsed in the yellow headlights through the veil of falling snow, before the side of the jeep struck the fragile machine, hurling the rider into the darkness, crushing the frame beneath the rear wheels.

Dragging the mangled bicycle with it, the jeep spun in a half circle, until its headlights flared back across its own erratic tracks in the snow. Alexander Trenton shouldered open the door and got out uncertainly. In the numbing cold, he stood searching the darkness beyond the headlights. Then he moved forward, breaking into a run. Jumping the twisted remains of the bicycle, he slithered down the steep camber of the road to where he saw a dark, still figure in the snow.

He had time to register stockinged legs above leather boots, a fur coat, a faint, surprising scent of perfume, before the dark bundle moved and the girl lifted her head.

He helped her into a sitting position, her back against the post of an unlit street lamp.

"I didn't see you," he said. "The jeep was already in a skid."

She nodded, her eyes closing.

"Are you all right?" he asked urgently. "Nothing broken?"

"I don't think so. I'm too cold to be sure."

"I'll help you up." He raised her, but her legs slid helplessly beneath her, like a foal's, until she steadied herself against him and the lamppost.

"The bicycle," she said. "Is it damaged?"

He pointed to the wrecked machine.

"Oh, no!" Tears rolled down her cheeks. "Oh God, no."

"I'm sorry, comrade." He helped her toward the jeep. "I'll do my best to replace it."

She climbed painfully into the passenger seat. "Replace a bicycle?" she said. "Where in Moscow will you find someone who'll part with one?" She shivered violently.

Trenton walked around the jeep, dragged the mangled bicycle into the gutter, then climbed into the driver's seat. "It can't be that difficult to find a bicycle," he said.

She looked at him disbelievingly. "Are you new in Moscow?" she asked.

He shook his head. "I'll take you home," he said. "To my home. We can talk about the bicycle over some hot tea."

"Some hot vodka would suit me better."

He smiled. "There's that, too. I'm glad you're not hurt," he said.

She nodded, still thinking of her lost bicycle, doubting his ability to replace it. Now that her mouth was less drawn with cold and shock, he noticed how young she was, not much more than twenty. Blond, with pretty, regular features, she had an irrepressible air not often found among young women in Moscow.

He started the engine and eased the jeep around in the right direction. The girl had taken a cigarette from her pocket and lit it, exhaling slowly, closing her eyes again. Then she half turned in her seat, wide-eyed in an effort at wakefulness.

"Who are you?" she said. "A man driving about in the middle of the night in an army car? But not in uniform?"

"I work in a ministry," he said, peering at the road ahead. "My name is Alexander Trenton."

"You are not a Russian? A Balt perhaps. Or a Karelian."

"I'm a Russian."

She inhaled the smoke from her cigarette. "My name is Katya."

"You work a night shift, Katya?"

She nodded. "Without a bicycle I have an hour's walk home."

Off the Arbat, he turned the jeep through a gateway in a wall flanked by crumbling stone columns. The splintered remains of wooden doors hung from the gateposts. She watched him as he turned off the engine. "Is this where you live?" she asked suspiciously.

"It's the back entrance," he said. "This way we can get upstairs without waking the concierge."

She made a face. "An apartment with a concierge! You must be an important man at your ministry."

"Not really." He got out of the jeep and picked his way around through the rubble scattered across the courtyard.

She was already standing beside the jeep. A light in an upstairs window threw shadows across the paved yard. "What is this place?"

"This is the courtyard of the old Moscow Variety Theater. The theater itself hasn't been used since tsarist days, but there are some apartments above the auditorium."

"I see." She was staring at the one permanent resident of the courtyard, a life-size statue. It was made of carved wood, the bloated, childlike features still recognizable despite the years of relentless Moscow winters which had split the figure in two from head to breast, as if it had been the victim of some savage Gothic attack.

"It's Queen Victoria." He came forward to stand beside her. "An English Queen."

"I know," she said.

For a moment, she stared up at the grotesque face. "Are you married, Comrade Trenton?"

"Yes."

"But your wife is away with the children."

"There are no children. And my wife is upstairs in the apartment. I brought you here to try and sort out the question of the bicycle. That's all."

"Then I apologize."

He led her through a small door at the far side of the courtyard and up a cast-iron staircase. Shreds of plush curtains hung from brass rails on each landing. Through the openings, Katya could see into the old auditorium. The seating had long ago been ripped out for firewood, as had the boards of the stage itself. The ceiling, once curved and gilded, now sagged on rotting laths or, in parts, had collapsed entirely into the auditorium.

"I live in the old theater director's apartment above the auditorium," he explained. "For these days, it's quite grand."

"I live in one room," she said. "But then, I'm lucky. Some of my friends, even with families, have room corners only."

"Room corners?" He frowned.

"You are unfamiliar with room corners, Comrade Trenton?"

He shrugged.

She looked at him quickly to see if he was mocking her. A government official who could show humility was too much of a rarity to take for granted. "A room corner," she said, "is a quarter space of a large room. Sometimes it has a plywood partition, sometimes just a few bits of cloth hanging from a rope, like washing on a line. Four people may live there in a space of not more than ten square meters."

"I knew they existed before the war," he said carefully. "I imagined by now they had been done away with."

"You *are* new to Moscow, comrade," she said. "I can tell."

"Since the war I've been serving abroad," Trenton said. "Before the war I lived on Cherkassy Street. Which part of the city are you from?" he asked.

"Red Presnya," she said. "Do you know why the old Presnya suburb was called *Red*?"

He nodded. "It was the first workers' district to rise against the tsar."

"More accurately, Comrade Trenton, the workers rose in protest against the living conditions. I've heard it said that at that time they sometimes lived two or three families to a single room. Imagine!"

They had stopped on an iron landing. "You're young," he said sharply. "You don't understand."

"Many people living in Presnya today also find it difficult to understand."

"Katya," he said, "I'm a stranger. It's not wise to talk like this to strangers."

She nodded slowly. "Not to strangers who live in grand apartments once occupied by theater directors."

"Not to any stranger," he said. "I'm an officer in the Ministry of State Security."

"The Cheka." She stopped, holding tightly to the bannister. "The MGB, yes."

She smiled fearfully. "I never thought . . . you don't look like a policeman."

He nodded briskly. Taking the keys from his pocket, he unlocked the shabby, peeling door before them. "It's not all that grand," he said, "as you'll see."

They entered a wide corridor with four doors leading off it. "You have *four* rooms. For only your wife and yourself?"

"My mother and my stepfather live with us. Or strictly speaking, we live with them. He's an important official in my ministry. It's his apartment."

"The same ministry—you mean he's a policeman, too?"

"Yes."

"Alexander," a man's voice called from the farthest room, "is that you?"

A door opened, and Petrov stood in the doorway. "You're late," he said. "I expected you back an hour ago." Then, staring past Trenton to Katya a half pace behind him, "Who's this?"

"I had an accident," Trenton said. "I knocked this young comrade off her bicycle. I brought her home to find some means of compensating her for the damage done." He turned quickly to Katya. "This is General Pavel Semyonovich Petrov, my wife's uncle."

"Compensation?" Petrov's head came up, as if he were stretching his neck.

"A bicycle is priceless to a late-shift worker."

"Worker?" Petrov stared insolently at her.

Katya returned his stare. "I work in the south of the city, Old Stables, past Pavelets Station, comrade. In Perlinka Lane," she added defiantly.

"Perlinka Lane?" Petrov was suddenly smiling broadly. Trenton looked at him, puzzled. "Step into the other room, comrade," Petrov said to her. "I must have a word with Alexander."

Katya stepped through the doorway, and Petrov leaned forward and pulled the door closed behind her. "Well, how did it go?"

"Very well."

"No threats from Jackson?"

"A minor attempt at bluster. But the brigadier general, Jones, knew there was no point in fighting it."

Petrov stood, the collar of his uniform jacket open, thumbs hooked into the flaps of his breast pockets. "Nicely handled. No Foreign Ministry huffing and puffing. I'm happier Jones is out of the way. Much happier . . ."

"How is Xenia?" Trenton looked toward the bedroom door.

"She asked to see you the moment you got back," Petrov said. "Have a word with her—I'll look after the young comrade."

Trenton turned back down the corridor and entered the bedroom. The light in the wicker-basket shade was still on. His wife lay sprawled across the bed, facedown, fully clothed. The tang of lemon scented the air—it was lemon vodka she favored.

Trenton crossed to the bed and rolled her onto her back. The liter bottle on the table by the window was half empty. "Xenia," he said. He shook her shoulder, but there was no movement other than the regular rhythm of her breathing. He glanced down at her thickening waist, his mind filled with images of the slender girl in the other room. Unable, for the moment, to bear the thought of undressing his wife, he took a blanket and spread it over her. Then he turned and left the bedroom.

His stepfather was standing in the corridor. "How is she?"

Trenton shrugged. "As anyone would be with half a liter inside them. She's asleep. I'll put her to bed later, when I've taken the girl home." He looked past his stepfather and frowned. "Where is she?"

"I threw her out," Petrov said.

Trenton looked at him in angry astonishment. "You threw her out? In this weather? Onto the streets?"

"Onto the streets." Petrov nodded. "Where she comes from. Old Stables in Perlinka Lane is an army whorehouse," he said. "Your pretty young pickup is a *whore*."

CHAPTER
2

Laughing, the five young men in MGB uniforms walked along the brightly lit corridor. Between them and the swinging doors of the canteen ahead, a young woman in a similar uniform jacket, but with a trim skirt above her polished black boots, swayed her hips outrageously. She turned, laughing as well. "I've been to New York," she said. "I know how a real hooker walks."

"You'd do well there, Natasha Petrovna," Roy Morosov said. "You could make a fortune in Times Square and bring us back mountains of watches and chocolates and nylon stockings for our wives."

She pushed open the canteen door, and the five young secret-police officers inhaled the aroma of Polish smoked ham and eggs cooking.

"How long were *you* in New York, Vassily?" Alex Trenton asked his friend.

"Six weeks; not more," Vassily Nozenkov said. "But I had just married Zoya; I was missing her like a madman and had no inclination for painted ladies."

"You had an inclination for painted ladies in Stalingrad," Trenton said. "You remember that picture of the girl from an old copy of *Yank* magazine you pinned up in every cellar we occupied?"

"That was different." Vassily joined the breakfast line. "That was a mascot. A good-luck charm. We're both still here, aren't we?"

Roy Morosov was telling a story. "Embarrassing," he said, with his cheerful laugh. "I was grunting this lad, really laying into him with the rubber truncheon, and between gasps for breath—I'm smoking too much of these—I'm tossing the questions at him, and he's squealing like mad but denying everything. Then suddenly there's a complete change and he's singing like a canary . . ."

Natasha Petrovna was already laughing. "Don't tell me," she said.

"You've guessed, you lovely bitch." Morosov put his arm around her and hugged her. "Wrong man! Had to start all over with the lad next door."

"How's Zoya?" Trenton asked Vassily.

"She's fine. She sends much love to you. Asks when you're coming over to see our new apartment."

"And the twins?"

"If they can't learn to sleep more, I'll never make promotion to senior captain."

With their trays, Alex Trenton and Vassily drifted to a separate table. As they sat down, Trenton glanced across at the table where Roy Morosov was settling down with the others. "Morosov asked for a special meeting with me this morning," he said.

"I know." Vassily bent his head over his ham and eggs. "What was it about?"

Trenton paused. "He thinks some material was wiped off the recording of your meeting with the American, General Jones."

"Seemed complete enough to me when they ran it back," Vassily said, his mouth half full.

Trenton drank some coffee. "Roy thought the missing lines were at the end. He says he believes the final turns of the cylinder had been wiped clean."

"Deliberately, you mean."

"Deliberately," Trenton said.

Vassily's hand was shaking. He put down his fork and began to cough nervously.

Trenton watched him.

"For God's sake, Alex," Vassily said when the coughing had passed, "you don't think I did it?"

"Why would you want to wipe the recording? You were there under orders."

"What did you tell Roy?"

"I told him I'd put my boot up his ass if he as much as mentioned it again. I told him the bonds of trust between officers of the MGB are sacred. He likes that stuff."

Vassily's head came up slowly. "I don't have to say thank you. Not to you."

"No . . ." Trenton looked at him levelly. "No, you don't have to say anything. But for Christ's sake be careful, Vassily. Roy was right. I reran the cylinder before I wiped it clean. Completely clean this time."

They finished breakfast in silence. Against the background of what had passed between them there was nothing else to say. When Vassily left, with a touch of his hand on his friend's shoulder, Trenton lit a cigarette, and unbuttoning his breast pocket, took out a worn copy of the poems of John Donne. He opened the book, as he always did, to the stained flyleaf. In a faded handwriting was the inscription: Charles Trenton, Harvard, Eliot House, 1912. He had seen a photograph of his father once, where, he no longer remembered. It was a sepia head-and-shoulders portrait of a young man in his early twenties, posed in profile, the chin raised, a slightly cold confidence emanating from the line of the mouth. Trenton smiled to himself. He thought of his dead father much more of late. Of his own American origins. He wondered, briefly, whether he was technically even a Soviet citizen.

So Vassily had used the staged contact with the American general to make a real contact . . . It was true that he had never been the same since he had served in the interrogation teams in the Ukraine just after the war. He had come back a changed man. This is not real soldiering, Vassily had said. Beating people in bloody cellars. But as always, Trenton had cut him short. Too many pictures, too many experiences came to his own mind to make it safe to talk. Even to Vassily Nozenkov.

It was easier not to think. He closed his eyes, the book open on the table in front of him.

* * *

Brigadier General Hal Jones walked rapidly across the apron at the old Moscow airport. His aide, Jack O'Sullivan, at six feet tall still four inches shorter than his chief, found it hard to maintain the pace without sucking in uncomfortable quantities of freezing, gasoline-laden air.

"The interesting thing about the man," Jones said, "is the extraordinary quality of his English. He spoke with a totally *impeccable* New England accent. Maybe a phrase or two here and there is a little old-fashioned, stilted even. But for Christ's sake, Jack, he did not *learn* that accent."

"You think he's an American?"

Jones launched himself across the tarmac toward the waiting Pan Am Stratocruiser, glittering silver and blue in the pale morning sun. "I don't know *what* I mean, Jack."

"I've run every possible check at the embassy," O'Sullivan said. "We have two hazy photographs of him, both with General Petrov. Beyond that, we've no record of his name or of secret-police details. Nothing."

"He doesn't behave like a new boy, Jack. He's too confident. Too sure of his position."

"Don't let him get to you, General," O'Sullivan said. "He dumped you this time, but this is just round one."

"Maybe," Jones grunted.

The young stewardess at the bottom of the ladder stood unflinching in the cold Moscow blast. "General Jones." She smiled a professional welcome. Slightly more than just professional, Jones considered.

"And Major O'Sullivan," Jack O'Sullivan said, marveling not for the first time at the way Jones achieved immediate contact with a pretty girl less than half his age.

"Welcome aboard, General," the girl said.

"I tell you, Jack," Hal said, looking down at the girl from the top of the aluminum steps, "getting kicked out of the Soviet Union isn't *all* bad news."

Five hours later the Stratocruiser landed at Copenhagen and turned onto runway West 3 to taxi toward the terminal. In the small first-class cabin, General Jones talked with the young stewardess as she stood near the door of the flight deck.

"But we know nothing about each other," she said, smiling.

"We know we've both got three or four hours in Copenhagen—time to have dinner together."

"That's hardly knowing anything about each other."

"You know I'm a tremendously important officer in the U.S. Army. And I know you're at least five feet nine in your nylons. I like tall girls."

The stewardess laughed. "What about your fellow officer?" She nodded toward O'Sullivan. "Shouldn't you be having dinner together?"

"I'm of American-Danish descent," O'Sullivan said. "I have an old Danish grandmother waiting for me with a whole tray of pastries."

"So it's all right then?" Hal unclipped his seat belt. "Drinks at the Skybar as soon as you're clear."

The girl smiled. "Aye, aye, General," she said.

Half an hour later they sat opposite each other in deep club armchairs in the airport bar.

"Tell me about yourself. And call me Hal, for God's sake. None of this general nonsense."

"You got your notebook ready?" the girl said.

"I've got a hell of a good memory."

"Okay." She uncrossed her legs and leaned forward to take her drink from the glass-topped table. "My name is Sarah Black. I come from Cambridge, Massachusetts. I am nineteen years old. I am technically the ward of a certain unlovable congressman and his so-so wife. No, that's unfair," she interrupted herself. "Jennifer's not bad. Harry is unspeakable."

"Forget Harry," Hal said. "What do you mean, a ward?"

"It means until I'm twenty-one years old I can't lay hands on my own money. That, duckie, is why I work. That, and to meet sexy generals and to get away from Harry."

"That's the story of your young life?"

"No, I was educated, if that's the word for it, at a crummy but expensive girls' school at a place called East Grinstead in England. There, I fell in love for the first time—with my field-hockey mistress. Unfortunately, my feelings were fully reciprocated. I was expelled, aged sixteen, and sent to a finishing school in Switzerland, where I dabbled quite enjoyably with my first male lover, a Swiss clock maker. I lost my virginity to another Swiss, this time a banker. That year I also lost both my globe-trotting parents in a midair collision over Gary, Indiana."

"Enter Jennifer and Harry."

"Yes. Harry planned for me to work in his office in Washington. I told him to go screw himself and found myself a trainee stewardess job with Pan Am. I chose Pan Am because I thought the powder-blue uniform suited my complexion."

"It does," Hal said.

"My taste in men runs to tall, muscular, tough-looking, graying generals." She lifted her glass and eyed him evenly across the rim. "What do you like?"

He stood up and stretched out a hand toward her. "You." She took it and he drew her up. "I like everything about you," he said. "Except maybe your tendency to be shy, retiring and unforthcoming."

She stood close. "You haven't quite put your finger on it, but I know what you mean. Let's say I make a big, big effort and say exactly what's on my mind. That I'm not hungry, but I do want to screw."

He smiled. "Could an officer and a gentleman say no?"

The inner courtyard beyond the entrance to the Kremlin's Tegem Palace was traditionally used as a parking area for the limousines of the highest-ranking ministers in the land. It had also become, because of its surrounding high, windowless walls, a recognized safe place for the highest to meet. Only here did they feel out of sight, out of earshot of Joseph Stalin. Only here did they have an excuse—the location of their cars—to meet together.

Tonight, as the snow drifted lazily down, the members of the Politburo of the Soviet Union stood in a group around the chairman of the Kremlin medical specialists. Doctor Weber shoved his gloved hands into his overcoat pockets. A small man, he was even shorter than Khrushchev. Malenkov, in his black woolen *shapka,* seemed to tower over him.

"There have been two new developments, comrade members of the Politburo," Doctor Weber told them. "The first is that all nine Kremlin specialists examined Comrade Stalin this morning."

"What conclusion did you come to about his state of health?"

Malenkov asked hurriedly, the words spilling out overanx-
iously. Khrushchev and Marshal Bulganin exchanged a glance.
Molotov remained silent, watchful of them all.

"We were unable to reach a collective decision," Doctor
Weber said. "Doctor Lenneman and Doctor Fogel both consider Comrade Stalin to be a sick man. They asked for the
opportunity to make further tests."

"And Comrade Stalin's reaction?" Khrushchev asked.

Weber allowed the ghost of a bitter smile to rest on his lips.
"Comrade Stalin's reaction," he said, "was to arrest them both."
His voice rose. "And he has now ordered the arrest of the
other comrade doctors who had examined him. Including myself."

The politicians were silent, shuffling their feet in the snow.
"It's cold out here, Mother of God," Khrushchev said, making
a half movement toward his car.

"Comrades," Weber said desperately. "I appeal to you. On
behalf of my colleagues as well as myself." He stepped toward
Molotov as the oldest present. "Comrade Molotov . . ."

"There's nothing I can do," Molotov said. "You fool—what
influence have I got?"

Khrushchev, Bulganin, Voroshilov were already moving toward their limousines.

"Comrades . . . please . . ." Weber lifted his hands in sup-
plication.

Only Malenkov remained where he was. "The sickness you
believe Marshal Stalin to be suffering from . . ." he said, his
black eyes glittering. "It's a physical affliction, is it?"

"I would think so, comrade," Weber said eagerly. "He suf-
fers great pain."

"Where?"

"The head, neck, shoulders."

"And what does that mean?"

Weber shook his head. Diagnosis on a freezing street corner
was not a familiar situation for one of the most distinguished
doctors in the Soviet Union. But he knew his diagnosis would
affect his own life, as well. "It could be a prelude to a heart
attack. Angina, perhaps. Pain radiating toward the throat. It's
possible the comrade marshal has already suffered a mild
heart attack. If so, he requires immediate treatment."

Khrushchev and Bulganin had returned to Malenkov's side. "Immediate treatment," Khrushchev said. "Or what happens?"

"I cannot be held responsible," Weber said, reverting to one of the empty commonplaces of his profession. But even as he spoke, he knew he *was* being held responsible. "I beg you, comrades. You must help me and my colleagues."

"Marshal Stalin's health is, of course, a matter of great concern to us," Voroshilov said portentously.

"Especially considering the grave responsibilities he shoulders on behalf of us all," Bulganin added, as the Politburo members turned their backs upon the doctor and moved to their cars.

"Comrades . . ." Weber appealed to them. "If Comrade Stalin is to be helped," he said with a desperate rapidity, "he must be treated . . ."

A car door slammed closed. Then another. An engine purred, and Khrushchev's Packard pulled away. Within seconds, Bulganin and Malenkov followed. Then the old guard, Voroshilov and Molotov. None wanted to speak with the others. None dared, even if they wished, to think of the fate of Doctor Weber and his colleagues.

CHAPTER
3

The two friends paced the long central alley of the Bulkansky Cemetery. The old gravestones on either side were humps of snow; the dark cypress trees shuffled in the wind like old men.

"I wanted to say good-bye," Vassily Nozenkov said. "After all we've been through together, I could not leave without saying good-bye."

"You give too much trust," Alex Trenton said fiercely.

"Not to you."

Trenton bit his lip. "You know the world we live in . . . for God's sake take care, old friend."

"Will you come with me?"

Alex stood in the middle of the path. Slimy black leaves were plucked up by the wind. "I'm a Soviet citizen, Vassily," he said. "If I'm anything at all I'm a Soviet citizen. I don't have the same freedom of choice as a born Russian like yourself."

Vassily nodded slowly.

"You're clean at this end," Alex continued quickly. "But you know we have a Washington operation the Americans call Iron Cross. Someone is passing information. Move quickly, Vassily. Before someone in Washington can point the finger at you."

"It's why I asked you to meet me here," Vassily said. "We're leaving tomorrow. I'm to drive south with Zoya and the twins.

In the Caucasus, the Americans have people working for them. We'll cross into Turkey."

In the fading light, the two men shook hands. Then they parted, taking separate ways back through the long line of trees.

Alex passed through the cemetery gates and started along Bulkansky Street. Behind him he could hear the footsteps of his friend crunching through the snow.

Women passed him in twos and threes, heavily swaddled against the cold, tramway workers from the Bulkansky depot on the corner. Young or not so young, their faces had the raw, blistered appearance of so many Moscow women. Encumbered by thick padded coats, they stomped like workingmen through the snow. The image of Katya entered his thoughts, a tang of scent, an outline of thick blond hair. He stopped on the street corner as Vassily passed him with a mumbled farewell. He knew he could not go back to the office, or home to watch Xenia slide gracelessly into drunken oblivion. He thought again of Katya, and turned away as Vassily Nozenkov disappeared in a dark flurry of snow.

Deep in his overcoat pocket, Alex thumbed the greasy surface of the ruble notes. The man facing him in the dimly lit doorway registered Alex's civilian clothing and shook his head. "The Stables are for officers only," he said. "If you're new in Moscow, comrade, have a quiet word with your union organizer. He'll put you onto the right place."

"I'm an officer." Alex drew out his internal passport and thrust it at the man. "Captain of the infantry. Medically discharged. Now MGB."

The gatekeeper's breath tumbled into the night air. "Apologies, Comrade Captain," he said, his head down, studying the document under the archway light. "Stalingrad front, eh?" he added. "My son was there. Came out without a scratch, thank God."

Trenton withdrew the wad of ruble notes from his pocket and counted off ten. The man took the bills and handed him a metal token stamped with a number. "Stalingrad," he said. "We set the Fascists back on their heels there, comrade."

Alex took the metal token and walked through the brick archway into the brightly lit stable block. Paint peeled from the planked ceiling, dark blue, red and gold. The cobbles were huge, rough-cut stones worn smooth by a hundred years of tsarist cavalry hooves. The line of men, thirty or forty junior officers in uniform, shuffled forward as their numbers were called.

It was still cold despite the two huge braziers burning in the center of the long room. Alex joined the end of the line. The door of each stable opposite was crudely painted with a white-washed number, perhaps thirty stalls in all. Alex gestured to the old man tottering past with a bucket of disinfectant. "Is Katya working tonight?"

The old man bent forward. The milky disinfectant heaved in the bottom of the pail. "Number twenty-four," he said.

Alex pressed a ruble note into the man's outstretched hand. The old man pocketed it and, producing a handful of metal discs, sorted through them until he found one stamped with number twenty-four. Trenton handed over his own disc and turned back toward the line of officers. Already, others were coming in behind him, men alone or in groups from the garrison barracks nearby.

The line moved forward. As a number was called, an officer would detach himself from the line and approach a stable door. The two-tiered doors would bang closed and the voice of a girl would echo across the ornately painted roof.

"Twenty-four," cried the peasant soldier with the white wooden baton, turning toward the line. Alex stepped forward. A middle-aged major was leaving the stall. Alex pushed past and let the door swing closed behind him.

The sides of the stall were boarded to shoulder height. Above that, strips of brown paper sacking divided one stall from the next. A bare bulb dropped light onto an iron-frame bed squatting at an angle on the cobbles. The girl stood with her back to him, brushing her hair in a mirror on the wall opposite the door. "Good evening, comrade," she said without turning.

He watched the blond hair curl at the nape of her neck. She was dressed in a shirt of white cotton, a dark green skirt and high-heeled boots of what seemed to be above-average quality for postwar Moscow.

"Take off your coat, comrade . . ." She turned toward him and stopped. "Comrade Trenton!"

He saw confusion in her face and wondered again if he should have come. "I wanted to apologize," he said. "Even from the Arbat it's a long walk home to Red Presnya."

She shrugged. "Before I had the bicycle I did it every night." Even as she spoke he knew her mood was changing, becoming more distant, more defiant. "All the same," she said, "someone could give policeman Petrov a few lessons in good manners."

His eyes turned involuntarily to the strips of sacking that separated them from the stall next door. A heavy grunting came through them.

She jerked her thumb toward the next stall. "Don't worry." She was laughing at him. "He's not listening and she's deaf as a tree."

She sat down on the bed and crossed her legs. "So you came to say you're sorry. Expensive apology. It cost ten rubles for a token."

He stood before her, his hands deep in his overcoat pockets. "I had no other way of contacting you. I brought a replacement for your bicycle."

Her foot stopped swinging. She leaned forward, frowning. "You found me a bicycle?"

"Yes. I bought it from someone in my department. It's outside in the lane, hidden behind the old wooden sheds. Do you know where they are?"

"Yes."

"So . . ." He took his hands from his coat pockets and made an awkward gesture.

Her eyes were on his face. "I don't understand," she said. "Why did you do it?"

"The accident was my fault. I was going too fast. I've done no more than even the account."

"But policemen who live in grand apartments with Pavel Semyonovich Petrov don't need to even accounts. At least not with people like me."

He stood silently.

Suddenly, she smiled. "I've made you angry. But I can still thank you for the bicycle."

"All right." He hesitated. "No bruises left from the other night?"

"No. The snow broke my fall. So you see, the account really is even."

"Yes."

"Except that you paid ten rubles for a token." Silently she began to undo his overcoat.

"No, Katya . . ." he said, but made no movement to stop her.

She sat back on the bed drawing him toward her by the lapels of his open coat. "Still," she said, "I don't quite believe you are a Russian."

She had unbuttoned his fly and was rubbing him into an erection. She laughed. "A landowner's son, then. *That's* what I can hear in your voice."

"Yes," he said, straining toward her, "yes, I suppose I am."

He leaned over her, supporting his weight with the flat of one hand against the wooden partition. With the other hand he groped down beneath her shirt, into the warm cleavage between her breasts.

"Come along, my prince." She was looking up at him, mimicking with her mouth and clenched white teeth his own pleasure. "Come along . . . come along . . ." she said, speeding the rhythm of her movements.

When the spasm came, she released him and fell back on the bed, her arms stretched wide.

He looked down at her as he buttoned himself up. Her face had an unfeigned serenity, as it might, he thought, if they were lovers, if she had done what she did for love.

"Is something wrong?" she said. "Did I not give you pleasure?"

"Of course."

He reached in his pocket and felt the round metal disc. For a moment he kept it in the palm of his hand, unwilling to break what little illusion he could foster in this harsh place.

Hands behind her head, she was watching him closely. "Was your wife really unwell that night? Or did your stepfather say that to get you out of the way?"

"My wife's unwell most nights," Trenton said. "She began

drinking during the war when she served as a partisan officer. Who can blame her, the things she saw? But she never stopped. She has no life now outside a half liter of vodka."

"And your life?"

"I work. There's not a lot of time for anything else."

"Ha!" She sat up, unconvinced.

He didn't want to leave. "And you," he said. "Have you never been married?"

She stood up and came close to him. She was only a few inches shorter than he. "I'm eighteen," she said briskly. "I've no Moscow residence permit. In this job, the authorities turn a blind eye. It was *suggested* to me."

He was shocked. At her age.

"Perhaps," she said teasingly, "you didn't think things like that happened in the Soviet Union."

He tried not to think about who might be standing on the other side of the strips of sacking. "I know they do," he said. "They shouldn't, but I know they do."

In the cubicle next to them the grunting subsided into a low, long growl. She raised her eyebrows and pursed her lips. Between them, they were both aware, something still fragile was being forged.

"I would like to see you again," he said.

"Whenever you have ten rubles to spare."

"You know that's not what I meant."

"Perhaps." She seemed to hesitate a long time. "I don't work on Thursday night," she said.

"Thursday, then. Where?"

"Nine o'clock, Yaroslavl Station?"

"In the kvass bar?"

She nodded. "The prince and the beggar maid." She shot her hand out toward him. "Now, give me my docket."

"Nine o'clock, Yaroslavl Station." He let the metal disc roll into her palm.

She took it and raised it to her lips, blowing him a kiss. He smiled good-bye and lifted the wooden latch on the door. Passing out into the brightly lit stable, he saw a captain crossing toward stall twenty-four. He turned away, feeling a pang of something akin to jealousy as he walked back along the length of the line of waiting men.

CHAPTER
4

At the last stroke of midnight, the old man hunched over the desk pushed aside the antique globe and closed the geometry textbook in front of him. As the notes of the Kremlin clocks faded and were lost in the snow outside his window, Joseph Vissarionovich Stalin sat back from his writing desk. Fate had decreed this dark night to be the eve of his private birthday, and he was distracted with childish anticipation. He pursed his lips. His mood was greedy, lustful, impatient for diversion.

The problem he had struggled with had arisen at the Nineteenth Congress, held a few weeks before. One of the speakers, during the endless tributes and ovations, had stated that the Father of the Nation kept a benevolent watch over a land area on earth as large as the surface of the moon. Stalin had been pleased by the comparison and had made a mental note to check it. He had pursued the question in odd moments ever since. The area he ruled on earth was easy enough. He had simply added East Germany, Poland, Czechoslovakia, Hungary and Romania to the mass of the USSR. Rounded up, that came to nine million square miles, give or take Bulgaria. The surface area of the moon was a more daunting proposition. He could, of course, have asked one of his secretaries and had the answer in a matter of minutes, but he wanted to work it out for himself. The secretary might well lie to please him; he recognized that. So he had grappled with the mathematics of the surface area of an irregular sphere. Nothing was easy. It was not easy being the greatest living man. The phrase had been used by at least two speakers at the congress. The greatest living man. His face suddenly creased into a frown. Would it not have been more appropriate to have said the greatest man who ever lived? The greatest living man. Who said that at the congress? Voroshilov? Was that a subtle way of saying he was less than Lenin?

Stalin pondered the question. Lenin. The mere thought of the man made his anger rise like a great tide. What had he written in his so-called will? "Stalin is too arrogant, and this fault becomes unbearable in the office of general secretary. Therefore, I propose to our comrades to find a way to remove him from that position." Even after thirty years, the words cut like knives. He felt his whole body shaking with rage. He breathed out noisily. This would never do; he was allowing the past to ruin his peace of mind, to destroy his celebratory mood. After all, what did it matter now that he had risen to the pinnacle of prestige and power. Below him, the vast pyramid of the nation stretched in unending layers of authority, all at his complete command. The other great consolation, he chuckled, was that Lenin was dead and he was still very much alive.

His good humor restored, he reconsidered the question of Lenin and himself. Perhaps the answer was an article in *Pravda*. A logical analysis of the achievements of two men, carefully considered, totally unbiased (that was important). He might even produce a rough draft himself. Notes to be expanded by some carefully selected journalist. A Stalin prize for the right man. Where was that pen? He suddenly noticed it hanging limply in his hand. He considered a moment, and then wrote: "What enemy could deny the achievements of V. I. Lenin?" There could be no argument with that. Now to continue, but how to continue? A minute passed. Stalin yawned. He was finding it increasingly difficult to maintain concentration. He eased back in the chair, then casually wrote the numerals one to nine across the page. Every number, no matter how big or small, every calculation—the amount of grain in a harvest, the distance of the remotest star, the number of nails required to attach a sole to a pair of boots or to a million pairs of boots—could be expressed in terms of this simple row of lines and curves. In recent months he had found a growing fascination in figures. Numbers were clean, precise. Numbers could not lie or cheat or deceive or plot. He had taken to counting his steps along a corridor, or the pips in an orange, or the shining toe caps of a line of guards as he shuffled past, head bowed.

Minutes passed as he drifted between sleep and wakefulness. The pen he saw, the fat black pen, had half slipped through his fingers. Throwing it aside, he carefully filled his pipe, packing the bowl to the rim with the black, pungent tobacco he favored. He eased himself up from the secretary and crossed to the large rosewood desk. As he walked, his bare feet, with the weblike folds of skin between the toes, sank into the pale green carpet. The desktop was covered with open books, reports and maps. For long moments he looked down at the items on the desk, focusing on one and then another, no longer recalling what he was looking for. He was already prodding among the desktop litter with the stem of his pipe when he remembered the matches. Then he spotted the box on the floor between the legs of the padded leather chair. As he bent to pick it up, there was a sudden ringing in his ears, and a sickening sensation of falling swept over him. Clutching the side of the desk, he managed to pull himself upright. What was happening to him? But the feeling passed as quickly as it had appeared. It had occurred before. He tried to remember how many times.

For a full minute, he waited without moving, then prodded the matches out from under the chair with his bare foot. Still holding the desk for support, he gingerly stooped and picked up the box. This time he felt no discomfort.

Slumping behind the desk, Stalin discarded the unlit pipe and yawned again. He looked down at the piece of paper on his desk. On it he had scrawled the name "Kazatkin" in thick, black printed letters.

He reached forward and pressed the electric bell.

In his office along the corridor from Stalin's room, the marshal's secretary, Poskrebyshev, was awakened from a light slumber by the jangling of the wall bell. He stood up immediately as he had trained himself to do. He was not unaware of the amusement his name occasioned among the members of the Presidium. In Russian it suggested *cringing, servility*, but it was on just these qualities that he had built a career as one of the most powerful men in the Soviet Union. Ministers joked with him, deferred to him, tried even to offer him promises for the future. But he had remained totally loyal to Stalin. Only now, as he saw daily in his master those telltale signs of age and infirmity, did he begin to consider which way he might step. Both Malenkov and Khrushchev had made late-night suggestions, offered vague inducements.

Crossing swiftly to the anteroom, Poskrebyshev threw open the door. The man who leaped to his feet in alarm was in his early thirties, slight, narrow shouldered, sandy haired, with an air of nervousness about him.

"Doctor Kazatkin," Poskrebyshev snapped at him from the doorway, "Marshal Stalin will see you now."

The young doctor crossed the red Turkish carpet on legs he could barely control, bringing himself inadvertently to a halt too close to Poskrebyshev. The secretary hissed his disdain into the young man's face, causing Doctor Kazatkin to recoil, apologizing.

"Remember one thing," the secretary said, poking him hard in the chest with his index finger. "Under no circumstances refer to Marshal Stalin's health. Understand? He is always assumed to be perfectly well."

Kazatkin nodded rapidly. "I understand, comrade. But I am a doctor . . ." The secretary sneered away a decade's qualifications. "Under no circumstances," he repeated.

Turning, Poskrebyshev led the way down the corridor. At the end door, he knocked twice, bending forward to listen for the grunt that meant he should enter. Then opening the door, he roughly pushed Kazatkin forward, waited for a sign from Stalin that he himself should stay, saw none, and withdrew.

Doctor Peter Nikolaevich Kazatkin stood before Stalin's desk, unable to move, unable even to speak. He could think of nothing but the great white marble statue in Kazan Square. And here, standing at the desk before him, magically animated in the yellow light, the statue had begun to move.

It was almost twelve hours ago that the adventure had begun for Doctor P. N. Kazatkin, senior consultant to the Leningrad Neurological Institute.

A message had been left with his nurse that two men asked

to see him. When Kazatkin had questioned her, she could only answer that they were officials of some kind; she had no idea what they wanted. The doctor, a member of the Party and a passionate believer in the system, had a clear conscience. Nevertheless an official visit, for whatever reason, could not be taken lightly. He told the nurse to show them in.

When she had gone, Kazatkin crossed to the window. The snow was falling in blind, swirling clouds. From his third-floor window he could still make out the line of the Neva River and the buildings opposite. But to his left the Kirov Bridge had already disappeared into the gray-white storm of snowflakes.

He could see no way in which he had transgressed. But then he had friends who had disappeared in the last years who, he would have thought, were equally guiltless. He had never admitted this thought to himself before.

His nurse had known precisely what sort of officials the waiting men were. Kazatkin, too, by hardly more than a faint movement of her shoulders, had been left in no doubt.

What could the Cheka, the security police, want with him? His work was wholly nonpolitical. His research into the possibilities of self-diagnosis had no known Western parallel. It was an area he had developed himself as a young man during the great Leningrad siege. Throughout this interminable nine hundred days and nights, he had sat with the starving citizens of the city, listening to their last hopes, their last thoughts, their last dreams. Over time, reading the postmortem reports on this schoolteacher, that snow clearer, he had conceived the idea that the dreams of his patients somehow presaged their deaths. Perhaps, if they could be properly interpreted, dreams might suggest a diagnosis more accurate and conclusive than that made from the conventional examination of symptoms and tests.

Frightened now, he considered the papers he had written for the *Soviet Medical Journal*. Never had he suggested a mystery beyond rational comprehension.

His last paper was published less than a month ago. He could remember it word for word. There was surely nothing . . .

The nurse showed the two men through the door. Both wore dark blue overcoats, identical gray felt hats. Even the heavy shoes, he saw with dismay, were of identical make.

"You are required," they had said flatly, "to accompany us to Moscow."

Now, standing before the leader of the Soviet people, he was aware that on one level his brain continued to function. He noted Marshal Stalin's lack of height, the pockmarked cheeks, the apparently partially paralyzed left arm. But the words emanating from the figure behind the desk were lost on him.

"I said, Comrade Doctor, that I have read your paper."

Kazatkin's head jerked up. "On dreams, Comrade Marshal, my paper on dreams."

Stalin nodded, slowly filling his pipe. "Your theory interests me," he said. "Not the least because of the nature of my own dreams this last year."

Kazatkin nodded wordlessly.

Joseph Stalin circled the desk, prodding the tobacco into the bowl of his pipe. To his horror, the young doctor saw that the premier was barefooted; the toes splaying on the carpet were webbed. With a quick, jerky motion he averted his eyes.

"Are you a charlatan, Kazatkin?" Stalin inquired genially. "Or do you believe that a dream, or more, a number of dreams," he was speaking faster now, "a series of dreams, nightly even, can so haunt a man that they *must* have a significance."

Kazatkin shrunk away from him. "I believe, Comrade Marshal," he said, "that the subconscious, in certain circumstances, is perhaps capable of its own diagnosis."

"What circumstances?"

"Perhaps a cancer. Perhaps an enfeebled heart. It's a matter, however," Kazatkin said hurriedly, "of the correct interpretation being laid on the dream. The subconscious is like a gnome"—he laughed nervously—"a wicked fairy—a *bessy*, as we Russians say—misleading, dissembling the true knowledge which the body is communicating to it . . ."

Stalin grunted, wiping his nose with the back of his hand. Was the man a charlatan? he wondered. Somehow he didn't think so. The idea of a demon, a *bessy*, appealed to him. It was an attribute of genius: other men might struggle helplessly against the grinning maverick, but his, Joseph Stalin's, unique quality was to make a *bessy* of his own.

He nodded. As a theory of genius, it was not bad. The young doctor had clearly stumbled upon something.

"I dream," he said to Kazatkin. "I dream often. And you interpret dreams."

Kazatkin nodded, afraid.

"I am tormented by the prospect of sleep, Doctor."

"This is not unusual, Comrade Marshal," the doctor stuttered.

Stalin eyed him icily. "I am tormented because my sleep is plagued with dreams. With one single, recurring dream. I need the answer, Kazatkin. Give me the answer. I must know the meaning of my dream."

White-faced, Kazatkin watched the hooded, oriental eyes. Stalin's face loomed close, his warm, tobacco breath odorous on the doctor's cheek.

"Each night the dream returns . . ."

Silently, Kazatkin's lips moved in terror.

"Each night," the dictator said, "I dream I have five heads."

Secretary Poskrebyshev responded quickly to the bell. Opening the door of Stalin's room, he stopped dead.

Stalin was crouched beside his desk, hardly upright, like a cornered animal. The doctor was pressed back against the opposite wall, his teeth bared in terror.

With a movement of his head, Stalin indicated a scrap of paper on his desk. Poskrebyshev crossed the room quickly. On the paper, in Stalin's hand, was written Kazatkin's name. The secretary frowned and looked toward his master.

Half turning, Stalin stood over the desk. With the wet stem of his pipe, he drew a brown tobacco stain across the doctor's name. "Now," he whispered. "In the courtyard below. Where I can see it done."

It had stopped snowing, and the crust on the pavements was already freezing hard. Alexander Trenton walked at a slow, careful pace. He knew the way well enough through the half-derelict southern part of the city. Streetlights were rare, usually confined to corners where they cast pale yellow pools of light at the intersections of long streets of dark-shadowed high walls and shuttered factories.

In almost an hour he had passed no one. But as he began to inhale the carbolic reek of the Lakraska varnish plant, he knew that he was over halfway, and that the lights would become more frequent now as he approached the center of the city.

At the bridge, two blister-faced women pushed wide brooms at the heaped snow. Their heads were wrapped in flowered cloths, their legs bound with rags. They paused to watch as Trenton approached. He lifted a gloved hand in greeting, and one of the women smiled in reply.

The pavement here was well lit by the ornate cast-iron lamps crested with the double-headed eagles of tsarist days. At the center span of the bridge, he paused, leaning on the frozen iron rail. Across the city, the clocks began to strike. Below him lay the huge expanse of the Moskva River, which mirrored for at least half the year the somber gray tones of the shabby run-down city that sprawled along its banks. But in November, with the first real frosts, the river was transformed into an ice-white highway, spacious, pristine, clear of the slicks of oil and floating rubbish that disfigured it throughout the summer. The effect of the pristine river on Alexander was therapeutic. High on the bridge, he could feel the anesthetizing bite of the wind off the frozen water. Below, to the south, the view of the city blanketed with fresh snow appeared almost wholesome, like a postcard.

Following the Kremlin wall along the line of the Alexandrovski Gardens, Trenton promised himself he would not stop, would not look up at the one window high in the Pleshny Palace behind which Joseph Stalin was reputed to work. On a late summer evening, a small crowd of visitors or soldiers could always be seen staring up at that rectangle of light, hoping for a glimpse of a shadowy figure moving back and forth across the room. No one remembered how that particular window had come to be chosen. Certainly there had never been confirmation from the Kremlin. But there had never been denial either. And the myth had persisted.

It had begun to snow again as Trenton reached the Trinity Gatehouse, thin drifting flakes that swirled and danced around the battlements of the Kremlin wall.

As he passed, almost without his realizing it, his eye had turned toward the window. As ever, it was lighted. But now a figure stood looking down. Trenton stopped abruptly. At this distance, he had no certainty that it was Stalin. But the figure seemed, in silhouette, stocky, not tall. And his arm was raised, crooked, as if holding a pipe to his mouth.

He had never seen Stalin before, if this was indeed Stalin. Or at least he could not remember having seen him before. Alex's mother had recounted a thousand times their meeting with the young Red Army commander in Georgia when Alex was a child. But he remembered nothing. Nothing but a priest and his comic, puppet jerk on the end of a gallows rope.

He shuddered in the raw wind and stamped his feet. The figure remained at the window, and the thought crossed Trenton's mind that he could lift his arm and wave, perhaps even elicit some response from the unapproachable figure. But he felt no affection for the man. Fear, certainly. Respect? Perhaps a grudging respect for his ruthlessness and power. He considered what he did feel, what was uppermost among his feelings, and he lifted his arm. His gloved fist was clenched, and he shook it in anger at the dark shape in the window. In pathetic retribution for so many deaths, so many shattered dreams.

From somewhere over the Kremlin wall there was a snow-muffled sound, like a car backfiring. As if in response to Trenton's gesture, the figure moved, turned away and left the window. In the courtyard below Stalin's window, two men took away Kazatkin's body, dragging it toward a dark doorway. Watching from the corner, under the single courtyard lamp, Secretary Poskrebyshev noted the parallel lines in the snow made by the Leningrad doctor's heels.

CHAPTER
5

Gopak. The full significance of the military operation's code name was well known to Western analysts. As early as November 1946, intelligence agencies in Washington and London had received the first drafts of the Soviet battle plan for an attack on Allied forces in the British and American zones of Germany. Later, further drafts were pirated to the West. In its most recent version, Paris and the French and Belgian Channel ports were targeted as the primary objectives. They were to be seized by the two and a half million men of the Sixth, Fourth and Seventeenth Soviet Shock armies in a dash for Paris that would take but three weeks. The casualty rate was unimportant; only the successful completion of the mission mattered. In the preamble to *Gopak*, written, it was believed, by Stalin himself, Soviet Air Fleets II and IV were to be sacrificed, in a diversionary maneuver, to the far superior Allied air forces.

While the main elements of the plan became clear early on, the *purpose* of *Gopak* remained obscure. The United States had the atomic bomb. What nation would dare to test America's military superiority?

It was President Truman who realized the answer. It was Stalin himself who had devised *Gopak*. *Gopak* was the first strategy based on the theoretical reluctance of nations to use the new atomic weapons.

Gopak, Truman told the Pentagon's analysts, could bring the Soviet army to Paris. At that point the Soviets would negotiate for peace. While the U.S. could destroy the Soviet army with atomic bombs, they would have to destroy Paris as well. Stalin seemed willing to risk an atomic strike against Russia herself in the belief that the U.S. would be reluctant to massacre millions of Soviet citizens.

Gopak, Harry Truman told his generals, is a viable military strategy. No one but a madman would take the risk to implement it. But if a madman—and here Truman emphasized the word—*did* implement it, he might, depending on the United States' response, win the whole of Western Europe to the Channel coast.

What was essential, military experts realized, was to find out what the top Soviet military officers thought of *Gopak.* In the years to follow, a considerable part of Western intelligence efforts were directed toward assessing senior Soviet officers' reactions to the plan. They knew Marshal Zhukov thought *Gopak* was insane, suicidal. But he had been forced into retirement for his lack of support. Others, less internationally known generals, had simply disappeared when they voiced a lack of enthusiasm. Some were known to have been executed. The man who was most important, though not most senior in the Soviet hierarchy, was Soviet Chief of Staff General S. M. Shtemenko, who had not made his position on *Gopak* clear. Short, stocky, with a self-confidence that bordered on arrogance, the fifty-five-year-old Shtemenko was an enigma to Washington intelligence analysts. What would his reaction be if Joseph Stalin ordered his chief of staff to activate planning for *Gopak*? Would he refuse the order? Would he sabotage the order? Or did he feel, as some Soviet generals undoubtedly did, that the Red Army could take Paris and the Channel ports before America implemented an attack with atomic weapons? And that after that, the ball would be in the American president's court?

Where did Shtemenko stand? Each year a new evaluation of the Soviet general's response was drawn up in Washington. But as Soviet attitudes to the West in the 1950s became more antagonistic, no further information was available to help Western intelligence experts.

Later that night, following the courtyard execution, a call was placed to the Soviet chief of staff, who was asleep in bed with his wife.

"Always, throughout my life," a familiar voice slurred, "I've loved dancing."

Shtemenko listened to the familiar breathy laugh that followed.

"General Shtemenko . . ." There was a long pause.

"Comrade Stalin . . . ?" Shtemenko said.

In the silence that followed, Shtemenko's wife, Irina, watched her husband.

"Comrade Stalin, this is Chief of Staff Shtemenko at your orders . . ."

Sounds of a Ukrainian folk song, sung in an old man's cracked voice, came over the line. Shtemenko held the telephone toward his wife. Irina Shtemenka frowned.

"Mother of God," Irina whispered. "He's drunk."

The singing stopped. Suddenly, Stalin's voice boomed over the line. "General Shtemenko . . . where are you? Why are you hiding from me?" His voice rose in anger, then grew quieter. "Of course you're not hiding." For seconds the breathy laughter again issued from the receiver.

"Shtemenko . . . will you dance with me, Shtemenko?" Stalin's voice whispered down the line.

Shtemenko waited.

"Will you dance . . . ?" The madman's voice crooned a Kiev folk melody. "Will you dance? All, all Ukrainian lads love to dance the *Gopak*."

"The *Gopak*," Shtemenko said.

"All, all Ukrainian lads," the voice sang, "love to dance the *Gopak*. Love to dance the *Gopak*."

"Comrade Stalin," Shtemenko said, "does the comrade marshal mean to order *Gopak*?"

"Love to dance the *Gopak* . . ." the voice trailed away. The line buzzed and clicked.

Shtemenko replaced the receiver. His wife was sitting up in bed now, watching her husband.

"Irina," he said slowly. "I want you to pack a case and leave immediately. Drive to your grandmother's dacha in Kovets."

"Why are you sending me away?" she asked, a hand on his arm. "What has Marshal Stalin ordered?"

"It's possible that by tomorrow morning he will have forgotten," Shtemenko said.

He got out of bed and left the room to find a glass of water. When he returned, Irina was sitting on the side of the bed. She watched him while he sipped the water. "I've never seen you like this before," she said. "Are you afraid?"

"No." He paused. "I don't think so."

"You must tell me," she said. "What does Marshal Stalin mean? What is *Gopak*?"

"*Gopak* is a code word," he said slowly. "With it, Comrade Stalin has just placed me in charge of a surprise attack on Western Europe."

CHAPTER
6

Hal Jones was not a desk general. A professional soldier who had seen action with "Vinegar" Joe Stilwell before the war, Jones had shipped to North Africa in 1942, fought in Italy in '43 and jumped into Normandy on D day with Maxwell Taylor's 82nd Airborne. By the end of the war, considered at thirty-five too old to be in the field, he had accepted a posting to OSS. From there he had moved to intelligence, after a course in Russian studies at Cambridge, England. In the years that followed, he had become one of the most effective field officers in U.S. counterintelligence.

The fact that he was skirting middle age did not diminish the pleasure he derived from the company of younger women. Sarah Black, young, pretty, eager for a more worldly sophistication, equally enjoyed the company of older men. The happy discovery of their common interests in Copenhagen had led them, within a week or two of Hal's return to Washington, into an erratic and cheerfully casual relationship.

Unpredictable and eccentric, Sarah Black would ring at Hal's Georgetown apartment at any time, day or night, that caught her fancy. Sometimes she would totter in drunk from a party, looking for someone to listen to her unending litany of troubles with her guardian, Congressman Harry Hunter. At other times she would walk in, stripping off her clothes as she made her way straight for the bed. She was an overly rich, not overly interesting girl, as Hal discovered, but not one whose deficiencies extended to the bedroom. What they had, Hal admitted ruefully to himself, fell far short of a meaningful relationship, but since his arrival back in Washington there had been too many official meetings for him to look farther afield.

Nevertheless, he had to admit that there was *some* justification for the way she behaved. By the laws of caprice that too often seemed to determine such things, Hal had found himself thrown together with Congressman Hunter in weekly meetings of the powerful so-called Hay-Adams committee, in informal but influential military-political briefing sessions on intelligence matters. Harry D. Hunter was the vice-chairman of the committee. Half an hour into his first meeting, Hal's sympathy for Sarah had enormously increased.

The tone of their relationship had been set with the first question Hunter had addressed to Hal. "General," he had said, leaning forward, "could you explain to us how you allowed yourself to be forced out of the Soviet Union less than a month after you arrived there?" Though still in his thirties, Hunter was pink-faced and heavily jowled.

"In Moscow, Congressman," Hal said, "that's one of the risks of the game."

"I don't regard counterintelligence as a *game*," Hunter snapped.

"Nor, in anything but terminology, do I," Hal drawled, his pale blue eyes fixed on Hunter. "It's my *life* on the line out there."

"All right, General, I understand that," Hunter said, backing off. "But as you are aware, there is a major leak somewhere in the government that's supplying the most sensitive top-secret information to the Soviets. And I personally, along with certain members of the Senate, want results."

Hal nodded. It was depressingly obvious that Hunter planned to use the committee to promote the career of Congressman Harry D. Hunter. And behind Hunter stood the powerful figure of Senator Joe McCarthy.

Afterward, in the old-fashioned walnut-veneered elevator of the hotel, Major Jack O'Sullivan made one of his rare attempts at advising his boss. "General," he said cautiously, "can I tread, for a moment, on your private life?"

"Sarah?"

"And Uncle Harry. Does he know you're humping his niece, or ward, or whatever she is?"

"I don't know, Jack. Sarah could have said something."

"If she has, he could make it difficult for you."

"I'll remember your advice."

The elevator bumped gently on the ground floor. "I haven't given you any advice," O'Sullivan said.

Hal smiled. "You never do. Maybe that's why I take it so often. Come on, I'll buy you a drink at the Cascade Club. You can forget you're a married man for half an hour."

The night's snow had cast a becoming white mantle around the shoulders of the statue of the English Queen Victoria. Her crown sparkled with frost. From the far side, opposite her split cheekbone, the statue projected a certain plump majesty.

Alexander Trenton, letting himself out into the theater courtyard, glanced past the statue; it was early morning and still an hour or two from full daylight. The electric globe over his head shone palely. Alex turned to relock the door. In the shadow beyond the statue, he heard movement. He turned with more curiosity than alarm.

Zoya, Vassily Nozenkov's wife, stepped forward. She seemed to have shrunk within her fur coat. Before he could speak, she said: "Vassily didn't come home last night."

Alex knew Zoya as if she were a sister. With Vassily, Zoya and he had served together through the unbelievably cruel winter of 1942 and survived to see victory in 1943. All three of them had given their lives a thousand times in defense of their country. Alex had been best man at their wedding and had stood with them and drunk champagne under the great memorial in the Lenin Hills. He had gotten drunk at their celebrations and stood as witness at the naming of their twins.

They stood a yard or two apart in the freshly fallen snow. He wanted to say it meant nothing: that there were a thousand possible reasons Vassily might have been delayed, but Zoya had been the wife of an MGB officer far too long. "Have you called the Lubyanka?" he said.

"I telephoned at five this morning. Roy Morosov is the duty officer." She paused. "He refused to speak to me."

Alex stepped forward and hugged her to him.

"He wouldn't speak to me at six or seven either," she cried into his shoulder. "We both know what that means."

"I'll find out what's happened," he said.

"You know what Vassily was about to do?"

Involuntarily, his eyes darted toward the door.

"He was trying to get us all to the West."

From a long habit of remaining silent in the face of dangerous news, Trenton said nothing.

"Please, Alex, find out where he is."

Alex nodded, dry mouthed. "As soon as I learn anything, I'll come to the apartment."

"He's been arrested," she said, staring at the ground. "I know it."

"Perhaps not. Perhaps—"

She raised a gloved hand to silence him. "As soon as you find out anything, Alex . . ."

He watched her hurry through the sagging gates. She turned briefly, without waving, and disappeared in the direction of the Arbat.

Hal Jones liked his apartment. It was in a large, older building constructed in the optimistic days immediately after World War I. The bathrooms had large brass taps on bathtubs and basins; the eight-paneled doors were a rich polished mahogany. The apartment consisted of living room, two bedrooms and an office—which the Security Section from Langley had ruined with a steel-plated door, steel-shuttered windows and a steel-mesh inner lining. Hal couldn't stand working in the office—he used it as more of a vast walk-in safe.

The alterations to the office were the only real signs of Jones's occupation, although there was a .38 pistol concealed in the overstuffed chair (another expensive Langley security measure) and a radio "panic button" under the bookcase. But to all appearances, it was simply a roomy, comfortable Washington apartment, with a spacious kitchen big enough to eat pancakes and eggs in the morning after. Girls liked the place.

Emerging from the shower, Hal Jones glanced at the carriage clock he had bought years ago in Moscow. If he phoned Sarah now, she should be back from the airport.

He dialed from memory.

"Jennifer Hunter speaking."

"I'd like to speak to Sarah, please," he said, hooking the telephone under his chin.

The woman's voice at the other end was cool rather than hostile. "Sarah's away at the moment," she said. "She had to fill in for another girl on a flight to Lisbon. She won't be back until Tuesday."

Hal tried to guess the woman's age. Fifty, maybe. Those carefully modulated tones made it difficult to be sure.

"Who shall I say called?"

Hal was certain she already knew. "My name is Jones," he said.

"Mr. Jones," she confirmed, pausing for him to give his first name.

"Mr. Jones," he repeated flatly. "I'll call again when she gets back. Or perhaps you could have her call me."

There was silence on the other end of the line. He imagined Mrs. Harry D. Hunter shifting from one foot to the other the weight of her sizable rump.

"Mrs. Hunter?"

"I'm still here."

"I said, perhaps you could have her call me."

"I heard you," her voice was patient now, as if explaining to a child. "I just wondered why a brigadier general should choose to call himself *Mr.* Jones."

"My apologies. There seemed no point in putting the record straight. Sarah would know it was me. As I gather you did."

"Yes," she said, "Sarah's told me about you. You met on a flight from Moscow, I believe."

As he waited for what was coming next, he stretched out and poured himself a large Glenmorangie malt whisky.

"I don't know you, of course, but Sarah has spoken well of you."

"You make it sound like a funeral oration, Mrs. Hunter."

She laughed—a surprisingly pleasant laugh. "I didn't mean to." She paused again to change the tone. "There is, of course, a very great difference in your ages."

"That's so." He let the smooth malt roll over his tongue.

"As her guardians, General, we are required either to approve or disapprove of her friends."

"Yes . . . ?" The flavor of the malt exploded deep at the back of his mouth. He wondered if he should just hang up there and then.

"For your information, I have not, in fact, told my husband about your friendship with Sarah."

"I appreciate it," he said, lifting his eyebrows to the mouthpiece of the telephone.

"Of course, my husband would not approve."

"Is that so?"

"I'm sorry to be saying all this to a complete stranger, General, but believe me, I'm doing it for Sarah's sake. Frankly, she and my husband have not been on the best of terms recently."

"I'm sorry to hear that, Mrs. Hunter." He finished his whisky. "Just what is it you're trying to say."

"I think you know, General." He could almost smell her expensive middle-age perfume, Tarascon by Borgueil or some such.

"Yes," he said, "I'm well aware. Perhaps you could give her the message to call me anyway."

At the other end, the line clicked dead.

CHAPTER
7

The MGB secret-police officers, some in civilian clothes, some in green MGB uniforms with red collar tabs, trooped down the stone staircase toward the basement, talking of families, new postings, the latest scores of the Moscow soccer team on its European tour.

Roy Morosov glanced at himself in the huge, ornate mirror on the middle landing. "You know," he said to Alex, "when I was at the Frunze Military Academy, I was a talent spotted by a Moscow Dynamo coach."

Alex grunted and moved on down the staircase.

Roy Morosov leaped two steps at a time to catch up with him. "It's true. At the Frunze we had the best academy team in the whole army. I played left fullback. I'm left-handed, you see." He made a series of violent beating movements with his left hand. "Anyway, I turned down the opportunity. The director of the Frunze said I was already singled out for the MGB."

None of the officers was more than mildly curious about why they should have been summoned to the basement of the Lubyanka police building on Dzerzhinsky Square. Most knew only the office sections or interrogation rooms where they worked; perhaps there would be a political lecture in one of the lecture halls.

Only Alexander Trenton in the group of twenty or thirty officers was uneasy. Detaching himself from the others to descend the staircase beside Pavel Petrov, his stepfather, he detected a certain grim satisfaction in the older man's signal to join him. Alex had known Petrov long enough to guess that it meant some score was to be settled, some wrong about to be righted.

"The lecture rooms are to the right, Pavel Semyonovich," Alex said, pointing to the corridor at the bottom of the stairs. Following more senior officers, the young MGB officers were already flowing left toward the area where the heating furnaces were installed.

"We're not going to the lecture rooms," Petrov said with a tight smile.

"May I ask what this is all about?"

"You'll know soon enough." Petrov stopped at the foot of the stairs, his face turned up toward Trenton's. "And incidentally, stay away from that girl. I got a report on my desk from the Old Stables office. You were there."

"I replaced the bicycle I ruined."

"If an MGB officer wants a woman, he doesn't have to go to the Old Stables. Stay away from her. She's a semi-illegal in Moscow. I've an important future mapped out for you, Alex. Perhaps even very important. But it doesn't include whores from Perlinka Lane."

Entering the furnace room, Petrov joined the group of uniformed colonels standing apart. Trenton looked around to see whom he knew and drifted toward a small group of administrative officers who stood beside a great mound of coke that rose almost to the ceiling of the basement. The furnaces themselves, six enormous iron monsters dating from the tsarist days when the building served as the offices for the All-Russian Insurance Company, stood, three glowing red, three unlit, along one wall of the room.

"Did General Petrov tell you what's up?" Roy Morosov asked. "Everybody on our floor has been very secretive about it."

Trenton shrugged. "I know no more than you do."

"Techniques of document burning?" Morosov whispered, as

the door of one of the huge furnaces was hooked back with a long iron poker.

Trenton watched the fury of the blazing coke as the draft was opened by one of the overalled stokers.

"Comrade General, officers of the security services," one of the colonels began. He stepped forward across the carpet of coke dust. The younger officers fell silent.

"Comrades," the colonel continued in a lower voice, "you all know former MGB Captain Vassily Pavlovich Nozenkov. I have brought you down here because each one of you knew him personally, worked with him, perhaps even knew his family." He paused. "The traitor Nozenkov has been interrogated and has confessed to having sunk to the lowest possible level of degradation. He is guilty of making contact with the American embassy. He is guilty of initiating moves to leave the Soviet Union illegally. He is guilty of offering secret information to the American enemy."

The colonel hesitated. Looking down, he pushed a piece of coke back and forth with the toe of his polished boot. "I could speak to you for hours about the infamy of this man, this imperialist agent, Nozenkov. But actions speak louder than words . . ."

The colonel turned toward the back of the basement. Through an open door, uniformed men were dragging forward a crumpled figure in prison shirt and loose cotton trousers. He was barely recognizable any longer. His head rolled backward on his shoulders, and Alex could see the bruises which distorted his face, the shapeless nose, the sunken, haunted eyes.

"Actions, comrades, speak louder than words," the colonel repeated. "Rubbish should be incinerated."

At a quick jerk of the colonel's head, the two uniformed men lifted Vassily Nozenkov off his feet and rushed him forward. The prisoner's hoarse cry echoed among the piles of coke as his body was propelled through the furnace door. For a moment, the opening spat and crackled angrily, then the shape of the body was obscured in leaping flame. One of the stokers slammed the furnace door closed.

Alexander Trenton stood in sick silence as Petrov led the

staff officers toward the stairs. One by one, the junior officers turned away. Nobody spoke as they climbed the stairs and dispersed through the pale green corridors of the Lubyanka to their own offices and their own thoughts.

"I come here," Brigadier General Jones said, "to look at the girls."

The bearded man in the black overcoat sitting next to him at the bar of Washington's Cascade Club raised his hands, palms upward. "What Amazons," he said, watching the show girls cross the restaurant.

"A girl has to be six feet tall to get a first audition," Hal Jones said. "But once accepted as a Snowdrop Girl, she becomes one of the queens of Washington. Politicians want to take her to dinner. Industrialists send her gold trinkets, embassies like to have her at their parties. And even our own congressmen have been known to be interested."

"Ah." Jacob Vishniak nodded gently. "Now I understand your interest in Snowdrop Girls, General Jones. Your interest is not quite what it seems."

"Not quite," Jones conceded, smiling. "But I try not to be too stuffy about my work."

For a few moments they watched the two girls in their ankle-strap heels, half a foot taller than the waiter who was taking their fur coats.

"The Irish redhead is Theresa O'Leary. They say she works for the French embassy." Jones pointed vaguely in her direction with the stem of his pipe.

"And does she?"

"If she does, she's two-timing the Canadians."

Another girl came down the steps of the sunken bar. From her height, the silk dress she wore and her hip-length silver fox fur, even Vishniak recognized her as a show girl. For a few moments, she stood at the bottom of the steps, imperiously surveying the men at the bar. Her eyes lingered for a moment on General Jones and passed on.

Hal turned his back to her.

"One of yours?" Vishniak said.

"You're very quick, Professor," Hal said, picking up his glass.

"So, Jacob," he continued in a low voice, "what has the Jewish underground got for me on life in the Kremlin today?"

The barman served the drinks and removed their old glasses. Vishniak took up his whiskey sour and spun slowly on his bar stool. The dancer in the fox fur, he noticed, had joined the other girls at a corner table. "For Russia's Jews, these are bad days."

"I see attacks on Jewish cosmopolitanism in every edition of *Pravda*. It's almost beginning to sound like the old Nazi paper, *Der Sturmer*. But why?"

Vishniak sipped his drink. "I wouldn't like to say I knew," he said. "In particular, it would be dangerous to think of it in terms of one man's anti–Semitism."

"Even if that man is Stalin himself?"

Vishniak moved his broad, round shoulders inside the black topcoat. "An atmosphere is being created. Today in Moscow, no senior figure in the government or army feels safe. A member of the Presidium this winter would have more chances of being shot in the snow in some prison courtyard than of dying of a heart attack."

"What is Stalin up to, for God's sake?"

"Hal," Vishniak said carefully, "it is perfectly possible that the Soviet Union today is in the hands of an uncontrollable lunatic."

Hal Jones pursed his lips. "I know you, Jacob," he said slowly. "You're not a man to run scare stories."

"Thank you for your trust."

"I believe you, Jacob. But I'm not sure to what extent I can persuade my government. I know your sources are good, but there are many well-placed American experts who believe the Jewish Intelligence Center—and Jacob Vishniak, its director—have a vested interest in exaggerating anti–Semitism in the Soviet Union. They see you as liable to exaggerate *any* aspect of Stalinist terror."

The old man nodded. "I've thought of this problem. Before I came to meet you tonight, I held a meeting with my committee. I have been given their permission to reveal to you one of our principal Kremlin sources. I have just one condition: that you restrict this information to only those with an *absolute* need to know."

Hal hesitated. "All right."

The old man stroked his beard. "A number of senior Soviet functionaries have Jewish wives. One of them, unknown to her husband, has for the last two years supplied us with information on the highest possible level. She is the wife of the Soviet Foreign Minister, Vyacheslav Molotov."

"Jesus! We're spending millions of dollars on gathering information, and the Jewish Intelligence Center, operating out of three dusty rooms above Mike's Delicatessen, has a direct line to Molotov's wife!"

Vishniak smiled. "Not bad, would you say?"

"Not bad, Yakov," Jones said in Russian. "Not bad." He thought for a moment. "Does your contact say anything about the new American administration?"

Vishniak shrugged. "Perhaps it's hard for Washington to accept, but at the moment the change of administration is not uppermost in the Presidium's mind."

"What is?"

"The state of Joseph Stalin's health. The question Molotov, Beria and Khrushchev are asking themselves is will he live long enough to commence with his plans."

"And they are?"

"Who knows? A purge of Red generals? A purge of the government? A break with Red China? Even the invasion of Yugoslavia. No one knows. Stalin keeps his own council. He's a terrifying contradiction—evil, calculating and possibly now in an advanced stage of mental illness."

"What do you know about his health, his physical health?"

"He's seventy-three years old. Vastly overweight for a man who's only five feet four inches tall. He drinks excessively. Still smokes, although he's been trying to give it up for the last year. He sleeps badly, mostly fully dressed on a couch in his office. But now there's a new development. About ten days ago a doctor was called to the Kremlin from the Leningrad Neurological Institute. His specialty was interpreting dreams as an aid to diagnosis. He was shot in the Kremlin grounds immediately afterward."

"Jesus! What was the diagnosis?"

"God knows." Vishniak slipped off his stool. "I must go. I have one further item for you, however."

"The most important of all, if I know your Jewish sense of theater."

"Perhaps," Vishniak said. "We don't yet know what it means."

"Go on."

"General Shtemenko, the Chief of Staff of the Soviet Land Forces, has disappeared."

"Arrested?" Hal sat bolt upright on his bar stool. "Shtemenko arrested?"

"Disappeared. For the moment that's all we know."

CHAPTER
8

The sudden heavy fall of snow had blunted the cold edge of the winter evening, bringing thousands of Muscovites out onto the streets to watch the fireworks celebration. Over Red Square, explosions splintered the sky, and cascades of man-made stars showered the rooftops of the city. Katya tucked her arm casually through Trenton's as they walked together along Krasnoprudnaya Ulitza.

"So you really are a prince," she said, amused. "An American prince."

"Not a prince. My grandfather was more like a minor count in tsarist days."

"But you really come from a landowning family in America?"

"Apparently. For what it's worth."

"And your father, the count, is he still alive?"

"He died many years ago."

"Leaving all his lands to his only son?"

"You're a romantic, Katya. By the time he was born, the lands had been sold."

"But even without the lands, he was still a count. Count Trenton?"

He smiled. "There are no counts or princes in America."

"Ah . . ."

"In reality, Katya, I am an officer working for the State Security Ministry, who has a tyrannical boss and an alcoholic wife. And who should not be out to see the fireworks in Red Square with a very pretty girl like you."

She took off her glove and, thrusting deep into his overcoat pocket, found his hand. "Did you especially want to go to Red Square?" she asked.

"Where else?"

"Perhaps I should take you to the Kalpretta," she said thoughtfully.

"The Kalpretta?"

"You don't know it?"

"I remember that, until it was evacuated at the beginning of the war, there was a Kalpretta machine-gun factory."

"The same. The Kalpretta is my favorite place in Moscow."

"Then we should go."

For a few moments she was silent. "What is it, Katya?" he asked. "Is something wrong?"

"No," she said slowly. "No. I'm just wondering about the Kalpretta."

"If you'd sooner not go . . ."

"Perhaps first," she said carefully, "we should go to Anton's."

He smiled. "There are places in Moscow I know nothing of. What is Anton's?"

"You'll see," she said mysteriously. "It is hard to get in unless you know people."

"And what happens there?"

"Exciting things," she said grimly. "All manner of exciting things."

"Do you want to go?"

"Perhaps we should," she said. "Then afterward we'll see if we would enjoy going together to the Kalpretta."

He understood that it was some sort of test. Though how the test might work, he could not guess. They ducked through dark alleys and crossed strips of wasteland where men crouched around fires in the bitter night and lifted bottles of spirit to their mouths. Katya led him past the derelicts without comment.

At last they entered a long, low hut, and Alex found himself in a large, smoke-filled room. Opposite him, at the far end of the room, a huge oil drum was set on its side on rough legs. A chimney had been welded to it at the back and a hinged door cut into the front. The oil drum glowed red-hot, radiating a fiery heat into the room. Katya led him to the long, rough bar. The men lifted a hand to greet her, then stared hard at Trenton. There were few women.

"What kind of bar is this?" he asked her.

"Men gamble," she said.

"On what?"

"On almost anything."

"Gambling is illegal under the 1937 Constitution."

She looked at him, not contemptuously but in a kindly, exasperated way. "You have a great, great deal to learn," she said. "We should buy a drink," she continued, in a low voice. "It's our entrance ticket."

"We could just go."

She shook her head. "No. Not yet."

From under one of the tables a chain rattled, and a large, blunt-nosed dog appeared, growling. His owner jerked aggressively on the chain, which Trenton could see was strapped to his wrist, and the dog slunk back under the table.

"Let's have half a liter, barman," Katya said. Trenton registered the arrival of another man. He was tall—head and shoulders above the crowd—and his glance was keen-eyed, unlike the sullen, absent looks of the others. He wore a fur hat and a woven poncho. Slamming the door loudly, he shouted over the clamor, "All right you filth, you can stop the prancing."

As the noise subsided slightly, he went on, "Listen, rabble, we've got a real fight for you tonight."

The crowd quieted and parted in deference to the newcomer. Trenton looked with astonishment at the man's companion. Next to the newcomer was a dwarf, no higher than the man's hip, dressed in a sleeveless leather jerkin. Around his neck was a thick leather collar. His face and arms were hideous, torn and disfigured with massive scars. A recent wound, still black and shiny, traced a jagged contour around the line of his jaw. As the two men approached, Trenton noticed the customer with the dog get up quickly and drag the growling animal over to a table near the red-hot oil drum. The two men seemed to command the attention of the room without effort.

"Let's have some vodka, comrade." The big man addressed the barman loudly. A rumble of approbation stirred among the men at the bar.

"For the smart fellows, I'm taking bets now." The big man scanned the faces around him challengingly.

As the crowd drew round the strange pair, offering their ruble notes, the man with the dog called out to the tall man from his seat by the stove. "Glad to see you, Zvov." His tone was artificially convivial. "I thought you must have backed out tonight."

The big man responded quickly. "I'd be throwing money away, wouldn't I, Pavel?"

The man with the dog looked down at his big hands and absently rattled the heavy chain strapped to his wrist, as if contemplating the answer. From the shadow under the table, the dog looked up at its owner peevishly. "We'll see, Zvov, we'll see," the man said.

The atmosphere in the fetid, smoke-filled room was charged with tension. Trenton and Katya sat quietly at the far end of the bar. As they watched, the dwarf crouched down on all fours and began to scan the floor with his hands, as if looking for something he had lost. Every now and then he stopped at a spot and looked around the room, obviously trying to commit the place to memory. Trenton guessed that he was checking the floor for uneven patches, in preparation for a fight. But what sort of a fight? A wrestling match between the dwarf and the burly man with the dog? It seemed unlikely the dwarf would stay on his feet long, despite his obvious strength.

At the bar, the dwarf's companion signaled for silence and bellowed across the room, "Stand back, you rabble—give the contestants room to show their paces."

The crowd shouted enthusiastically back at him. Only the man with the dog and a few supporters who had gathered around him remained silent.

In the long room, the men pushed back against the walls. The center was now clear, except for two huge wooden posts at opposite corners, which supported the wooden roof. Next to one of the posts, the dwarf stood preparing himself, while Zvov collected the final bets. The dwarf produced a bottle of yellow oil and offered it for scrutiny to the onlookers before rubbing it into his arms and neck. Then he moved over to the far post and placed the bottle next to it. Finally, with the help of his companion, the dwarf buckled a wide leather belt around his waist and attached himself by a short chain to the post. As Zvov drew back to his place behind the dwarf's corner, the tiny brutish figure crouched down on his heels and stretched his arms out in front of him, rubbing his hands together. Then he ran forward suddenly, testing the tension of the chain, and was pulled back sharply as it reached its full length at the center of the room. His face was set in some hideous expression of satisfaction. As he returned to his original position and crouched on his heels, he shouted over the buzz of talk, "Right, Pavel—I'm ready for you!"

Men stepped quickly aside as Pavel came forward, dragging the dog behind him. Trenton heard the terrifying sound of the dog snarling frenziedly as it was restrained on its chain. As he again looked over at the dwarf, now poised on his knees, arms held out in front of him, Alex realized with horror what the contest was to be.

"Ready, dwarf?" Pavel shouted gruffly. "Once I let him go you'll have to be fast as lightning."

The dwarf nodded, staring in front of him, licking his scarred lips. In the background, the dog pawed at the floor. As Pavel pushed quickly toward the center of the room, men shrank against the wall and the animal leaped forward, straining against Pavel's hold on the chain. The big man checked the animal fiercely and dragged it toward the post opposite the dwarf. Deftly he released the strap on his wrist and wrapped it around the post.

The dog attacked first. Alex stared in horror as the dwarf recoiled from the rush and pulled back quickly out of the animal's reach. He could see now that the chains had been measured so that each contestant could retreat just out of reach of the other to regroup. The dog sprang forward immediately, eager, bloodthirsty. Then the dwarf attacked, fists clenched, punching with incredible power at the dog's face and neck. The crowd in the small room roared at the fury of the attack, and Zvov passed among them, collecting more money, shouting obscene encouragement at his companion. The audience roared again as the dog drew first blood, a deep gash in the dwarf's forearm. The dwarf drew back again, taunting, and the dog hurled itself to the full length of its chain. The links snapped noisily against each other with every attempt. Behind the lunging animal, its owner stood quietly with a bowl of vinegar in his hands, watching.

The glass in Alex's hand was empty. He looked toward Katya, and she stretched out her hand and rested it on his arm. But her face was as determined as ever.

The fight was now reaching a climax. A human scream cut the quiet in the bar. The onlookers began to chant loudly in support of the dwarf, stamping their feet on the wooden floor, but Alex could guess, from the desperate fury in the dwarf's cry, that the dog was winning. He looked at the barman, who shrugged.

He felt nausea rise in his stomach. Again the dwarf let out a terrifying scream. In the sudden silence, the snarling of the dog and the clattering of its claws on the wooden floor filled the room. Then there was a sudden thud, and another. The men began to roar again, and Alex, despite himself, twisted in his chair to watch. The dwarf was on his feet before the dog, shaking its neck and head with a series of perfectly executed blows. In the bizarre atmosphere of the wooden hut, Trenton watched the dog reel, stumble forward and collapse, while the bloodstained dwarf fell upon it, his overlarge hands throttling it to death.

Outside again, crossing the strip of wasteland, Katya walked apart from Trenton, her hands deep in her pockets. "What did you think?" she asked.

"I was sickened," he said. "As you expected me to be." His anger caused a tightness in his throat. "Do you enjoy that depravity?"

"No."

"Then why do you watch it? Why did you take me to watch it?"

"Watch what?" she asked airily.

"You know what I'm talking about."

"But how can such a scene exist, comrade?" She leaned toward him with mock earnestness. "Such depravity, as you so accurately describe it, cannot exist in the Soviet Union. De-

pravity, after all, is the result of the contradictions of a cap-
italist society. Did we really see what you imagined tonight?
Did we see all this is the capital city of the Soviet Union?"

"You are crazy, Katya," he said vehemently. "Stay away from
there."

She nodded, almost bowed. "Yes, Comrade Captain."

They walked on against the drift of people. Whole families
pushed by them, their heads turned toward the eruptions of
light over Red Square. His anger began to subside. In its place
was a feeling of perplexity.

"Do you love your mother?" she asked suddenly.

"I suppose so," he said cautiously. "She is not a simple
woman. People don't have simple reactions to her. Even me. I
admire her, but I know there are many things about her not to
admire."

"And the decision to stay in Russia, was that one of the
things you admire—or not?"

She had removed her hand from his pocket. He looked at
this slender blond girl walking a pace apart from him. Was she
really only eighteen? What sort of life experience had enabled
her to force to the surface in ten minutes all the doubts that he
had kept hidden for so many years?

He made one further attempt at evasion. "It's too far away to
admire or not to admire. She simply decided to devote her life
to the Revolution."

"She devoted *your* life, too."

"Yes," he said slowly. "Yes, she did."

"And are you grateful, Alex—or not?"

She stopped, and he slid to a halt, turning to face her. Com-
ets trailing fiery tails rose in an arc, exploding brightly against
the night sky. "It's wrong of me to ask these questions," she
said, "knowing you so little. And yet how else can we know
each other better?"

Perhaps if he had not been drinking most of the day he
would have drawn back there. Perhaps if he had not seen Vassily Nozenkov hurled like trash, living, into the furnace, he
would have silenced her. Perhaps if he had not been softened
up by the horror of the fight at Anton's . . . Instead, he spoke
words he had never given voice to before, even in his furious
arguments with his mother, Vanessa. "I'm a Party member," he

said recklessly, "but beyond that, what I am I don't know. How can anybody know, living in today's Russia? Since the war, I've seen the dead laid out in rows by the wayside. I've seen whole villages, townships marched off to hard-labor camps. I've seen innocent people punched and flogged. Today I saw a friend . . . executed. We still live in tsarist Russia, Katya. We live under the Red tsar."

He watched her face soften into something warmer than a smile. With her arms, she encircled his waist, hugging him to her, her mouth warm against his cheek.

"Will you take me to the Kalpretta?" he asked her.

"Where else would we go," she said, releasing him, "on the night of Joseph Stalin's feast day."

Turning off Krasnoprudnaya Street, Katya led Alex Trenton into a maze of alleys between the railway and the Yelockhovsky Cathedral.

Occupying the whole of the street corner, a shattered brick-and-steel structure rose gaunt and deserted. Fireworks played across the sky behind the broken walls.

"This is the Kalpretta?" he said.

"Do you like it?"

He waved his gloved hand in bewilderment. "I expected some Palace of Sport and Culture. A remote, little-used Gorky Park."

"How long have you lived in Moscow?"

"Since I was a child," he said.

She laughed up at him. "But then princes live such sheltered lives."

They were entering now a narrow brick alley. Beyond the end, he could hear the sound of locomotives being shunted in a not too distant freight yard. Suddenly, a heavy man's shape was silhouetted against the pale light at the end of the narrow alley. The man picked his way toward them and bade them a courteous good evening as he passed.

"Katya," Alex said, "for God's sake where is it we're going?"

"Patience, your honor," she mocked him. "Patience, Comrade Prince."

She was leading him by the hand now, first through a brick archway and down a half-flight of steps. A man and a girl were

bargaining on the stairway as they passed. Other people
emerged from deep shadow, carrying sacks on their shoulders
or struggling across the debris with heavy suitcases. Somewhere not far off, it seemed to Alex, he could hear music.

Katya stopped before a heavy wooden door that seemed to
lead into the heart of the Kalpretta factory. Opening it, she led
Alex down past shallow alcoves that held candles and lanterns
which threw soft yellow light on the brick vaulted roof. The
music was louder now, and the sound of voices rose toward
them. From the noise, there were not a few people but dozens,
perhaps hundreds.

They passed through the doors at the bottom of the stairs.
To Alex, it was a fittingly extraordinary climax to an extraordinary day.

A gigantic cellar stretched out in front of them—lantern lit,
smoky—a vast market crammed with people. Line after line of
stalls festooned with clothing, vegetables, old furs, bicycle
parts, books, windup record players, secondhand boots, clocks,
icons, bric-a-brac, vodka, hanging sausages . . .

For a few moments, Trenton stared in astonishment. Katya,
beside him, laughed.

"What in God's name is this place?" he said.

She took his arm and plunged into the crowds. "The Kalpretta Market," she said. "It's where the soldiers bring their
loot from occupied Germany. You can buy anything here," she
told him proudly. "Things you haven't seen in a shop since
long, long before the war."

Trenton looked around at the Moscow *babushkas*, ordinary
housewives and their husbands, soldiers, young people hand in
hand . . . "But aren't all these people worried about the authorities?" he asked. "This is an illegal market, it's a crime
against the state to buy and sell like this."

"The authorities!" She shrugged contemptuously. "They
know of the Kalpretta. It suits their purposes. It gets goods
circulating in the system. I wouldn't mind wagering there's a
Kalpretta Market in every city in the Soviet Union."

A group of perhaps twenty or thirty people stood at the
planked bar. Each one, Trenton noticed, wore a stall-holder's
apron with a money pocket sewn across the waist. They
seemed to be of all ages, some barely more than children, oth-

ers in their early twenties, yet others in their fifties and sixties. Munching sausage and drinking vodka from half-liter bottles, they exuded a cheerful, almost gypsy air, their banter laced with insult, their laughter loud and uninhibited. It crossed Alex's mind that not since the end of the war had he seen a gathering in Moscow as relaxed as this.

"These"—Katya embraced them all with a gesture—"are my friends."

She moved among them, kissing cheeks and shaking hands. Behind her, Trenton found himself similarly engulfed, kissed robustly, a bottle thrust toward him and a fat end of sausage pushed into his hand.

"Alexander, eh?" said a fourteen-year-old, his face streaked with grime, wearing a leather cap and tattered clothes, something out of Dickens. He washed down his sausage with a great gulp of vodka. "I'm Nico."

"You have a stall here?" Trenton asked tentatively.

"No," the boy said proudly. "I carry my stock with me. I'm known as Nico the watch man." He pulled from inside his ragged coat a leather belt to which was attached a dozen scratched and dented watches. "For a friend of Katya, I could let you have one for eighteen rubles."

"I have a watch, thank you, Nico." Trenton eased his sleeve back to let the boy see his watch. "But something you can tell me as a friend of Katya: Who are all these people?"

"We're all the same," the boy said. "Just market people. Mostly we're orphans who started coming down here to deal a clock or a pair of boots or whatever we could lay hands on. Anya, the girl next to Katya, she's a general's daughter, so she says."

"Is she really?"

"Perhaps. It wouldn't be the first general our comrade uncle in the Kremlin has sent to Siberia."

Trenton looked at the sharp-tongued boy in surprise. "That's not the sort of thing you say to strangers, Nico."

It was the boy's turn to look surprised. "You're a friend of Katya's," he said.

"And that's enough, is it?"

"Of course." Nico grinned cheekily.

By the time Katya came back, dancing had started to the

music of a battered piano. "I'm sorry I left you," she said, "but I had a little business to transact."

"Nothing for me this week?" Nico pushed forward. "I pay the best price in the Kalpretta."

"That's not what I heard from the last contact I gave you," Katya said with a grimace. "Twelve German watches, and you offered a thief's price."

"Well." Nico shrugged defensively. "He'd stolen them himself, hadn't he?"

She took Trenton's arm and led him to a trestle table.

"I don't understand this talk," Alex said. "What is it you do for these people?"

They sat down and he pushed his half-liter across to her.

"At the Stables," she said, "I meet officers just back from Germany or Czechoslovakia. They have Western goods— watches, furs, blankets. I put them in touch with dealers here at the Kalpretta," she said, laughing. "It's a free-market system."

Trenton shook his head. "I had no idea such things were done in Moscow."

"Many things are done in Moscow that were never mentioned in the Nineteenth Party Congress. Here," she said, with that sudden change of pace he had begun to associate with her, "American cigarettes. Take them."

She dropped a pack of Lucky Strikes on the table. Alex picked up the gleaming red-and-white cellophane-wrapped package. He knew they were worth twenty rubles or more on the black market.

"I can't take these."

"Take them," she said. "A present."

"Katya. . ." He fiddled with the package in his hand. "How did you come to be in Moscow?"

"You mean what am I doing in Moscow without a permit, a *propiska*?"

"Yes."

"My parents brought me to Moscow. My father was a senior Party official in charge of recruitment in Latvia at the end of the war. He did so well he was invited to Moscow. A promotion."

"And?"

"He fell from grace. One night he didn't come home."

"He was arrested?"

"Nobody ever said. My mother spent weeks with all the others at the Central Committee Office asking for information. But there was none. Then she began to write letters. To very senior people my father had worked with. And one day she was arrested for an economic offense. Profiteering, they said."

"How old were you?"

"I was twelve. They took me to a state orphanage. I learned a lot in my two years there. How to lie and steal, and much more. When I was fourteen I decided the Kalpretta was my home."

"You ran away?"

"I drifted away. The orphanage was chaos, hundreds of children without documents, some even without names. The sons and daughters of the war dead and the others, the thousands and thousands who had simply disappeared. It wasn't difficult to leave."

"So you came to the Kalpretta."

"And later, much later, to the Old Stables."

He opened the pack of Lucky Strikes and passed her one. She took it, inhaling as he lit it for her.

"We're both foreigners, in a way," she said.

"Do you want to go back to Latvia?"

She looked at him, her gray eyes narrowed under the line of her eyebrows. "I want to leave the Soviet Union," she said. "I want to go somewhere, anywhere, that is not part of the Soviet Union."

"Be careful, Katya," he said. "Even here there could be people who report to the militia. There are people like that everywhere."

"What more can they do to me?" she said wildly. "They've taken my parents. They've taken my country. In return they've given me the dignity of labor the constitution guarantees every citizen—in the Old Stables at Perlinka Lane."

"I'm not by any means sure this is a wise move," Hal said as he and Sarah mounted the marble staircase.

"It's Jennifer's birthday, and I'm expected to be here," Sarah replied. "When you see the guests, you'll understand why I need help."

She opened the double doors onto a long, opulently furnished room peopled with even more opulently attired guests.

"Before we do anything, I want you to meet Jennifer. If there is an ally in the enemy camp, she's it."

She left Hal and pushed quickly through the cluster of guests. For an instant he lost sight of her. But in a moment she returned, drawing by the hand a woman in her early forties, dark haired and full figured, in a flame-colored silk dress. It took Hal a moment to register that this tall, elegant, beautiful woman was Sarah's guardian. In that moment Sarah had disappeared among the other guests.

"So you're the tall, handsome, gray-haired, debonair lover," Jennifer Hunter said.

"If you say so," Hal agreed.

She smiled. "It's a pleasant evening. Lots of old friends. I'm happy. I'm in no mood to do battle."

"Good." Hal steered her to a corner of the room. "Because any belligerence I might have had is slipping away fast."

"Why might you have felt belligerent?"

"Well, Mrs. Hunter, I don't like being taken for a lecherous gun-slinging cowboy from the wrong side of the river. At heart, I'm really a very decent fellow. Not at all unlike your friends."

"Put up your six-shooter," she said. She had a very charming smile. "You've made your point."

She turned and signaled past the curtaining to a part of the room blocked from Hal's view. "Sarah didn't get you a drink."

"She was too anxious to introduce me to you."

The butler came forward, carrying a tray with two glasses of champagne. Not much less than Hal's height, he had the perfectly composed butler's face. He bowed slightly, proffering the tray.

They each took a glass. "For reasons that are now unclear to me," Hal said, "I had the impression that you were fat, ill-favored and fast on the way to advanced middle age."

"That's because you've been listening to the Washington gossip about my handsome young husband marrying me for my money," she said coolly.

He lifted his glass. "I don't think any man would need an ulterior motive to marry you," he said.

"You've embarrassed me," she said, blushing. "That's the nicest compliment I've received tonight."

Their eyes met briefly. "I like you, General Jones," she said, any reserve she had had falling away.

From across the room, Congressman Harry Hunter moved toward them. His face was pale, his forehead clammy with too much drink. "General Jones," he said, coming to a halt in front of his wife. "I have just heard some very disturbing news." He looked toward his wife. "Do you mind leaving us, Jennifer?"

"If you're going to talk state secrets."

"I'm asking you to leave me with General Jones, damn it," he said. "What I decide to talk about is my own business."

She turned to Hal. "Please excuse me, General," she said. "Please excuse both of us," she added grimly, before she turned and walked rapidly across the room.

"You have a beautiful wife, Congressman Hunter," Hal said.

"Keep your compliments to yourself," Hunter said furiously. "I've just heard from Sarah that you've been dating her."

"That's true."

"Don't imagine I can't see the attraction," Hunter said.

"Then spell it out, Congressman." Hal leaned toward Hunter menacingly. "Spell it *out*."

Hunter backed away. "Doonan," he called to the butler. "Show General Jones out, please. And we will not be receiving him again."

The butler came forward, his face impassive.

"I want you to leave, Jones. Now," Hunter snarled.

"I'll say good night to Sarah and Mrs. Hunter, if that's all right."

"It's not all right." Hunter turned back to the butler. "Throw him out," he said, his voice loud enough for the nearest group of guests to turn and stare at them.

The butler nodded toward the door. "If you don't mind, General?"

Hal turned his back on Hunter and strode out quickly onto the landing. The butler followed Hal down the marble staircase. In the black-and-white-tiled hall, the butler stopped. "Maybe you'd like a drink with me before I throw you out."

Jones hesitated, then grinned. "Don't you have to look after the guests?"

"Screw them," the butler said.

Hal nodded. "In that case, fine."

"I guess you don't recognize me," the butler said, leading the way downstairs.

"No, I don't."

"No reason why you should. I was a divisional HQ clerk when you commanded a regiment of the 82nd Airborne."

"In Dorset. Afterward in Normandy. You did the big drop?"

The butler's apartment was in the basement of the old house, a large, untidy sitting room with a bedroom, bathroom and kitchen arranged off a small hall. "Yup. I did the big drop," he said. "You drink bourbon, General?"

"Never."

"Scotch?"

"Thanks."

"My name's Doonan," the butler said, pouring whisky. "Don't ask me how long I've worked for the bastard."

"I'm impressed with your sense of loyalty." Hal took the scotch Doonan had poured.

"He's a bastard, a sniveling, cowardly son of a bitch. Now I've said my piece. You'll get no more out of me, however hard you try."

"Does he pay well?"

"He's a cheap, arrogant, pompous mother," Doonan said. "Beyond that, my lips are sealed."

"What about her?"

"She's an angel. You know, General, she really is an angel."

"Angel enough to keep you here?"

"No, I don't stay for her. I stay for him."

"That sounds ominous."

"It is ominous," Doonan agreed. "Let's talk about old times instead."

It was over an hour later when Hal left. The butler's regally composed face now presented a loose-lipped grin. His wing collar had burst in response to the finger constantly tugging at it. He looked a long way from the imposing figure of a couple of hours ago.

"Thanks for the drinks," Hal said as he took his coat.

"Anything for the 82nd." Doonan failed to struggle from his chair.

"One more question." Hal paused at the door. "If I were to ask Mrs. Hunter out to dinner tomorrow night, where would your respected employer be?"

"Thirty thousand feet up over Denver, Colorado," Doonan mumbled. "Or thereabouts. He's making a two-day trip to Los Angeles with Senator McCarthy, his main man."

Hal nodded. "Thanks." He smiled. "Stay where you are. I'll see myself out, James."

CHAPTER
9

The Packard limousine of Nikita Khrushchev was checked through the Borovitsky Gate entrance to the Kremlin, and proceeding ahead, turned left into Cathedral Square. In front of the Ivan the Great Bell Tower, five or six similar Packards were parked. Beside them, a group of six men stood in a tight knot, which broke apart as Khrushchev's car came to a sliding halt.

In the back of his car, Nikita Khrushchev threw aside the lap robe that covered his legs and let himself out before his chauffeur could reach the rear door. Beneath the heavy fur hat, he saw, his eyes half-closed against the wind, that all the senior members of the Presidium had arrived: Malenkov; Bulganin; Voroshilov; Lavrenty Beria, chief of secret police; and Molotov, the veteran Foreign Minister.

"What has happened?" Khrushchev asked as he approached. "I received a message saying it was urgent that I come early. It's going to be a long night as it is," Khrushchev said irritably. "What's important enough to make it even longer?"

Foreign Minister Molotov took Khrushchev's arm. The others moved into a tight circle around them. "We have just heard that General Shtemenko has disappeared."

Khrushchev pulled his arm free. His face puckered in the

biting wind. "General Shtemenko has disappeared?" He turned to Beria. "Arrested? Has he been arrested?"

"No," Beria said.

The sharp cut of the wind was forgotten. Nikita Khrushchev stared ahead at the snow-laden stonework of the bell tower. Nobody had mentioned the possibility that the Chief of Staff of Soviet Land Forces had defected to the West, but he knew it was uppermost in each man's mind. Every Soviet military secret, every item of contingency planning—force levels, reinforcements, training standards, organizational weaknesses, new equipment—was known by General Shtemenko. Stalin would demand people's heads. Beria, of course, would have to bear primary responsibility. He controlled the borders, the actual physical constraints on a defector trying to leave the Soviet Union.

Khrushchev turned to the police chief.

"He's disappeared. It's been three days since he was last seen at army headquarters. I've placed his entire staff under arrest as a precautionary measure."

"His family?"

"I've had them arrested too, of course. They were on their way to the country, to Kovets. They appear to know nothing."

"You've questioned them personally?"

Beria nodded. "And his staff. All they know is that General Shtemenko was ordered to the Kremlin to see Comrade Stalin sometime after midnight on Tuesday. Stalin knows nothing of the Shtemenko disappearance."

"Ah . . ." Khrushchev nodded toward his feet.

"He will have to be told, Nikita," Beria said. "We thought you . . ."

Khrushchev's head came up. His right hand flailed the air. "Me?" he shouted. "It's a security matter, a police matter. It's your responsibility, comrade," he told Beria.

"Or Bulganin's." Beria turned to the short figure beside him. "As Minister for the Armed Forces."

"Yes," Khrushchev said. "Bulganin's."

"Of course," Molotov agreed.

Ice drops had formed on Bulganin's goatee. His eyes moved imploringly from one member of the Politburo to another.

"Those in favor?" Khrushchev asked. Every man but Bulganin raised a gloved hand. "Then it's agreed"—Khrushchev dropped his hand to his side—"the comrade Minister for the Armed Forces will inform Joseph Vissarionovich of the disappearance of the Soviet chief of staff."

The reception had been in progress for almost two hours. Stalin had moved among the recently elected members of the Presidium, receiving their congratulations. But at the supper table, he had scarcely touched the food and his mood had slowly clouded once more. He was seated at the head of the table. Behind him the orchestra was playing a folk dance from his native state. It conjured up a distant memory, two traveling musicians playing by the light of a blazing fire, while he, as a boy, stood on the edge of the village square watching the festivities. The men of the village had started to dance, the moving figures silhouetted against the bright red and orange of the flames, everyone clapping their hands with the beat, everyone smiling. Honest enjoyment, earned by hard-working people.

And now another year was being celebrated. The last year of his life. The Leningrad doctor had told him. So be it.

But first there was work to do. The faint hearts must be removed. His eyes flickered along the line of Soviet generals. General Shtemenko, Chief of Staff of Soviet Land Forces, was not at the table. He made a note to ask someone why. But first, a vital change must be made without exciting suspicion. His eyes rested on the aging General Peslovsky, commander of the First Shock Army. For a moment, he studied the general's flabby jowls and small, soft hands. His deputy commander sat next to him, a shaved-headed, ruthless man. A man much more to Joseph Stalin's liking.

Abruptly, Stalin stood up. Voices stopped in midsentence; knives and forks were suspended halfway to the mouth. "Mikhail Pavlovich," Stalin said, leaving his place and rounding the end of the table. The commander of the First Shock Army began to rise. Reaching the general, Stalin rested an arm on his shoulder, pressing him back down into his seat. "Mikhail Pavlovich, you're looking tired. When did you last give yourself some leave? Answer me truthfully, now." He was smiling genially, but his slant eyes were narrowed.

Peslovsky looked up, his rounded face held at an angle. "Leave, Comrade Marshal? Six months ago. Eight perhaps."

Stalin stood over him, nodding thoughtfully, stroking one end of his mustache. "Mikhail Pavlovich, you have the Winter Maneuvers coming up next month, the biggest winter exercise since our forces entered Germany. But you're looking tired. In need of a rest."

"I'm fit, Comrade Marshal," Peslovsky protested. "I've never been fitter."

Stalin leaned heavily on him. "We men in important positions in the state must watch our health. Take some leave. Now. A month in Sochi at your dacha. Six weeks, even. The Crimean air will do you good."

Around the table, every face was turned toward them, every brain racing to interpret the new development.

"Comrade Marshal," Peslovsky said, awkwardly half turned in his chair, "I cannot command the First Shock Army from Sochi."

"Then let others do it." Stalin smiled his black-toothed smile. "You have a deputy. Come back in six weeks' time." He gave the general a playful smack on the head and waddled back to his seat. "Leave tonight," he shouted across the table. "As soon as the party's over."

One by one, the others began eating again, quickly, timorously, like uncertain schoolboys in the presence of an unpredictable headmaster.

In the tiny apartment off Sverdlovsk Square, the twins were sleeping peacefully in the deep alcove. "You must leave before it gets light," Alex Trenton told Zoya. "Travel on your internal passport—it won't have been rescinded yet. Go to your father in Stalingrad and tell him Vassily is dead."

In a dark, flowered dress, she paced the small room, nodding as he spoke. "Of course you'll decide yourself what you tell your father. But my advice is not to burden him with too accurate an account of events."

"I understand," she said, stopping in the center of the room.

"I mean to imply nothing, but as a senior official, he will be able to operate more effectively if he believes you innocent."

"I understand," she said again.

"Now take a sheet of paper. Sit down at the desk. Write this letter to my stepfather, Pavel Semyonovich. He will know you were involved in the attempt to get to the West, but at the same time he would relish the thought of having someone as important in the Volga party as your father indebted to him. It's a minuet, a gavotte. We all dance it, Zoya."

"Except in my case, and"—she nodded toward the alcove—"in their case, it's less of a gavotte and more of a dance of death." She crossed to the desk and took a pen and paper.

"Dear Pavel Semyonovich," Trenton dictated to her. "I have to report to you the absence for the last two nights of my husband, Vassily Pavlovich, who of course is one of your officers, working directly under your supervision in Dzerzhinsky Square. I make this report in nothing less than a spirit of Revolutionary concern. For some weeks he has expressed ideas which have verged on the unacceptable. One does not have to be a graduate in diamat to see that some of his views are directly hostile to dialectical materialism. I am, in short, deeply worried, first and foremost about his loyalty to the Soviet state, and naturally, too, about his loyalty to his Soviet family—myself and his two children.

"I myself, as a defender of Stalingrad and a holder of the Order of Lenin, feel that the best person to deal with this matter is you, Pavel Semyonovich. I have decided to take the children immediately to the Stalingrad oblast, where, as you no doubt know, my father is the major general commanding the Iron Division stationed there and a senior Party officer."

She finished writing. "What if your stepfather discovers you came here tonight?"

Trenton shrugged. "It doesn't matter, Zoya." He crossed to the desk and put his arm around her. "As I said, it's a gavotte we all dance."

"Even Pavel Semyonovich?"

"Especially him. That's how he's got so far in the whole filthy system."

From his place at the table, Stalin let his eyes wander slowly from one face to another of the senior Presidium members. Molotov, his Foreign Minister, kept his head low over his plate, as well he might with a Jew wife. Next to him sat a giggling nonentity with a goatee; however had he risen to be Minister for the Armed Forces? Then Beria, a fellow Georgian, at least, but growing too powerful now as commander of the Cheka. And Khrushchev, built like an Ukrainian bull, a peasant still, more cunning than he liked to appear.

Nikita Khrushchev, aware of Stalin's heavy-browed scrutiny, forced a smile of acknowledgment, wondering whether to propose the first toast. In that moment Stalin confirmed his prey for the night.

"It is time you gentlemen refilled your glasses. Bring some bottles to the fire." Stalin's teeth showed briefly as his lips pulled back in an ugly smile. He stood up, leading the gathering away from the table. The group followed hurriedly, many still chewing their last mouthfuls; Beria, who habitually ate with his fingers, wiping his hands on a hastily snatched up napkin. They kept together, united momentarily in their recognition of the viciousness of the leader's mood.

"Now, comrades, members of the Politburo, I suspect you have prepared toasts and speeches to flatter me. True?" Stalin became more animated as he plotted his own amusement. They watched him without moving. Only Molotov, concealed at the back of the group of ministers, allowed himself the luxury of a moment's inattention. If he had read the signs correctly, it was to be a long, brutal night. In this mood, Stalin sought a victim, not the company of a few puppet companions in play. He sensed also it was not to be his turn. He turned his attention back to Stalin as the dictator named his prey.

"Comrades, no speeches tonight, I beg you. Instead I have entertainment for us. Tonight we shall have music. Nikita Sergeyevich"—he turned suddenly to face Khrushchev—"you will help us, I'm sure."

Khrushchev stiffened.

"For your pleasure tonight," the dictator shouted theatrically, "revered members of the Politburo, our much-loved Nikita Sergeyevich the Cossack will dance the *Gopak*."

Nikita Khrushchev stepped forward slowly into the open space before the fire. Out of the corner of his eye, he caught Malenkov's sly smile. Beria, standing next to Stalin, affected a joviality which sat chillingly on his murderous face; he began to clap his hands in time, his head thrown back in affected abandon.

As Khrushchev began to stamp his foot to the music, he promised himself that Beria would pay dearly for this evening.

A willing performer in his younger days, Khrushchev was now approaching his sixtieth birthday, fearful as much of a loss of dignity before the younger Presidium members as of the exhausting, acrobatic nature of the dance.

Setting his face in a smile he raised his arms above his head, moving in a circle, snapping his fingers.

Stalin drained a quarter-liter tankard and threw it onto the table. As it crashed and rolled among the glasses, he reached out and shoved at Khrushchev's back. "Get into it, Nikita, the *Gopak*. Give us the *Gopak*!"

There was no escape now. Within the ring of chanting men, Khrushchev circled and leaped, clicking his fingers above his head, stamping and kicking in time with the heavy musical beat. The sweat began to trickle down his face.

"You're a young man, Nikita Sergeyevich—but you dance like an ox," Stalin roared, clapping up the beat of the music, dragging the orchestra behind him.

Beria had slipped away and dimmed the lights, and the huge leaping flames of the fire umbered the circle of faces as the short, broad-shouldered Minister of Soviet Reconstruction kicked out his legs, arms crossed, squatting low in the punishing dance of the cossack villages.

Within the relentless rhythm, his consciousness was blunted to everything but the pain in his legs and the searing agony in his chest as he gasped for breath. Rolling and stumbling, crimson faced and wild eyed, he stamped and clapped and shouted hoarsely to the music, hurling droplets of sweat with every movement of his body.

Around him, the encircling, looming features of the others were unrecognizable, shapeless faces in the flickering firelight. Only Stalin remained in focus, inexorable, bending toward him, shouting the steps wildly, clapping, driving the tempo on.

In a dim corner of his mind, Khrushchev became convinced his heart was failing. He fell suddenly, heavily, tripping over his feet amidst the crescendo of urgent shouts from the audience. He lay still, eyes closed, playing dead like a trapped animal. Around him, the assemblage bayed, echoing Stalin's wild streams of jeers. "Up, up, up, comrade. Show us what cossacks are made of. Someone get him up. His politics have made him soft. He would never forgive us if we allowed him to stop now. The *Gopak* . . . the *Gopak*."

In the small of his back, Khrushchev felt a dull pounding. His shirt was sodden, and he could smell the reek of his own body. He strained helplessly against the tangle of his clothes, his body jerking with effort as he heaved himself onto his knees.

Stalin stood, feet apart, the right boot tapping out the rhythm, vigorously prodding the air with his pipe. Wartime memories flooded over him, evoked by the cossack dance. He had never been to the front himself, but each night he had watched newsreel film of his tanks attacking; his armies rolling forward; his generals grouped in spring woodlands, studying his orders.

His generals. Zhukov, Rokossovsky, Konev, Shtemenko . . . Joseph Stalin frowned. Beside him, intent on Khrushchev's last exhausted efforts, was Bulganin. The leader reached out and dug him hard in the ribs with the stem of his pipe. "Shtemenko," he snarled. "Why isn't Shtemenko here?"

Nikita Khrushchev knew he could last barely a few more seconds. He could no longer make an attempt to match the rhythm. His arms would scarcely rise above chest height. He stamped and watched the sweat spray from his forehead. Nausea engulfed him.

"Where is he?" Stalin screamed. "Where is Shtemenko?"

The music stopped abruptly.

"He's not here," Bulganin stammered.

"You oaf, I know he's not here." He turned on Khrushchev, swaying in the middle of the room. "Shtemenko, where is he?" he said quietly.

"General Shtemenko," Khrushchev's voice was a croak. "Comrade Stalin, General Shtemenko is reported absent from his post." Sucking great gulps of air back into his lungs, Khrushchev stared through misted eyes at his tormentor.

"Find him," Stalin spoke into the silence. "Find him and bring him to me . . ." He snatched the baton from the conductor's hand and hurled it across the room. Then suddenly he began to totter backward, reeling, thrashing at the air.

A hoarse scream of pain immobilized the Presidium members as the Soviet leader rolled to the floor, his right hand clutching the side of his face.

The guests stared down at the white-uniformed figure. The black boots were kicking feebly. His withered left hand opened and closed to the rhythm of a heartbeat. Saliva spumed his mustache.

CHAPTER
10

Brigadier General Hal Jones sat at the wheel of his jeep watching the big bomber's landing lights through the early morning mist as it touched down on La Guardia's reserved 01 runway. As the tail wheel hit the tarmac, the aircraft slowed until it rolled past him at taxiing speed. It came to a halt on the service apron next to a four-engined Liberator, high on the nose of which was painted a full-bosomed blonde captioned "Berlin Belle."

Unhurriedly, he put the jeep in gear and drove slowly toward the stationary aircraft. From fifty yards away he could just make out shapes descending steps let down from the belly of the plane.

He stopped the jeep and climbed out. The figures of the crew were heavily bundled in their flying jackets. The single passenger was tall, about sixty, in black homburg and long dark overcoat. As he walked toward him, Jones hoped he had not brought Charles Trenton to New York on a wild-goose chase. He extended his hand. "Professor, I'm Hal Jones."

Charles Trenton's face was pinched with cold, his gray mustache already dampened by the mist. "Glad to meet you, General Jones," he said, staring past him toward the low prefabricated huts beyond the jeep. "Where are you keeping him?"

Hal pointed to the two American MPs standing guard at the entrance to the farthest hut. Another pair of guards sat in an open jeep. Two more patrolled on foot.

"How did he get here?"

"I don't have full details yet. Through Berlin, I guess." He pointed to the Liberator. "My first report came from Camp King reception center in Frankfurt. He arrived there during the night and was shipped straight out by the same plane."

"He hasn't identified himself?"

"Not yet."

"How's your Russian?" They were walking toward the hut.

"Not up to your standards."

Charles Trenton grunted. "His English is good enough, if I recall."

"I'm sorry to have brought you to New York in the middle of the night, sir," Hal said, in an attempt to be conciliatory.

"Oh, I'm well paid enough," Professor Trenton said. "And of course this sort of thing's a lifelong hobby. The truth is, I would be put out if no one called on me. Even in the middle of the night."

The guard saluted and held open the door for them to enter. Inside, the room was warm and brightly lit. An army lieutenant got up from behind a trestle desk and offered them coffee. The professor removed his hat and coat and lit a cigarette. Coffee in one hand, cigarette in the other, he came close to a dry smile. "Well, Jones," he said, rocking back on his heels, "shall we go in and talk to your man?"

Jones finished his coffee and nodded briskly. Already he found himself objecting to the professor's desiccated air, his subtle assumption of superior rank, despite the fact that his status was no more than that of a civilian advisor—although admittedly the most knowledgeable Kremlin specialist the U.S. possessed.

"You still doubt my identification, Professor?" Hal said, leading the way toward a door at the far end of the reception area.

"Frankly, yes."

"Whatever he is, let's just hope he's important enough to have dragged you all the way from Charlottesville." Jones twisted the handle and pushed open the door. A stocky figure in dark-gray civilian suit was asleep in one of a dozen armchairs scattered around the room. He awoke at the noise of the opening door and stood up, frowning, running a hand over the thin strands of dark hair that covered a balding head. Jones looked at Trenton and made no effort to conceal a smile. He knew by the professor's face that he was right.

Charles Trenton inclined his head. "My name is Professor Trenton. I represent the United States Government. General Jones you've already met. You are General Semyon M. Shtemenko, Chief of Staff of Soviet Land Forces. Perhaps you recall our meeting during the war when I was chairman of the Anglo-American Strategic Materials Commission in Moscow."

The Russian nodded slowly. "Yes," he said.

Hal glanced at Professor Trenton. Nothing in the man's lined face revealed the fact that Shtemenko was without question the most important Soviet defector the West had ever received.

Shtemenko looked around at the unpainted, prefabricated walls of the hut. "Where are we to conduct our discussions, gentlemen?" he said in English. "Somewhere more agreeable, and more *secure*, than here, I hope."

"We have a secure house just outside Washington," Hal said. "We'll be taking you there this morning."

"You mentioned discussions." Charles Trenton looked at him from under his heavy gray eyebrows. "What sort of discussions do you have in mind, General?"

"I must make my objective clear," Shtemenko said. "I am not here to ask for asylum."

"You're not exactly here on an official visit, either, General," Hal said.

"I am not without a great deal of official backing, however, General Jones."

"May we know the extent of your backing?"

"Most of the Soviet General Staff."

"If you are not asking for political asylum," Professor Trenton said, "your hope is to return."

"My *intention* is to return," Shtemenko said firmly. "My object is to communicate certain information to you. And to ask for your cooperation. When you hear the nature of the information, you will understand that only a Soviet officer of the most senior rank could have undertaken this mission."

Charles Trenton glanced quickly at Hal Jones. The interrogation was not going in the direction he had imagined. "Let's begin," he said, "with the information."

"First the background," Shtemenko said, pausing, pulling at his underlip. "I've no doubt that both of you gentlemen are aware of the present power structure in the Soviet Union. It resides solely with Marshal Stalin."

"This hardly represents a change over the last twenty years," Charles Trenton said.

"I'm not here to debate the nature of Soviet power. I offer my statement as a fact, that is all."

"We accept that fact," Hal Jones said. "Go on, General."

General Shtemenko pursed and relaxed his lips. "The *Vozhod,* the sole leader of my country," he said flatly, "is mentally unbalanced." He paused. "Again I offer a statement not as an opinion but as fact. I do not propose to humiliate myself before Westerners by giving you examples—the information I bring is sufficient. Joseph Stalin is dying. He has perhaps six months to live. His condition appears to be a tumor of the brain. Normal medical certainty is impossible. He has murdered one doctor and arrested every Kremlin specialist who has treated him in the past. They too are about to be murdered. Nevertheless, certain medical information has reached the Soviet army."

Hal leaned his long body against the wall and fumbled for a cigarette, his eyes never leaving the intense, tortured face of the Soviet general. He could see the effort General Shtemenko was making to fight the humiliation he felt. Charles Trenton stood silent, his lower lip just occasionally moving under his gray mustache.

"So," Shtemenko continued, "the *Vozhod,* a leader who is terminally sick, in madness believes himself and his country *omnipotent.* And he intends to prove it." Shtemenko turned to General Jones. "One week ago, as chief of the Soviet General Staff, I was ordered to initiate Operation *Gopak. Gopak* is the Supreme Military Council operational plan for the invasion of Western Europe. It requires bringing Soviet forces to fighting status within two and one-half weeks. In eight days' time, gentlemen, six Soviet Shock armies will attack West Germany.

Their objective is to take Paris and the Channel ports in France and Belgium within twenty-one days."

In the long silence that followed, Hal Jones pushed himself off the wall. "I guess the reason you're here, General," he said, "is that the Soviet High Command believes the attack will fail?"

"No, General Jones, we are not convinced of the failure of *Gopak*. But we recognize the West's superiority in aircraft-borne nuclear weapons, the American Strategic Air Command and the British V-Bomber force. Your staffs equally recognize our immense superiority in conventional arms in Europe. The Soviet army believes *Gopak* would take us to Paris in twenty-one days. We also believe that Moscow, Leningrad, Kiev, perhaps Berlin, Frankfurt, Paris itself would be reduced to radioactive cinder by the U.S. by then. *Gopak* therefore must be prevented."

"How?" Charles Trenton's voice was sharp, unnaturally high. "A rebellion in the Soviet army?"

Shtemenko shook his head.

"How then?"

"With some cooperation from the West," Shtemenko said carefully, "the Soviet army will undertake the assassination of Joseph Stalin."

CHAPTER
11

From the top of the hill, the skaters could see the pale orange glow over Moscow. Bundled in enormous furs, they skated across the ornamental lake in pairs or small groups. On the balustraded stone terrace, braziers threw flames into the dark sky, and on a stone jetty pushing out into the frozen lake, fur-coated servants turned roasting suckling pigs on a row of iron spits. The party for the tenth anniversary of the Battle of Leningrad at the country dacha of the MGB was regarded as one of the best in Moscow. The skating, interrupted for hot spiced vodka and suckling pig, would continue until just before midnight. Then the distinguished guests and the specially selected female "hosts" would retire to the elegant nineteenth-century dacha for the banquet, the toasts and the all-night party which would follow behind closed doors.

Alex Trenton sat on the stone balustrade, watching for his mother. He had seen enough to catch the reek of privilege about the event: the obsequious servants offering stoops of hot vodka; the new Western-made skates straight from their boxes and blue tissue wrappings; the huddle of chauffeurs, carelessly tossing great chunks of suckling pig to the loose-chained dogs. It was a far cry from the German front, where men and officers (junior officers, at least) shared the same dangers, the same rations, the same patch of frozen earth floor in a shattered *izba*. Out on the frozen lake, he saw Pavel Semyonovich Petrov extending his arms to receive a figure gliding in an elegant arc toward him.

"Vanessa," Petrov said as she stopped, spraying ice shavings before her, "you put these young army tarts to shame." He clasped her in his arms. "There's someone sitting alone up there. I think it's Alex." Petrov felt for the warmth of her body under the layers of fur.

She allowed him, as she always did, a moment or two of familiarity before pushing his hand away. "Let's call him over."

"In a moment. Come with me." He linked arms with her, and they skated together to the far end of the long balustrade.

A servant appeared immediately, leaping over the coping. "Vodka, Comrade General?"

"Two." Petrov removed a glove and handed a steaming pewter mug to Vanessa. Taking another for himself, he skated off toward a stone bench against a bank of alders, thick-rimmed with frost.

With a deft movement of her skates, she glided after him, the mug held high.

"Well?" With her free hand she threw her fur hood back and ran her fingers through her thick red hair. Her face was still handsome in middle age. "Don't be coy with me, Pavel Semyonovich," she said. Her tone was that of an aristocratic New Englander, the accent impeccably Russian. "What is all this about?"

"Listen to me, Vanessa," he said. "I have a task for Alex, in Washington."

"You're transferring him to the embassy in Washington?"

"No. He will go as an illegal."

She sucked in her breath. "So it's dangerous."

He remained silent. Then he said, "Yes. Very dangerous."

"You could not extend him your protection? Find someone else?" She let her arm rest on his shoulder.

Petrov shook her off angrily. "Of course I could." He took a long draft of the hot vodka and sprayed it out as it burned his mouth. "I have thought carefully, Vanessa. This evening Comrade Beria called me to see him." He paused. "Yes, of course there are others I might have chosen."

"Then why didn't you?"

He hesitated. "It's a gamble," he said slowly. "This is something that could lift us all—Alex, you, me—to the very top."

She watched ambition work his facial muscles like an emotional disorder.

"There'd be no barrier," he said sibilantly, "no barrier for any of us. A colonelship for Alex. A place on the Central Committee for you . . ."

"And for you?"

He smiled. "I might even take Comrade Beria's place," he said slowly.

"Minister of State Security?" Her voice was awed.

"When Comrade Beria moves on. Why not?"

"What is this mission you're planning for Alex?" she asked slowly.

He shook his head. "I've said enough already. It's dangerous. It's vitally important." He paused. "It could bring . . . the highest rewards."

"And you think Alex is the man?"

"Yes." Petrov nodded. "I think he is. Sometimes, I don't mind admitting, I am not entirely sure what goes around in his head. He visits a prostitute in Perlinka Lane to replace her bicycle. And at the same time, he can work as coolly and efficiently as any man in my department. He's chalked up some real successes since he's been back with me." Petrov nodded, pursuing his own line of thought. "Yes, he's the man. He speaks perfect English . . . and while he's not a *regimental,* even so . . . he's a crack shot and a good officer . . ."

For a moment they stood in silence. It was, he recognized, her tacit consent.

"First, there's a serious issue to be resolved," Petrov said.

"An issue between us?"

"No, between you and your son. He must know the truth about his father."

"Why?"

"Because, if he's not told, he may find out in Washington and try to make contact."

"Rubbish."

"I cannot jeopardize the mission, Vanessa," Petrov said slowly. "My instructions come direct from Comrade Beria. Do what I tell you. Do it now."

She turned away. With casual skill, both hands deep in the pockets of her fur coat, she skated thoughtfully across the lake.

From the balustrade, Alex Trenton watched his mother approach. Was it no more than a fierce determination to ward off old age that kept her young as she was? Or were New England women physically like that? People from the southern Soviet Union, he had noticed during the war, aged more rapidly than the northern Slavs. New Englanders were a northern people. Perhaps all their women retained this extraordinary youthfulness into their fifties. He walked down the steps onto the ice, and she came to a stop in front of him.

"Where are your skates?" she said, frowning. "Were you not offered any as you came in?"

"Vanessa"—he took her by the arm—"I told you I'm not staying. I'm here because my comrade stepfather told me to be here."

Her chin came up peremptorily. He recognized the movement as an indication of her displeasure. "Pavel Semyonovich says you're having an affair."

"I only wish the Cheka were right for once."

"Don't be childish. What's her name?"

"There's no affair, Vanessa. If there had been, her name would have been Katya."

"Her family name?"

"That I don't know."

"A pickup, I suppose."

"A pickup," he agreed flatly.

She shrugged, glaring at him angrily.

"What does Petrov want?"

"I think he plans to offer you a promotion."

"He could have done that at the office. Why did he want me to come here?"

Servants struggled down the bank and set up a coke brazier on the ice. Vanessa removed her gloves and held out her hands to the glowing coals. She was silent while a pair of canvas chairs were brought for them, along with mugs of spiced lemon vodka.

"To Joseph Stalin." She raised her drink. "Many more long years to him." She watched her son.

"To the next hundred," he repeated flatly and drank the spiced vodka. "So what's all this about, Vanessa?"

"Pavel Semyonovich asked you here because he wants me to tell you something. To fill you in on some information about your past."

"Something you hadn't told me?"

She looked hard into the sputtering fire. "It's about your father. Your internal passport records him as having died in Georgia in 1921."

"Of cholera."

"Yes."

"He didn't?"

"No. He's still alive."

"What! And you've known all this time?"

"Your father *left* us," she said. "An American warship arrived in Batumi. Your father returned to the United States."

"You mean he refused to stay in Russia."

"Yes."

"There was no cholera?"

"Yes," she said. "But it was farther north. The cholera was a convenient fiction," she said without a hint of apology. "The surgeon's cut. Clean. Small boys can be incurable romantics."

"Their mothers, too."

"Don't be foolish, Alex."

"You lied to me about my father's death. What else did you lie to me about?"

"I will not be interrogated by *you*, Alex."

"Not even for Comrade General Petrov?"

"If you want this job, you have to know what happened to your father. Otherwise I wouldn't have brought it up."

"Why does Petrov want me to know?"

"To get your documents straight. It's an important post."

"What happened to my father? After Batumi?" he asked.

She shrugged. "I believe he left the consular service when he divorced me. Afterward he took up an appointment at Harvard."

"Harvard?"

"My dear boy, Harvard is a university for the sons of the rich and powerful. Your father was a considerable linguist. When he was in Russia, he was frequently taken for a Russian. After some years he became a senior professor at the University of Virginia. He has been very successful."

"Did he ever marry again?"

"How would I know?"

"You must have been in contact with him."

She waved her gloved hand dismissively. "A few letters after he left for the United States."

"That's all?"

"I object to your tone, Alexander."

"If there's more, perhaps Petrov can tell me."

"Sit down," she said. "I can tell you whatever you want to know."

He sat down. Fumbling in his coat pockets, he took out a pack of cigarettes, and removing his glove, he leaned forward to light one from the glowing brazier.

"After the divorce," she said, "I lost touch with your father. I moved from Moscow to become a shock worker in the Ukraine."

"Part of the time I was with you," he reminded her. His stomach turned over at the memory of the gaunt faces of the starving peasants as they, the Party activists, dug the last bushel of wheat from under the floor of the peasants' homes, or dragged away the hidden family cow. When the whole murderous farce was nearly over and the Soviet state had stolen the farms from the peasant owners, Joseph Stalin published an article in *Pravda*. He entitled it "Dizzy with Success." Its appalling cynicism in the face of millions of dying peasants had destroyed Alex Trenton's enthusiasm forever. But from then on, as a soldier at Stalingrad and on the Kiev front, he had told himself he was fighting for the poor, battered millions who were victims of Stalin's great tyranny. Never for the corrupt system and the despot himself.

Vanessa Trenton pursed her lips. "Your father was here in Moscow during the war," she said.

Trenton rocked back in astonishment. "You saw him here?"

"Yes. He was head of the Anglo-American Strategic Materials Commission. It was at the time you were on the Leningrad front."

"You saw him and never told me?"

"There was no point."

"Of course not. As far as I was concerned he was already dead."

He knew that if anything hurt her it was to be in the wrong. To be seen to be in the wrong. "Did he ever marry again?"

"I can't imagine why, but yes. Precisely the sort of inane creature you'd expect. All blond curls and perfect teeth. Younger than him."

"You met her?"

She sighed impatiently. "She was here in Moscow as your father's secretary. Yes, I met her. Of course I met her."

"Do I have half brothers or sisters?"

"No."

"Is that the truth, Vanessa?"

"She left him before you had a chance of a sibling, my dear boy," she said. "I believe she ran off and committed adultery with a circus strongman."

"Is that the truth?"

She shrugged.

"And my father, how long did he stay in Moscow?"

She hesitated. "He was here several months. More, probably. A year."

"In 1944?"

"1943, 1944."

"Two years."

"Yes," she said wearily. "Almost two years altogether. He came twice."

"With his wife each time?"

"No. The second time alone."

"Did you see him often?"

"Yes," she said. "Quite often."

He stared at her in silence. She smiled a small, tight smile. Defiant pride.

"You picked up where you left off," he said, his voice rising. "You began again, *despite* the new wife."

She smiled that smile of supreme confidence which he knew well. Which always somehow managed to carry him along with it. "A dull husband. And an even duller lover."

"You bitch, Vanessa." He was laughing in spite of himself. "You dreadful bitch."

*   *   *

Turning into the long snow-swept street of factory buildings, Katya hunched over the handlebars of her bicycle and drove the wheels across the crackling ice. She was within a few hundred yards of home now, and again her anticipation lightened the strain of the nightly ride home from the Old Stables. It was two days since she had seen Alex Trenton; any night now she might return and find a note waiting.

With her eyes on the patches of crusted snow ahead, her mind turned over the problems that had preoccupied her since she had last seen him. Or more accurately since Anna, her neighbor and friend, had mentioned it a few days later.

Prostitution was to Katya a simple fact of life. It enabled her to remain in Moscow in a strange semilegal limbo. It earned her a little money, and through her contacts with officers with goods to sell, it earned sufficient money for her to live. She had had a few minor romances, mostly with boys from the Kalpretta, and the Old Stables had never stood in her way. But Alex Trenton was different. A man like that, Anna had insisted, would not be able to tolerate her life at the Stables. Even though he had come to see her there.

Braking carefully, Katya controlled the skidding wheels and brought the bicycle to a stop. Lifting the machine until the crossbar rested on her shoulder, she carried it across the street and into the courtyard of a half-ruined office building. Before the war it had been decided by the Moscow city council to convert the offices of the Leningrad–Moscow Rail Freight Company into an air-cadet school. But the project had been abandoned, or indefinitely delayed, and now a hundred or more people like herself, living on the fringes of Soviet legality, occupied the rooms, paying rent to no one other than an occasional bribe to the local militia station.

Locking her bicycle in a shed, Katya entered the huge, dark entrance hall and ran across to the crude set of pigeonholes which the occupants had hammered onto the wooden paneling. Moonlight fell from the great circular window above the door. She stopped. Her pigeonhole was empty. She turned miserably toward the staircase. She had no reason to expect a note. Yet still . . . perhaps tomorrow. Or the night after that.

Or perhaps her friend Anna was right after all. A man like Alex could not find her prostitution tolerable.

The staircase was dusty and uncarpeted. In harder, wartime winters the mahogany bannisters had been torn out for fuel. She started up the stairs to her room off the first landing. Of course it was true that the mail delivery was totally unreliable. One of the girls at the Stables had received a letter from an aunt in·Siberia that had taken over two months to reach her. And winter delivery times in Russia were always so much slower than the summer. She was, she told herself, a fool to think that a letter was possible this soon.

Reaching the landing, she turned toward the door. A man was slumped on the flight of stairs above her, hunched in a greatcoat. In Moscow, where thousands were still homeless, there was nothing unusual about a drunk on the doorstep.

As she delved in her pocket for her keys, she could hear the man's regular breathing. She moved quickly to the door, trying not to wake him. But with a grunt and a cough he changed position. Only then, as the greatcoat collar slipped from his face, did she realize it was Alex.

In the half-light of the landing, she stood in front of the slumped figure, her heart racing. She reached out a hand.

"Alex." She shook him gently.

He grunted.

"Alex, it's me, Katya."

He shook himself and came awake, smiling up at her. "It's not too late to call?" he asked.

She knelt on the stair beside him and threw her arms around him. Burrowing through the damp cloth of his greatcoat collar, she kissed him on the mouth. For all the sexual experience they had shared, they had never kissed before.

Still holding one another, they got to their feet. "Just tell me one thing, Alex. How much time have you got?"

He laughed. "It used to be a joke among soldiers, you know. Always the first question when you got home is, When do you go back to the front?"

"Please," she said. "Tell me if you can stay tonight."

"I've lots of things to tell you," he said. "Later."

"Yes," she agreed quickly. "Come inside."

She took out her keys and shone a flashlight onto the lock.

"You must be frozen," she said. "Listen," she dropped her voice, "I have some American coffee an officer brought from Berlin. I was saving it for a celebration."

The door swung open, and she switched on the light. It was a single room, large, high ceilinged. "Spacious enough for a commissar," he said, still yawning.

"Shush . . ." She pulled the door closed.

His first impression was of a warmth and color rare in Moscow apartments in that time. Although the room was furnished with old pieces from the pre-Revolutionary past, mostly of worn leather and dark-stained wood, she had nevertheless managed to add some color in the form of a strip of carpet and a length of bright wall hanging.

"Do you like it?" she asked.

"Very much," he said. "What I don't understand is how you have a place like this without a Moscow residence *propiska.*"

"Nobody in this building has a permit," she said. "Most of them have a workbook or a *karacteristika.*"

He took off his coat and threw it on the bed.

"Light a fire," she said, "while I make the coffee. I have a bag of real coal there."

He crumpled newspaper and threw it into the grate, piling broken box wood on top. Behind him, she had a small gas stove.

He placed pieces of coal in the flames. When he stood up, he saw that she was watching him intently. He spun around, one knee bent under him. "I wanted to see you again," he said.

A slow smile spread across her face. "I'm very pleased to hear it," she said. "Perhaps it's not entirely proper to say how pleased I am."

"Why should it not be entirely proper?"

She shrugged, her face clouding now. "I must not forget that you are an MGB officer. And I am a semilegal . . ." She could barely bring herself to add, "working in the Old Stables in Perlinka Lane."

Between them, the fire blazed, slowly spreading warmth through the room. On the gas stove, the American coffee bubbled.

"Katya," Trenton said carefully, "I have to leave Moscow shortly."

The pain spread slowly across her face. "You are leaving Moscow?"

"They are sending me to America."

"America!" She sat abruptly on the arm of one of the leather armchairs. She was looking down, her face hidden from him. "It's as far away as the moon," she said.

He reached out a hand and touched her hair. "I find I hate the thought of leaving you."

She looked up. "America, Alex. It's your own country. Will you come back?"

"Of course."

"When?"

"I shall be back within a month."

Her face lightened. "If I were you"—she tried to smile—"I would not come back, ever."

"You would stay in America?" he said slowly.

"You know I would."

"Even if I were here, in Moscow?"

Her gray eyes met his. "You have no right, Alex, to play games with me. If I were lucky enough to go to America, why should I care about leaving you here in Moscow?"

"Because I love you," he said levelly. "What do you say to that?"

"I say you're mad," she said somberly. She took his hand and pulled him down on the strip of carpet in front of the fire. "Alexei," she said, "after the night at the Kalpretta, I'd hoped that perhaps we might have a light love affair. But even that, my friend Anna said, would be ruined by the Old Stables."

He crossed to his greatcoat and took something from the inside pocket. When he turned he was holding a thick brown envelope.

"What is that?" She was looking at the envelope.

He came forward and placed it on the table between them.

"What is it?" she repeated.

He looked at her across the table. "I'm not sure," he said, "whether I even have the right to offer it to you."

She stretched out her hand cautiously, as if the envelope were booby-trapped.

"Open it," he said.

She took the envelope and pulled open the flap. Inside were

documents and a slender book with soft cardboard covers. "A residence permit," she gasped like a child on Christmas morning. "A workbook and *karacteristika*." She was fighting back the tears.

"You must choose," he said carefully, "whether you want to use them."

"Whatever I choose," she said, "Perlinka Lane would always lie between us."

He took cigarettes from the pocket of his uniform shirt and gave her one. Pulling a piece of smoking wood from the fire, he lit her cigarette, then lifted the flame to his own. "During the war," he said, "I met men who were in love with girls from their villages. They had known each other sometimes since they were children together. Usually their families knew each other or were already related by marriage. Perhaps that is the best foundation for two people to come together. I don't know. I know that for people like us, without family, without background even, such a coming together is not possible. We have to seize what we see before us."

She sat beside him and stroked the back of his head. "Even if we *can't* see before us?"

"Yes," he said, "even then."

She laughed nervously.

"Don't laugh at me." He cupped her slender chin in his hand. "Or I won't bring you nylon stockings back from America."

Kneeling, she threw her arms around his waist. "Bring yourself back, if you can bear to," she said. "That's all I want from America now."

Behind them, the coffee boiled over, and the precious liquid ran hissing over the stove.

CHAPTER
12

Alexander Trenton awoke with a start. Wiping the condensation from the train window with the edge of his hand, he looked out over a waste of sand dunes topped with rusted barbed wire. From Hungary, he had been smuggled by MGB border specialists into Vienna. From Vienna, the United Nations displaced-persons identity card he had been given carried him across Europe to France. Now, beyond the sand dunes was the cold grayness of the English Channel. As the train began to move again, a signboard inscribed CALAIS-MARITIME slipped slowly back past the window. He stood up and took his bag from the netting rack, then hesitated by the window as the train gathered speed. The dunes were beginning to flatten out now and give way to brick warehouses and marshaling yards. Huge sea gulls dived and banked between stationary freight trains.

Behind him, the compartment door slid open. He turned to see the conductor standing in the doorway. "Calais-Maritime, monsieur," the man said. "Are you catching the Dover ferry?"

"Yes."

"It leaves in half an hour's time. The name of the boat," he added carefully, "is the *Arromanches*."

The hair lifted on the back of Trenton's neck. The man had spoken the first half of the recognition signal.

"I was given to understand it was an English boat," Trenton said, repeating the reply he had been given in Moscow.

The man nodded, then stepped back to look each way along the corridor. Coming forward into the compartment again, he delved into his leather bag.

"Your passport, monsieur." He handed Trenton a stiff-backed dark-blue Canadian passport. In the cut-out window on the front cover was written the name R. D. Blackburn.

"One hundred pounds sterling, Monsieur Blackburn." The conductor handed Trenton a thin packet of bills, white fives and smaller blue-green one-pound notes. "And one thousand American dollars."

The train had come to a stop. Past the Frenchman's shoulder, Trenton could see the lights of the ferryboat rising above the concrete station buildings. "When you arrive in Victoria Station, take a taxi to London Airport. Your American visa is in the passport with your round-trip air ticket to New York. I am instructed to order you to make all possible speed to your rendezvous in Washington. Bon voyage, Monsieur Blackburn." He stepped out of the compartment. "All change," he shouted down the corridor. "All change—Calais-Maritime, all change."

In Congressman Harry Hunter's office, everything conspired to muffle sound. The windows were double glazed, the carpet thick, the furnishings soft and heavy.

"I'm not empowered to answer that question," Hal Jones said carefully.

The faint hum of the central heating system rose like the sound of a distant swarm of bees, then subsided gracefully.

"I repeat my question," Hunter said. "You informed the committee that General Shtemenko has defected. Why did he take this step?"

"I must respectfully decline to answer that question, Congressman. I was specifically ordered by my superior officer, General Bolsover, to give no further information."

"Your superior officer has no authority to stop you from giving any information this committee requests."

"He has over *me*, Congressman," Hal said. "I don't claim to know my way around the Constitution of the United States.

But the army, I know. At the moment, as far as I'm concerned, what General Bolsover says, goes."

Harry Hunter stood up angrily. "The clear implication is that the members of this committee are not to be trusted."

"Someone is not to be trusted," Hal said. "In the last year or so almost every piece of information relating to Soviet defectors to the West has somehow made its way back to Moscow. That's pretty worrying, Mr. Hunter. Especially to potential Soviet defectors."

"The Un-American Activities Committee of the United States Senate has required you to brief me fully on all developments relating to defection and defectors. Do I understand you are withholding information on General Shtemenko?"

Hal got slowly to his feet. "Yes, sir, I am."

"I warn you, I intend to take this up with General Bolsover immediately."

"Save yourself time, Mr. Hunter," Hal said, his patience suddenly exhausted. "Take it up with the president himself, for all I care."

A day later, Alex Trenton found Washington's Union Station, in the cold light of early morning, a confusion of neon advertising signs, swarming with people and dozens of foods stands and gift shops. Two passing policemen gave him a moment's acute anxiety; a newsboy selling copies of the *Daily Worker* caused him to veer sharply away at the very thought of being seen buying a Communist newspaper.

He found it difficult to come to terms with the strangeness of the setting, and yet the familiarity of the language. Two women hurrying past spoke in accents similar to his mother's. The advertisements carried comprehensible slogans for totally unknown products; lights flashed theatrical details; billboards offered to improve his memory or height or muscles. Crossing the station forecourt to the bar, he ordered a cup of coffee and carried it across to a table in the darkest corner of the room. He was a Soviet illegal in Washington at a time when, as Moscow had warned him, American counterintelligence activity was at its peak. Perhaps his easy progress through customs and passport control at New York's Idlewild Airport had been misleading. Perhaps an FBI agent had already been assigned to follow him.

His eyes passed back and forth across the room. At 12:20, a man in his early thirties finished his drink and began to walk toward the swinging doors. Then, as if seeing Trenton for the first time, he turned and came toward him, extending his hand in greeting.

Alex leaned forward to shake the contact's hand. Looking into the face above him, he was struck by the man's piercing eyes.

"Mr. Blackburn," the man said in heavily accented English, sitting down at the table, "I've been watching you since you arrived. You're clear."

"In a station, it's hard to be sure."

"Of course. But watching and waiting is my job."

"You have a message for me."

The man nodded. "The target arrived in America about an hour ago."

The word hit Alex with the power of an electric shock. "Target? I know nothing of a target."

The wolf eyes flinched. "Of course not. It is not normal to detail the assignment to an illegal until he has actually arrived in the West. He is at his most vulnerable to exposure while passing through immigration and customs, crossing frontiers. It would be short-sighted to give an illegal vital information before it is necessary, would it not?"

Alex saw the pale scalp below the black hair gleaming with brilliantine. "Call me Sobotkov. Rank, major," Sobotkov said suddenly. "I'm your backup officer. You can rely on me implicitly. At this moment the unknown is where the Americans are holding the target."

"Who is the target?" Trenton asked slowly.

Sobotkov hesitated, pursing his lips with disapproval. "A senior officer who has defected to the West."

"How senior?"

"It is unnecessary for you to know more at this moment. When we know where the Americans plan to hold him, we will contact you. Go to the Chelverton Hotel just outside the station. Check in as Blackburn. You will be given room 707. Behind the cupboard you will find a briefcase. In it a pistol and silencer. You are familiar with the weapon from your training at Kalmudstan."

"That was a long time ago."

"Your record shows you achieved Marksman A Class. You also received additional training last March. I trust you're not *too* rusty."

The Chelverton was a small, run-down hotel with leaking gutters. The sounds of trains shunting in the yards behind reached room 707 where Alex stood looking down at the gleaming oiled metal of the Tokarev 7.62 mm lying on the bed. He had always believed that his mother's influence with Pavel Semyonovich Petrov would protect him from this. From the time when being an MGB officer stopped being an international game and became serious—beatings, assassinations, the death of friends like Vassily. To kill a man. That was now his ticket, his passport back to Moscow, back to Katya. To kill a man.

CHAPTER
13

The sign on the gilt-topped wrought-iron gates of Manor Grange read: DEPARTMENT OF AGRICULTURE, RESEARCH AND DEVELOPMENT STATION. The winding gravel drive between the winter starkness of the lime trees was immaculately kept. At the far end of the drive lay a 1920's manor house with long casement windows. There was no sign of experimental greenhouses. But there was no sign either of the fifteen guards who, day and night, patrolled the grounds.

In the first-floor library, General Semyon M. Shtemenko sat at a long polished table, his back to a wall of books which rose to the ceiling. On either side of him sat Professor Charles Trenton and Brigadier General Hal Jones. Opposite them were the three most important figures in the NATO organization, men whose influence outranked the Secretary General's and even that of the NATO commander, General Matthew Ridgway, himself. The Standing Group of three senior officers was in permanent session in Washington. General Eli and Air Marshal Elliot represented France and Britain. The chairman was President Eisenhower's trusted World War II associate, General Omar Bradley.

Beyond them, ranged around the long table, were their deputies and assistants. General Bolsover, Omar Bradley's deputy, had already apologized to the Standing Group for asking them to come to Manor Grange. General Shtemenko's security, he had explained, made it impossible to hold the meeting in Washington itself.

The Soviet general wore a new shirt and a new off-the-rack suit, replacing the ill-fitting Russian suit he had been wearing at La Guardia earlier that morning. He had bathed and shaved; the effects of many sleepless hours in the air were indicated only by a slight darkening under the eyes. To Hal, he appeared tough and confident. The awesome responsibility of the men now assembled in Manor Grange was to decide whether or not he was also telling the truth.

"As I understand, General," Bradley began, "you are asking that we recommend to President Eisenhower that, despite all the evidence of a Soviet military build-up in Germany, we should take no preemptive action."

"Correct."

"And the reason the United States should take no preemptive atomic action against your forces is that the Soviet army is preparing to depose Joseph Stalin."

"That is the situation," Shtemenko said. "I don't have to underline the personal risks I have taken to bring you this information."

Bradley's face creased as he looked around the table. Fifty years old, born in Clark, Missouri, Omar Nelson Bradley had been one of World War II's most successful Allied commanders. Biographies and military appraisals of the man had always stressed his monumental commonsense. He knew he had to make a far greater decision now than had faced him in over three years of war. His eyes rested on Jones. He nodded toward him. "Take the questions, Hal."

"Yes, sir." Hal turned to Shtemenko. "Compliance with your request for no preemptive action on the part of the U.S.," he said carefully, "obviously depends, in part at least, on the credibility of the arrangements to depose Marshal Stalin . . ."

"To *assassinate* Marshal Stalin," Shtemenko corrected him.

"To assassinate him." Hal nodded casually.

"First, the problem," Shtemenko said crisply. "Stalin is infinitely suspicious. He lives in fear of an attempt on his life. Nothing, therefore, in his existence is routine. Meals are served at odd hours, guards are selected in a random fashion and changed sometimes three or four times a night. Above all, there is the difficulty of getting into his presence."

"And this has been solved."

"Yes. Until last month the First Shock Army, which is to lead the attack on the West, was commanded by General Peslovsky. He was, in Stalin's view, too old and not sufficiently aggressive. He has been removed. In his place I have arranged for a young officer to be promoted to the position of general commanding First Shock Army. His name is Peter Voronov. He has many personal and patriotic reasons for hating Stalin."

"Is it arranged that he will be received by Stalin?" Charles Trenton interjected. He was looking down, staring at the cigarette burning between his fingers.

"Stalin has insisted on briefing Voronov personally."

"When?" Hal said.

Shtemenko shook his head. "It could be tonight. Or tomorrow. It could be barely a day or two before the attack is launched."

"In that case, it may be too late, General," Hal said. "If that attack is launched and the United States responds, Europe could be a mound of smoking rubble within one week."

"I realize that." Shtemenko nodded vigorously. He looked toward the three members of the NATO Standing Group. His eyes fixed on Omar Bradley. "I am asking for the U.S. government to wait for seven days. I believe by then Voronov will have gained access to Stalin. In that case, *Gopak* will be countermanded immediately. Within an hour, your intelligence reports will show the Soviet assault forces being pulled back from the border."

On the afternoon of his return through the driving rain from the meeting at Manor Grange, Hal's mind was churning too fast to think of Sarah Black, even as he let himself into his apartment and was met by a waft of familiar French perfume.

Closing the door behind him, he reflected back on the images of Charles Trenton's long, smoke-stained fingers, of the nervously aggressive tug Shtemenko gave his lower lip. All of them present that morning had been aware of being on the very edge of Armageddon.

"Hello, darling," Sarah's voice broke into his thoughts. "I'm in the bathroom. I hope you don't mind awfully—I had to force your janitor to let me in. I was caught a block away in a storm of Biblical proportions."

Sarah Black walked out into the living room completely naked, drying her hair with a bath towel. She looked through the open door to where Hal was standing in the hall. "You don't mind, darling, do you?"

"I do mind," he said. "I mind a lot. More than that, I'll make sure Dixon does not do it again. For you or anybody else."

She posed in the doorway, her body still tanned from her last Bermuda trip. "We *are* in a dreadful state this afternoon, aren't we? What happened at the office? Doesn't your four-star general understand you?"

"Get your clothes on," he growled, peeling off his overcoat.

She dropped back a few steps into the room, easing her body over the arm of the sofa until she lay on her back, her legs apart. "Give me a quick one," she coaxed. "Now. You'll feel much better afterward."

He threw his coat onto a chair. Walking over to a side table, he poured himself a whisky. Still half turned away from her, he said, "I want you out, Sarah. I want you dressed and out in three minutes."

She watched him, her face sullen, as he walked across to an armchair and sat down.

"Don't I get offered anything?" She brought her legs together with a slap of her inner thighs. When he didn't answer, she stood up, wrapping the towel around her. "No," she said to herself. "Evidently not."

Sipping the whisky, he was only vaguely aware of the exaggerated noises from the bathroom. Within a minute or two, she stood before him in a wet coat, a Hermès silk scarf tied in her damp hair. "I can see you're awfully busy," she said with heavy irony.

He stood up. "I am, Sarah, believe it or not—I am."

She was unmollified. "Well, I'm afraid you're going to be disturbed yet again. Another unwelcome visitor."

"A visitor?"

"When Dixon let me in, I used your phone to call my guardian. Jennifer. We were going to meet at the Vassar Club, you see. But since I was drenched, I asked her to pick me up. She'll be here in about half an hour. *I'll* be at the Vassar Club."

"Can't you phone her again?"

"She's already on her way, *duckie*." She turned and walked out. He sat down again as the front door slammed, hard. Already he was back in the library at Manor Grange, replaying the tense face of the Russian general as he spoke the unspeakable.

It took the best part of three large Glenmorangies before Hal Jones felt anything like normal again. Normal enough to think of Sarah, to suffer a faint tinge of regret that he hadn't acted on her invitation. No matter; he would call her. No emotion ever lasted very long with her. Perhaps he would phone the Vassar Club and have her paged. There was no action he could take about Shtemenko until the political decisions were made. Dinner with Sarah and cognac in bed would keep the terrors at bay. Or at least would help.

The bell rang, and he started from his sensual reverie, entwined with the dark threat of this morning. He arose from the chair, aware that he was exhausted. Going out into the hall, he opened the door.

Jennifer Hunter stood before him, a quizzical smile on her face. "Sarah asked me to meet her here."

"I know," he said, shaking hands with her. "She left a message to say she would be at the Vassar Club."

"I see." She hesitated. "From what Sarah said on the phone, I expected you to be out," she said carefully.

"I was."

"Now that you're back and Sarah's not here, I wonder if I could take up a few minutes of your time."

He stepped back and opened the door to let her enter the hall.

"Just a few minutes." She walked into the living room.

"Sure. Take your coat off and I'll get you a drink. What will it be?"

"If you have a gin and tonic . . ."

"I have."

She took her coat off and sat down on the sofa.

He mixed the drink, went into the kitchen for ice and came

back to see she was still sitting comfortably with her legs crossed, one hand on the arm of the sofa. Not a woman easily disconcerted, he decided. He also decided he liked her legs.

Handing her the gin and tonic, he topped up his own whisky and sat down opposite her. "How can I help you, Mrs. Hunter?"

"Perhaps, in fact, we can help each other, General Jones."

"You can help me if you call me Hal."

"Very well. Hal. I imagine you think you know a lot about Sarah?"

"Quite a lot."

"She had a bad childhood. Her parents were killed in an air crash, but long before that they'd already effectively abandoned her. She was placed in expensive private schools in Monaco, England, Switzerland. My brother was not a devoted parent."

"And after the air crash you tried to fill in, is that it?"

"I agreed to be her guardian, yes."

"You took on a wayward charge, Mrs. Hunter."

"Yes. A wayward charge. Add good looks and the promise of far too much money, and it's an excellent recipe for trouble."

"And that's what she's been to you and your husband."

"To herself."

"What does your husband think?"

Her head lifted slightly, before she regained control. "Don't ask me questions when you already know the answers."

"Do I know the answers?"

"Sarah must have told you."

"Her side of things, naturally."

"But you saw enough of my husband at the party to make up your own mind."

"Yes."

She took a deep breath. "To you, he's an opinionated man on the make."

"Is that your opinion, too?"

"Yes," she said coolly.

"That doesn't sound like a recipe for a long and happy marriage."

"No—I doubt we'll be drawing our retirement pensions together."

Hal watched her across the rim of his glass. She was, he felt, a hell of a strong woman. Not much like the guardian Sarah had described.

Jennifer Hunter smiled suddenly. "And what," she asked, "is a middle-aged American brigadier general, no doubt with a wife in Iowa, doing in Sarah's life?"

Hal shrugged. "No wife in Iowa. No wife, for that matter. I never quite got around to marriage. Too many postings in too many places. Sarah's fun. Spoiled, but fun."

Jennifer nodded. "What was your job in Moscow?"

Thinking about it afterward, he wondered why he had answered her as he had. But to hell with it, he'd thought. "I'm a spy," he finally replied. "A spook, as we say." Her face betrayed her surprise. "You look startled."

"Only because spies don't usually announce themselves."

"No," he said slowly. "Maybe it's just because I'm under the whip at the moment. Or have had too much whisky. Or I'm just feeling sorry for myself and the human race."

Again she smiled, the warmth lighting her face. "I won't ask you to confide in me."

"No, don't," he said somberly.

For a few moments she sat, her eyes down, looking into her drink.

"I've a feeling 'the big speech' is coming. Am I right, Mrs. Hunter?"

"Please call me Jennifer."

"Okay. Am I right, Jennifer?"

"Not the big speech. The big question. Are you sleeping with Sarah?"

He raised the graying line of his eyebrows. "Am I sleeping with Sarah? Yes, I am."

"Even now?"

"What do you mean?"

"Since she became engaged to be married."

"Jesus! When was that?"

"Yesterday. Will you believe me if I say he's a very nice young man?"

"Will you believe me if I say he might not have the best taste in wives-to-be?"

"I accept that. I know more about Sarah than you might

imagine. About her drinking and her sleeping around. But with this boy, I think she has a chance."

"Does *he*?"

"Is it really up to me to answer that? He wants to marry her. She seems to want to marry him. He's rich, so she can't play the money game."

"She knows lots of other games."

Jennifer Hunter put her glass on the side table and stood. "Marriage could make a great deal of difference to her."

"You're asking me to stop seeing her."

"I don't expect an answer. I've given you the facts. You must decide."

Hal helped her on with her coat.

She walked through into the hall. He followed, stopping in the doorway, one hand on top of the door, as the phone began to ring.

"Don't go for a minute," he said, turning to pick up the phone. "Hal Jones," he said into the receiver.

It was Jack O'Sullivan. "We've had a kind of funny call, sir," he said. "Completely American voice, gives his name as Blackburn. Claims he's Russian."

"A hoax?"

"Definitely no. He gave your name. As a reference, he said."

"Anything else?"

"Try this," O'Sullivan said. "He says he is a Soviet illegal. Just arrived."

"Go on."

"He claims to be here in connection with a senior Soviet officer, newly defected."

"Jesus Christ. Where is he?"

"He was speaking from a pay phone in the city. He is prepared to meet. But not until tomorrow afternoon."

"Where?"

"In Charlottesville."

"Are you serious?"

"*He* is, sir. I gave him six o'clock, the Bierhaus on Jefferson Avenue."

"I'll take it." Hal put down the phone.

"You've got things on your mind," Jennifer said. "I'll leave you."

"Before you go"—he touched her arm—"I'd like to ask you—would you have dinner with me?"

She paused for a moment. "Yes," she said, moving toward the door. "But only if you stop seeing Sarah."

"Ah . . . you're making a deal."

"Not a deal. But there *is* a price. If the price is too high . . ."

"No, it's not too high. Will you have dinner with me tonight?"

"Yes," she said slowly. "With pleasure."

Shortly after 5 P.M. on the following day, the two duty operators at the British Rhine Army 27th Signals Regiment, Sennelager, noted an increase in the series of oscillations of the recorder arm on their monitoring equipment. The captain in command of the unit, called in to interpret this apparent increase in radio activity among Soviet army units across the East-West border, concluded that a new Soviet formation, perhaps even of division strength, had moved into the area.

Reporting the development by telephone to 11th Armored Division headquarters at Padeborn, the captain watched the oscillations deepen as he waited for Padeborn to answer. By the time he had gotten through to the Divisional Signals Officer, he had begun to revise his estimate. Increase in radio activity among Soviet units opposite the 11th Armored Division's sector was now averaging twenty percent. It seemed, he reported tentatively, to suggest that up to two new Soviet divisions now occupied the triangle Neustadt-Detmold-Karlingen.

One hundred and seventy miles to the south, at the Anglo-American zone line, the 6th U.S. Army Radio Detection Unit was struggling with the opposite situation. The Soviet close-support Sturmovik fighter-bomber wing stationed at Dresden, across the East German border, seemed to have gone out of business. Or maybe it was just gone. That, at least, was the view of Captain Thomas R. Krivitsky, as he sat with the earphones over his cap listening to nothing but heavy static. Since seven that morning, he had not heard a single Russian pilot or controller's voice.

Removing the earphones, he placed a call to his colonel in Heidelberg. "I hate to tell you, Colonel," he said, "but there's still no sign of them."

"Could it be a radio-silence exercise?"

"Colonel, after a year of eavesdropping I know these boys like I do my own family. They don't fly for five minutes without asking instructions from Dresden control. If they're maintaining radio silence, they aren't in the air. My guess is that they've upped and gone."

The colonel lifted a pack of papers from his desk. "I have a noon report from British Rhine Army here," he said slowly. "They've picked up a big increase in radio traffic opposite their 11th Armored Division sector. They put it at up to two Russian divisions."

"Well, it's Winter Maneuvers season for the Soviets."

"Couple of other things from Joint Posts in Berlin too." The colonel tucked the telephone under his chin and leafed through the onionskins. "Movement going on up there too, Tom."

"Like I said, it's maneuver season."

"I'm going to forward it up to corps all the same," the colonel decided. "Dammit, I don't like the idea that a whole bomber wing has just given us the slip."

By late afternoon, the flow of information to SHAEF headquarters in Fontainebleau, just south of Paris, had increased to a small flood. Order-of-battle evaluators in timber huts in the grounds of the great palace were forced to conclude that a major redeployment of Soviet forces in East Germany was taking place. As yet they were unable to establish an overall *increase* in the number of Russian divisions or air support units. But new units were moving into the sensitive hundred-mile belt behind the East-West border, while other formations seemed, temporarily, to have disappeared altogether. The huge wall map in number 4-5 hut, normally able to offer full Soviet order-of-battle information at a glance, was now a confused mass of green pins, denoting unconfirmed units. Soviet field commanders' names, confidently displayed a few hours ago, were now removed from the board or followed by question marks. Urgent calls for an increase in photographic reconnaissance went out to USAF and RAF special units, but nothing could now be done until daylight, and meteorological units were already forecasting heavy morning fog.

The daily report was made up at 1930 hours each day and delivered in cipher by radio to all NATO governments. Today was the first time since the Berlin Airlift crisis that anyone could remember an occasion when the Supreme Allied Commander had signed it in person.

CHAPTER
14

A further fall of snow had been forecast for a week. Over the Chesapeake Bay, a leaden sky spread across the gray water and far out into the Atlantic Ocean.

In Charlottesville, Virginia, it was just warm enough for fog, but by late afternoon the fog was already freezing. Snow, it was predicted, would be here during the night.

Paying off the taxi, Alexander Trenton walked until he stood before wide steps leading to a white-columned building. To the right, he could see a lodge, a small office, behind the lighted window of which a man sat before a wood fire. No sign indicated that this was a university building. As he entered the gate, he could see that it gave onto a courtyard lit by wall lamps whose yellow light glistened in the thin fog. He paused, watching dark figures as they walked along the side of the court and disappeared through other archways or into the large pillared building in front of him. Had Vanessa not made her choice, not made the choice for *him* as Katya had put it, he imagined he would have attended an institution such as this, with its air of serene privilege.

He stepped forward and knocked on the lodge door. The man before the fire rose unhurriedly and slid back a window on the level of Alex's head. "Can I help you, sir?"

"I would like to see Mr. Charles Trenton." He found strange even the enunciation of the name.

The porter leaned forward and pointed across the square. "Right of the yard, sir. See a door in the center of the building? That's *J* staircase and the professor's office is on the first floor. J3."

"Thank you." Alex hesitated. "Does Professor Trenton live here?"

"Yes, sir." The frown was replaced by polite amusement. "Married professors have houses in the town. But since Professor Trenton is unmarried, he lives in. That's the way things are here, sir. Always have been."

Alex crossed the courtyard and passed through the archway on the far side. He found himself in a second lamplit courtyard, the buildings covered with ivy. Around him, lights shone from the mullioned windows, and from time to time the shadow of an undergraduate passed before him. Turning right, as the porter had instructed, he arrived at the stone-arched doorway marked *J*. The third name painted in white on a black board was Professor C. Trenton.

The stairs before him were bare oak. He climbed to the floor above. His mouth was dry, his heart hammering against his chest. He reached forward and knocked on the black-painted door.

A voice called to him to come in. He opened the door and stepped into an enormous book-lined room. A tall man, older somehow than he had imagined, dressed in a tweed suit, stood with a decanter in his hand, staring incuriously at him.

"You're Sapsford," Charles Trenton said. "You're late."

Alex shook his head. "No," he said, closing the door behind him. "I'm not Sapsford."

"No, Sapsford's tomorrow night." Charles Trenton replaced the decanter on the sideboard and turned back to face the stranger. Perhaps for the first time a faint sense of unease crossed his face. "What can I do for you?" he said to the silent young man at the door.

"I have a message for you," Alex said. "From Vanessa. She sends her greetings."

The old man was visibly startled. "From Vanessa?" His hand

was gripping the back of the chair. "From Vanessa—after all these years!"

Recovering himself quickly, he came forward across the room. "Forgive me," he said. "Do come in. May I offer you some sherry? Please take your coat off . . ." He turned back to the sideboard and took the decanter by its long glass neck. "You were in Moscow recently? At the embassy?"

"Not at the embassy."

"No? Introductions," the professor said, waving the decanter. "You know me, obviously. Charles Trenton. And you are . . . ?"

"I'm Alexander," he said as he stepped into the middle of the room.

"Alexander." Charles repeated the name softly. "Alex?"

"Your son."

"Alex . . ." His mouth opened and closed. "Alex . . . I don't know what to say."

"There's nothing to say," Alex said. "It was all a long time ago. I have no memory of you. You can have little memory of me. I was forbidden to come to see you. Vanessa forbade me."

Tears glistened in the old man's eyes. "At least," he said, "at least let us shake hands."

Reluctantly, Alex drew his hand from his overcoat pocket. His father's hand was thin and dry, squeezing compulsively. "Alex," he said. "Well . . . this is a shock to me."

Alex withdrew his hand.

"Sherry," his father said. "We must have a glass of sherry." He crossed back to the sideboard and poured sherry into two glasses. "You must tell me everything," he said. "About Vanessa. About yourself. You must tell me what you're doing here . . . Are you with the embassy?"

"I've come here, to America, to kill a man."

Charles Trenton looked at his son's set face. "To kill a man?"

"But I will not do it," Alex said. "I have decided to stay in America."

Charles Trenton nodded slowly. "I have some knowledge in these matters," he said. "I serve the American government as a kind of consultant. Perhaps you already knew."

"Until a few days ago I believed you died in Georgia. Of cholera."

"Cholera?" Charles smiled distantly. "Yes, good thinking," he said. "There was a most frightful cholera outbreak at that time. Sherry?"

"Do you have whisky?" Alex asked.

"Of course, of course. Whisky, that's what any young Soviet citizen wants when he comes to the West. I have a very fine malt." He poured two inches into a tumbler and handed it to his son.

"Don't you mind that Vanessa killed you off?"

He shrugged. "Not really."

"Did you write to her?"

"Oh, I tried to in the thirties. But those were such troubled times in the Soviet Union, Alex. Purges, a war looming. I saw your mother later, you know. In Moscow in 1944."

"She told me."

"Still beautiful. She always was. And happy, too, I think. She told me you were at the front. Stalingrad first and then the Ukraine. Sit down, sit down, my boy," he urged his son.

Alex, still wearing his overcoat, sat on the arm of an over-stuffed chair. "There's a girl in Moscow," he said, "that I decided I wanted to spend my life with. Now that's impossible."

Charles Trenton stood in the middle of the Persian carpet. The light from the wood fire flickered on his raised sherry glass. "Because you've made your mind up to stay in America?"

"Because I don't believe I can kill a man as the price of my happiness. And if I can't kill him, I can't go back."

"I won't disguise from you the fact that I know the name of the man you were sent here to kill. I've no doubt he is the man in whose debriefing I am involved."

"I have no wish to know the man's name," Alex said bitterly. "I might discover he is an eminently killable person. I might persuade myself that the price was acceptable. Low, even. But I know the price for me would still be one man's death."

"If you stay in the United States," his father said, "what do you imagine will happen to your mother in Moscow?"

"More important to me are others, one other, I shall never see again."

For a moment his father was silent. "You have grown into a cold young man, Alex. Why do you no longer care about your mother?"

"Because I've no doubt she knew the nature of the assignment."

"How could she know that?"

"It was given me by General Petrov."

Charles Trenton finished his sherry. "Why did you come to see me, Alex, after all these years?"

"Curiosity."

"And it has been satisfied."

"Yes."

Charles Trenton shrugged. "There's not much to me. I'm a fairly ordinary man."

"Perhaps." Alex got up and put his empty whisky glass on a side table.

"You're quite decided."

"To stay in America, or not to kill a man?"

"Both."

"Yes," Alex said. "Both."

"It's a course fraught with great difficulty, frequently great personal unhappiness," Charles Trenton said. "I hope for you, it will turn out differently." He paused. "You will come and see me again when you can, when your debriefing is over."

"Of course."

"They'll keep you a month or two somewhere, with interrogation sessions twice a day. But not too unpleasant." He paused. "Perhaps we'll even have a chance to get to know each other again."

Alex walked to the door. He offered his hand. "Good-bye," he said.

Again his father's thin, dry hand clasped his. "It's such a life," the old man said. "Such a hell of a life."

Alex turned into the Bierhaus on Jefferson Avenue and stopped just inside the door. The wooden booths that lined the walls were empty. One or two men sat at the long beaten-copper bar at the far end of the room. It wasn't difficult, even in the dim light, to pick out the long form of Hal Jones hunched over a drink.

For a moment Alex stood still, waiting it out until at least one of the other men at the bar revealed himself. Then a young man in jeans and red-plaid shirt lifted his eyes slowly from the sports paper he was reading. Alex smiled to himself and walked forward to the corner of the bar where Jones sat.

Slipping onto the bar stool next to the American, Alex watched him take a cigarette from a pack of Lucky Strikes and slowly light it.

"What happened to the moral relativism, Captain?" Jones said. "Did you decide we're nicer guys after all?"

Alex smiled grimly. "I don't grudge you your moment of triumph, General. We're professional officers, but a winning return match is still a triumph."

Hal signaled the waiter for two beers. When they had been placed before them on the table, he lifted his glass to Trenton. "Why?" he said. "Why weren't you prepared to go along with it?"

"I'm not an assassin—I'm not a killer."

"Did you know it was to be Shtemenko?"

"Shtemenko . . ." Through Alex's mind passed a mix of newsreel pictures of General Shtemenko inspecting troops, bending over maps, pointing across rivers in the direction of the next attack. "No," he said, "I didn't know who it was."

For a moment, Hal Jones watched him without speaking. The telephone on the bar rang, and the young man in the plaid shirt picked up the receiver. He spoke softly into the instrument, then looked up, nodding briskly to Hal Jones.

"You're in some danger yourself, Captain, you must know that," Hal said after a moment.

"If I'm worth killing, I'm worth protecting. You must have a safe house in Washington for someone like me."

"We have a central 'reception' center, yes. But it's occupied at the moment."

"The whole place is occupied?"

"By just one man. The general you were sent to kill. I'm not likely to put the hired gun in the next room to the potential victim—however much the hired gun claims to have reformed."

"You don't trust me."

"I'm working on it. But you still don't get the room next door." He slid off the bar stool and crossed the length of the bar to the phone.

"It's General Bolsover," the young man said in a low voice. Hal took the receiver. "Hal Jones here," he said.

In the White House, his chief, Lieutenant General Ted

Bolsover, was handed the receiver by his adjutant.

"Hal," Bolsover's voice was almost naturally flat. "Whatever you're doing, drop it."

"You want me back in Washington?"

"Immediately. It's decision time, Hal. Presidential briefing in two hours."

Hal hung up and stood for a moment, his hand resting on the phone. Then he lifted the receiver again and dialed. When Jennifer Hunter's voice came on the line, he gave his name briskly and cut across her expressions of surprise.

"A favor," he said. "I need a favor."

"Sure," she said cheerfully. "What is it you have in mind?"

"I'm in Charlottesville right now."

"Yes . . . ?"

"Sarah mentioned a place you have on Chesapeake Bay, an hour or so from Washington."

"I've got a cottage in Angleton."

"I'd like to borrow it."

"Sure," she said, less certainly. "But may I first ask who you're taking there?"

"Not Sarah," he said. "A man. A Russian defector."

"Good God!" she said. "You want him to stay *there*."

"Yes. He'll be under guard, and we'll have him out of there in a few hours."

"Well, of course," she said slowly. Her tone changed completely now, no longer flippant or uncertain, taking the urgency from his own voice. "But I'll have to drive over with the keys."

"Can you do that?"

"I'll leave right away. The address is 1633 Broadside. You can't miss it. Ask at the bar on the boardwalk."

"One more thing," he said, squirming to keep the receiver to his ear. "Can I ask you not to mention it to your husband?"

"Of course," she said crisply. "It's *my* cottage; I don't see what my husband has to do with it."

"I'll be there as soon as I can. You say I can't miss it?"

"A pretty little clapboard place with unpruned roses around the door," she said. "In summer, that is. At the moment, it's freezing, and the wind comes off the bay like a knife. See you there, Hal."

CHAPTER
15

Jennifer Hunter was making coffee in the kitchen when she heard the car outside. She listened to the car doors slam and the footsteps crunching across the snow. When the bell rang, she walked unhurriedly through the living room. She could see the towering, reassuring shape of Hal Jones on the porch.

When she opened the door, to her surprise and pleasure, Hal bent forward and kissed her lightly on the lips.

He came in and closed the door behind him. "I'm sorry to have to do this to you," he said.

She smiled. "It's worth it. What's happening?"

He sat for the moment on the arm of an overstuffed chair. "Almost everything," he said.

"A crisis," she said.

He nodded. "More than you could possibly know."

She reached out and slid a hand along his shoulder. "Tell me what you want me to do."

"I have to leave. I have a meeting in Washington in forty minutes." He put his arm around her waist. "I'll bring the Russian in now. I have a man outside on guard. Call, whistle, scream if you need him. But I don't think you will. I know the Russian. Maybe you could give them both a cup of coffee and a sandwich before you head back to Washington."

"Of course," she said.

He leaned down and touched the top of her hair with his lips. Then he walked quickly to the door, opened it and called to Trenton, outside.

The man who appeared in the doorway was in his thirties, his face lined with fatigue, his eyes watchful. "Come in," she said. "I'm just making coffee."

She expected the Russian to communicate in an awkward series of nods and smiles. But upon entering the living room, Alex said, smiling, "It's very kind of you to allow me to come here, Mrs. Hunter."

She stepped back in surprise. "I thought you were Russian," she said.

"I am. Or at least, I'm a Soviet citizen." He liked the way her eyes opened wide in unaffected surprise. He liked the warmth and opulent comfort of the cottage. He didn't care, he decided, whether she was part of the U.S. intelligence service or not.

The wind, cutting in from the bay, buffeted the rented Buick which drove slowly along the deserted boardwalk and turned onto the main square.

The snow lay thin but uniformly across the area between the clapboard courthouse and the low line of shops and houses. The Buick slowed to a halt outside the Angleton bar. A man got out and carefully locked the driver's door after him. Picking his way across the sidewalk, he entered the empty bar and smiled a greeting to the barman. Afterward the barman would remember that there was something about the stranger he had not taken to. When the coroner pressed him, he said it was the eyes. Something about the eyes that made the man seem to be flinching as he spoke.

He had bought a copy of the illustrated tourist map of Angleton on sale at the bar. He had ordered a beer and drunk it unhurriedly, studying the map. Perhaps five minutes later the man had finished his beer, thanked the barman and left.

After Hal Jones left for Washington, Jennifer made coffee and sandwiches and took them to the man on guard outside. Returning to the house, she poured coffee for Alex, too. "How is it you speak English so well?" she asked him.

"My parents are American."

"Both of them?" She frowned, not understanding.

"Yes. My father was a U.S. consul in Russia when I was a child," he explained. "We were overtaken by the Revolution."

Jennifer turned. "You were forced to stay in Russia?"

"No," he laughed. "My father took the warship home, and my mother decided to stay. In their relationship she was by far the stronger of the two."

She handed him a steak sandwich. "Why would an American woman at that time desert her husband for life in Russia? She was a believer, evidently."

He nodded. "Mostly in herself. I think she finds it genuinely difficult to believe that a thought she has could possibly be wrong or second-rate."

"And your father?"

"I had no memory of him. But this afternoon I went to see him. He is, not entirely coincidentally, a teacher of Russian, and I understand quite an expert on the Soviet Union."

"Did you like him?" She led the way back into the living room. "Did you like your father when you met him today?"

"I don't think so, no. I expected somehow to find he was weak, feeble."

"But he isn't?"

"No, I don't think so. I think, under his very polite manner, he's as arrogant and pigheaded as she is. I think he too finds it difficult to believe he has ever been wrong."

She finished her coffee. "I'm sorry," she said. "Had you hoped he'd be a friend?"

"Perhaps." He paused. "At this point in my life I certainly have need of friends."

She nodded slowly. "I know nothing about you or why you're here in the U.S.," she said. "But if I can offer you friendship, without disloyalty to my country, then I do so."

He stretched out his hand. "You're a remarkable woman, Mrs. Hunter," he said. "I would like to accept your offer."

In the small military briefing room in the White House, Hal Jones sat opposite his chief, General Bolsover, head of Military Intelligence Assessment. There was no one else present.

"The president," Bolsover said, "has been informed by the

Joint Chiefs of Staff of the defection and debriefing of General Shtemenko. President Eisenhower has been in touch with Prime Minister Churchill and other NATO leaders. In an hour's time the final decision will be taken by the National Security Council and the president as to our response to the USSR."

"That," Hal Jones said, "will presumably depend on the extent to which the president is convinced that Marshal Stalin has really ordered *Gopak.*"

"Exactly." Bolsover shifted his considerable bulk inside his uniform jacket. "Dammit"—he nodded toward the cigarette box lying among the leather-bound notepads on the desk between them—"give me a cigarette, Hal. I stopped smoking the day the last war ended."

Hal Jones opened the silver box and pushed it across the table.

Bolsover lit the cigarette and immediately forgot he was smoking it. "Let's first consider the movement of Soviet forces in the last two days. We are presently in the Soviet army's main winter maneuver season. All the radio activity reports, all troop, vehicle and aircraft movements so far could be the result of a vast Soviet exercise."

"Could be," Hal Jones said. "Just."

"Hal, we carried out exercises ourselves in the autumn," Bolsover said. "*Operation Counterstrike* had ten British and American armored divisions careering around Germany, not to mention French, Dutch, Danish and Norwegian infantry brigades."

"We warned the Soviets in advance," Hal said. "We gave them our order of battle and our restricted areas. If the Soviet army *is* engaged on a massive maneuver they're taking one hell of a risk not to cut us in. Sir," he added, in belated deference.

"Okay," Bolsover said carefully, "I will agree then that this *might* not be a straightforward Soviet maneuver. So we have, as I understand the problem, two possibilities. The first is one sketched out for us by Professor Trenton. He suggests that an attack on Western Europe may not be the object of the present troop movements. He does not rule out, however, the possibility of a Soviet housecleaning exercise, as he calls it, in Yugoslavia. His report, which I have here, suggests that the

Soviet movement *west* is a smoke screen. He feels Joseph Stalin is bluffing, that Stalin will agree at the last moment to call off *Gopak*, on condition that the West sits by and watches him invade Yugoslavia, his real objective."

"I understand his argument," Hal said carefully. "But I don't accept it."

"Why not?"

"Because it does not offer a reason for Shtemenko's defection."

"It does," Bolsover said, "in my view."

"Tell me how, General."

"Trenton believes the Soviet army may not have been told Stalin is bluffing. All they know is what we know—that a vast Soviet troop movement *westward* is taking place. Now, they are professionals. They know that in a war between the U.S. and the Soviet Union, the Soviet Union would almost certainly lose. Therefore, they send Shtemenko, the chief of staff, to beg for time while they depose Stalin." Bolsover paused. "What do you make of that?"

Hal nodded slowly. "I can't deny it's a possibility," he said carefully. "If that were true, it would be in our best interest to wait until Stalin reveals his hand."

"To do nothing. Exactly."

"You're asking me whether I agree with Trenton, or not?"

"Yes."

"The answer is I do not."

"Go on, Hal."

Hal Jones stared down at the leather-bound notepad. "We are being invited to believe that Stalin is bluffing and that Shtemenko, in ignorance of Stalin's bluff, has defected. The result of that defection, the theory runs, is to reinforce our fears that Stalin is poised to strike at the West."

Bolsover put out his cigarette and lit another.

"This afternoon, General," Hal continued, "I discovered that an MGB illegal had been introduced into the U.S. to assassinate Shtemenko. Now why would Stalin be so anxious to do that if Shtemenko's defection had suited his book as perfectly as Professor Trenton argues?"

"Jesus, Hal. In other words, you accept Shtemenko's story. You believe *Gopak* is not a bluff."

"I do."

"Is that the view that you want me to convey to the Joint Chiefs and President Eisenhower?"

"Yes."

Bolsover got up, again extinguishing his cigarette. "If he agrees with you, the president might order an immediate response. A preemptive strike against Russia's major cities. We are talking about ten million, perhaps twenty million dead."

"There's another way, General," Hal Jones said slowly.

"And that is?"

"Give the Soviets the time they need to get rid of Stalin."

Bolsover straightened. "Trust Shtemenko?"

"Yes."

"We're dealing with two separate factors, Hal. First, is Shtemenko's Soviet army truly willing to dispose of Stalin? Second, are they able to do so in time?"

Their eyes met across the desk. "We would be recommending to the president a terrible risk, Hal. If we ask for time for Shtemenko, *Gopak* each and every day comes closer to success."

Hal nodded slowly. "You asked me for my recommendation, General. I say we must take that risk."

Jones found his thoughts drifting with fatigue. The White House . . . he'd been here many times. Twice he'd had the honor to brief Harry Truman himself. Ike, of course, he'd known, if only slightly, from the European Theater in World War II. A general squeezed between the fussy, pompousness of Montgomery and the ugly arrogance of Patton; he was the only man in the world who could have kept the Allies together . . . The White House . . . a little scruffy, perhaps, after its long years of war and cold war. But he liked it as it was, he decided, a jumbled repository of American history. The telephone rang. A guard swung around in his chair. "Yes, we've got him here. For you, General. Major O'Sullivan."

Hal reached over the counter and took the telephone. "Hello, Jack," he said. "Are you at the cottage?"

"Hal . . ." O'Sullivan's voice came clear but hesitantly down the line. "I got stuck in the snow the moment I turned off the highway. A patrol car picked me up and got me to a farm where I could telephone the cottage . . ."

"Speed it up, Jack," Hal said easily. "You got through to the cottage?"

"There's been an accident. I'm afraid it's bad, Hal. A police lieutenant answered the phone there."

"Jennifer?"

"Jennifer's dead, Hal."

"Oh, Christ."

"The Russian, too. I couldn't get much from the cop. Can you call someone in the Met. Police Department there and get him to clear lines for you? I'm trying to get across there now."

"Right."

"I'm sorry, Hal."

"Thanks, Jack," he said.

He handed the telephone back to the guard, his face averted. Picking up his briefcase, he walked slowly back along the corridor. Afterward he could only remember the intense difficulty he had breathing.

It was nearly fifteen minutes before Hal got through, with the help of the White House MPD duty officer, to a Lieutenant Cogan at the cottage.

Cogan's voice, South Boston, was hard as a buzz saw. "Hallo . . . hallo. Lieutenant Cogan here."

"Cogan," he said quietly, "General Jones here. I need answers to some questions."

"Yes, sir."

"How was the 'accident' discovered?"

"A neighbor reported a rumpus. Maybe shots, maybe just someone chopping wood. Cold air does strange things to sound. We sent a man down, and he came back empty-handed. We sent another man down when the same neighbor called to say the place was on fire."

Hal Jones remained silent.

"You there, General?"

"I'm here."

"So the fire department deals with the fire. It's not much. Somehow it didn't take hold."

"And . . . ?"

"My man went through the place and found the bodies. I can't rule out robbery, but there's no sign . . ."

"How were they killed?" Hal asked.

"Messy," Cogan said. "Some sort of bludgeon."

"Wait a minute," Hal said. "How many bodies were there?"

"Two bodies, General. A man and a woman."

"And where did you find them? In the same room?"

"In the same room?" the lieutenant said. "They were in the same *bed*! The murderer caught the pair of them in the sack together." A strange sense of triumph came through in the lieutenant's voice. "Caught them right there in the sack together. It's a bitch, uh, General?"

"Yes, Lieutenant," Hal said as he hung up. "It's a bitch."

CHAPTER
16

President Eisenhower sat at his desk in the Oval Office in front of the television cameras. Seb Agnelli, the White House cameramen's lighting technician, dropped his hand in a signal.

"Fellow Americans," Eisenhower began. "Tonight we are on the brink of war."

The camera crew stared rigidly.

"The United States government has received information that Soviet forces are assembling for an attack on Western Europe. Every indication available to NATO reconnaissance suggests that the known Soviet war plan, code-named *Gopak,* has been initiated. Under Article V of our North Atlantic Treaty obligations, and because the government and the American people fully accept those obligations, an attack on Western Europe will, in any and all circumstances, be considered as an attack on the United States. I have therefore ordered our forces to a six-day level of response." Eisenhower paused. Resting his hands flat on the Jefferson desk, he continued. "Let me explain what that means. It means that preparations to resist attack begin immediately on land, sea and in the air. These preparations are both conventional and nuclear in their nature. From the ordering of the six-day response, one hour ago, only my direct intervention can halt or reverse the process."

Eisenhower stared into the camera with that grim, un-affected sincerity which had made alliances coalesce and re-calcitrant generals back down.

"The United States wishes the Soviet Union to be quite clear about this point. If the Soviet Union is not seen by American and Allied radio and physical reconnaissance to have aban-doned *Gopak*, then we shall be at war in seven days' time."

Eisenhower got up, nodded briefly to the crew and left the room.

Bolsover and Hal Jones followed among the aides and Cabi-net members who trailed out into the corridor.

"What happens now?" Hal opened the door to the military briefing room, and Bolsover led the way in. He made straight for the cigarette box, took one, lit it and turned to face Hal.

"That recording will be broadcast on all networks at midday tomorrow. The truth of the matter is that the response has already been ordered, giving the military *seven* days to prepare. We're on the road to Armageddon, Hal."

"Why the gap between the order and the announcement to-morrow?"

Bolsover inhaled deeply on his cigarette. Two hours had al-ready rededicated him to the smoking habit. "The President, in agreement with Prime Minister Churchill, decided to give the Soviet government a head start in initiating its plan to de-fuse the situation. But they also felt that we could not lose time. Response ought to be instituted immediately."

"You mean assassinate Stalin."

"Shtemenko says they can do it, Hal. Okay, they've got seven days."

The snow flurries swept around the dark shapes of the B-36 bombers as each emerged from its bomb shelter and taxied slowly, engines whining with the unevenness of start-up, onto the long runway facing out toward the North Sea.

In the eastern English counties of Norfolk, Suffolk, Cam-bridgeshire and Essex, the major part of the U.S. Strategic Air Command was on immediate readiness. On the night of 27 February 1953, white-helmeted MPs raced their jeeps from vil-lage to village, from pub to oak-beamed pub, assembling off-duty

ground crews and flying crews. The locals had seen nothing like
it since the days of 1944.

At Mildenhall, Greenham Common, Lakenheath and a dozen
smaller airfields, the B-36s lumbered onto the runways and took
off into the air with an ear-splitting roar of power. Once in the
air, they flew east into the freezing headwinds to describe vast
circles over the North Sea as they waited for coded commands to
open the document case every crew captain carried and to take
up the course heading that would direct them across the German
plain, eastward toward their assigned targets in the USSR.

In the Mediterranean, the sun was setting after a cool, sunlit
day. From the great Valetta Harbor on the island of Malta,
three battle cruisers, the aircraft carrier HMS *Eagle* and a de-
stroyer screen of the British Mediterranean Fleet steamed east
to an appointed rendezvous off Sicily with the United States
Sixth Fleet leaving the harbor at Nice.

Throughout Italy and across France, United States supply
squadrons began moving stores and ammunition toward the
German border. All NATO leave had been canceled; at the
Fontainebleau headquarters, planning staffs were assembled
around tables showing latest Soviet movements in the vast ad-
vance-to-contact operations that already involved nearly four
million Russian soldiers. From U.S. headquarters at
Heidelberg, armored units were activated to take up positions
deep in the snow-covered pine forests along the Czechoslo-
vakian border; reconnaissance units probed to the very edge of
the mined areas that cut great swaths through the Thuringian
Forest dividing East and West Germany.

Throughout Europe and the United States, in every U.S. base
from Greenland to Korea, American forces were placed on alert.
Although no operational order had yet come from Washington,
many feared World War III was virtually a reality.

"Okay, I'm just a nobody police lieutenant," Cogan said.
"But I am investigating a murder when all you military men
have stopped flashing your special permits at me."

O'Sullivan entered the cottage and stopped in the hall.

"Who else has been asking questions?" he said.

"There was a general in Washington. The White House, no less. He was on the phone twenty minutes ago wanting the gory details."

"You told him the two were in bed together?"

"I told him, Major. I told him the killer had busted in and caught them in the sack, no less."

O'Sullivan nodded bleakly. "Where's the bedroom?" he said.

"This way." Cogan ducked through the living room and into a passage. At the bedroom door, he stopped and turned, one hand high on the doorjamb, blocking the view into the room. "Nobody's fooling me on this one, you know that, Major," he said.

"Why should anybody want to fool you, Lieutenant?" O'Sullivan asked impatiently.

Cogan ran his tongue across his bottom lip. "This is my investigation. My story. However much Washington is interested."

"Step aside, Cogan."

"I've already given the press their first shot in the arm. They like an investigating officer who plays open with them."

"Step aside."

Cogan slid his hand down the doorjamb and turned to face into the room. O'Sullivan stepped forward and stood beside him.

The sheets of the large double bed were drenched with still-wet blood. The bodies of the man and woman tangled in the bloodstained sheets were turned back to back in fetal positions of helpless self-protection.

"Burst in," Lieutenant Cogan said, "and hit out at them like a crazy man."

Jack O'Sullivan stood in the doorway of the bedroom. "Have you identified the bodies yet, Lieutenant?" he asked slowly. "Did your shot in the arm to the press give any names?"

"The man's a mystery," Cogan said. "The woman's the owner of this little love nest. Wife of a congressman." The lieutenant smiled a dark-jowled smile. "Mrs. Harry D. Hunter, no less."

O'Sullivan walked across to the bed. The man had long dark hair. In death his face wore a silly smile. A face unknown to the major. O'Sullivan circled the bed to get a better look at the woman among the tangle of the sheets. He stood for a moment, grunting in surprise. "You've fucked up, Cogan," he said briskly. He was looking down at the blood-flecked face of Sarah Black.

"For God's sake, Hal, did you hear me?" O'Sullivan shouted down the phone.

"Yuh, I heard, but tell me again. After that you can go on telling me just as many times as you like."

"Jennifer's alive. So is the Russian."

"What happened, for Christ's sake?"

"Our man spotted a Buick cruising back and forth past the cottage, got edgy and made a quick decision to move Jennifer and the Russian into Charlottesville."

"But if it wasn't Jennifer and the Russian killed in bed, who was it?"

"The good news just ended," O'Sullivan said somberly. "The couple in bed was Sarah Black and an as yet unidentified male. They arrived after the others left. The killer caught them asleep, drunk out of their minds after balling and boozing all evening."

Hal realized he was nodding slowly to himself. "Sarah . . . ?"

"I said the good news just ended."

"Sarah." Hal repeated her name. "The poor kid. Jack," he added on a wave of exhaustion, "do all the right things and get back to Washington as soon as you can."

"You got a message for Jennifer?"

"I'm going to have a lot of messages for Jennifer."

"Funny thing is," O'Sullivan said, "I think she's expecting them."

CHAPTER
17

Perhaps Joseph Stalin conceded in his private thoughts that he would have preferred a year or two longer to launch *Gopak*. At the 1945 Moscow victory celebration, he had assigned 1955 as the year of the onslaught on the West. To attack two years earlier involved serious risk. To the viewer from the Kremlin window high in the Pleshny Palace, the risk was worthwhile. Stalin knew no future Soviet leader would ever possess the naked will to attack the West. *Gopak* was Stalin's opportunity for total European domination.

The Soviet army staff saw *Gopak* quite differently. Most of them had hotly argued *Gopak*'s feasibility with close colleagues a dozen times in the last year. The seizure of a West European front on a Paris–Brussels–Channel-coast axis represented a massive political gamble. Could the Soviet land forces take the major Western European cities with their population concentrations before the United States retaliated with atomic weapons? If so, Joseph Stalin was probably right in calculating that an American president would not order the destruction of Paris, Brussels, Amsterdam . . .

But most Soviet senior staff generals doubted that it was possible to seize Western Europe in one violent, headlong lunge. NATO forces had steadily improved their strength in the last two years. Their planned tactical response, a fast retreat to the

Rhine and a series of disabling counterattacks, had been practiced successfully by NATO North, using the British Rhine Army and NATO Center under U.S. command in the vast *Counterstrike* exercise of 1951. Many Soviet generals had watched *Counterstrike* with dismay.

In Germany, at that very moment, NATO officers were preparing grimly for war. They were soberly aware of the overwhelming numbers of Soviet forces. There were now twenty armored divisions, forty mechanized shock divisions and almost one hundred rifle divisions in position in East Germany. Against these one hundred and sixty divisions, the West could raise only the equivalent of thirty. French General Juin had that week insisted that the Soviet army *could* reach Paris and the Channel ports in twenty-one days. Only the Strategic Air Command and its atomic weapons, the NATO commanders believed, stood between them and utter defeat.

Both sides teetered on the fine line of terror.

Among the select few senior Russian officers who were fully aware of what was happening, most cast their hopes with General Shtemenko and Peter Voronov. Stalin had to die. But they reached *Gopak* minus 6 in the countdown, and the tension in the Soviet field commands in the towns and villages of East Germany visibly mounted. There was little drinking and no feasting. The few generals who knew of the plot found their thoughts turned toward Moscow, their ears attuned to the first jangling of the field telephone that would announce that Stalin was dead.

Along the straight, deserted road, the sound of the Mercedes engine broke the silent tranquility of the surrounding countryside. Conspicuous as a small black beetle on a white carpet, the car sped along the Pavlovsky Road beside a large expanse of frozen lake. In the distance, a setting red sun danced on the horizon. As it died, it seemed to draw in all the raw colors of the snowscape, leaving the lakeside pale, bereft, gentle in the evening light.

In the back of the Mercedes, General Peter Voronov, newly appointed commander of the First Shock Army, sat, one arm on the window rim, watching the sunset on the horizon. A spiraling column of blue smoke rose from a cigarette held be-

tween his fingers. Secretary Poskrebyshev had telephoned him
at his dacha that afternoon to tell him he was to be in Moscow
by midnight. An interview with Joseph Stalin had been arranged for two hours later; Voronov should bring all the necessary maps and charts which would enable Stalin to brief him
in detail on the first crucial six hours of the breakout.

But Peter Voronov was bringing with him more than maps
and data. His briefcase, which could be opened out to form a
field briefing table if laid on the hood of a jeep, carried in its
spine a long, slender steel bracing strut, one sharpened end
converted into a stiletto. Voronov had chosen the weapon himself. The problem of smuggling a pistol past the Chekist
guards was insurmountable. And he had no scruples about
using a knife. The fierce patriotism that motivated Peter
Voronov left him with no scruples at all. Stalin must be
stopped at all costs. He watched the cigarette smoke curling
through his fingers. The driver clicked on the headlights; the
wheels of the Mercedes hissed steadily across the snow. He
would be in Moscow in little over an hour. Time to eat and
perhaps take a small glass or two of vodka. He lifted his head,
aware that the car was slowing. Ahead there were moving
lights, men with flashlights.

The driver brought the Mercedes to a halt. Three cars lined
the roadside, along with eight to ten armed MGB men. The
leader was draped in a heavy fur coat, the collar masking his
face against the wind.

It was still not quite dark. They might have been, halted
here by the side of the road, a hunting party. Of course,
Voronov thought wryly as he was ordered out of the car, that's
exactly what they were.

Leaning against the car, Voronov tried to protest when the
man in the fur coat, whom he recognized as a Chekist senior
officer named Petrov, ordered him and his driver to stand side
by side against the rising snowdrift. Moments later, both Peter
Voronov and his driver were shot without ceremony. Afterward they were stripped naked and left on the snowbank for
the wolves.

CHAPTER
18

An onion-domed church cut from cardboard stood at the head of the snow-covered slopes, dominating the skillfully painted Austrian village on the backcloth. Falling snow filtered through twinkling lights. The chorus line, in ski caps and fashion goggles, high heels and fishnet nylon tights, twirled their ski sticks and yodeled prettily for the Cascade Club audience.

Jacob Vishniak swung around on his bar stool, away from the stage, as he caught sight of Brigadier General Jones entering the club.

"Caught you at it," Hal said, laying his hand on Vishniak's shoulder.

Vishniak smiled. "You're right," he said. "I'm developing a taste for the girls. My problem is, at five feet five, I barely reach their shoulders."

"Come and sit down," Hal said, turning toward a corner booth.

Vishniak followed him, his eyebrows lifted. "It's not like you, Hal, not to want to talk about the girls."

Hal nodded and signaled a waiter. "What will you have, Jacob?"

"Same as you. You know I'm not really a drinking man."

"Two scotch, no ice," Hal said mechanically.

Vishniak watched him as he lit a cigarette. "Did you find our lost general?"

Hal Jones hesitated. "Yes, we did. Pretty much as you predicted. He crossed at Checkpoint Charlie three days ago."

Vishniak locked his fingers together on the table in front of him. His head was bent. "Are you able to tell me why?"

"I'll tell you what I can, Jacob. Shtemenko was debriefed here in the United States on Thursday. He confirmed what you said—Stalin was no longer recognizably sane. He argued that the danger was such that he would have to be removed."

"Assassinated?"

"Yes."

The waiter approached the table and placed the drinks before them. The ski tableau was coming to an end with much high kicking and, by now, slightly strained yodeling.

"Assassinated by whom? An associate of General Shtemenko's, clearly." Vishniak answered his own question.

"Yes," Hal said carefully. "That's as far as I can go, Jacob."

"Let me try to go further then, Hal. Just a step or two. Was the name of this associate of Shtemenko's a young general named Peter Voronov?"

"Jesus Christ!" Hal swore under his breath. "How could you know that?"

"I've got bad news for you, Hal. Perhaps I don't quite know how bad. But Peter Voronov was shot on the road to Moscow last night."

Hal leaned forward heavily on the table. "You're absolutely sure of that, Jacob?"

"He was shot on Beria's direct order," Vishniak said steadily. "There will be no assassination of Stalin by Peter Voronov."

Hal pushed back his chair. "I'm going to leave you for a while, Jacob," he said. "I have to think. Have another drink, watch the show. But wait for me, okay?"

Vishniak looked at his friend's totally absorbed expression. "You take your time, Hal," he said. "I'll be here."

Leaving by the main entrance of the club, Hal walked through the light snow that was sprinkling down under the streetlights. He had not thought to pick up his hat and coat before he left the Cascade, but he walked on, with long, fast strides, oblivious of the damp and the chill in the wind that

came down Independence Avenue. He wished he could talk to
Jennifer. He knew it was impossible to talk to Jacob Vishniak,
or to Jack O'Sullivan or any other of a dozen service friends. A
plan began to form in his mind. If he got an okay, his plan
would have to be implemented right away. He supposed it
would mean, almost certainly, the death of Alexander Trenton. But it might be the only way of avoiding World War III. It
was his decision. One death, versus so many lives, and he
might even be able to save Alex. No excuses. No philosophy.
He would put it to Bolsover immediately.

He found himself walking north on First Street. At the Library of Congress, he stopped. Two patrolmen of the MPD
watched him from the other side of the street. His short gray
hair was plastered down on his forehead. Under the street-
light, he turned abruptly and, slowly now, his hands deep in
his pockets, began to walk back the way he had come, looking
for a phone.

Fifteen minutes later he was at the Cascade Club again.

"I've got a man, Jacob. And I've got the go-ahead to use
him."

Vishniak's eyes half closed as if stung with smoke. "Whether
he succeeds or not, you know he'll be made the scapegoat."

"I know."

"Russian?"

"Ex-MGB."

Vishniak smiled. "Perhaps you've put the right pieces together. But why should he do it?"

Hal Jones took a mouthful of his whisky. "That's the only
part of the jigsaw that doesn't fit yet. But I'm working on it. I
need your help, Jacob."

Vishniak inclined his head in assent. "Go on."

"For this one, I'm going to ask you to pull out all the stops,
Jacob. I know you've got help inside the Kremlin."

"Yes," the old man said through pursed lips.

"In the last resort, which way will your man jump?"

"He will save his own skin," Vishniak said. "What do you
want him to do?"

"It is impossible to smuggle a weapon into the Kremlin. In
return for a promise that his skin will be saved, would your
man help?"

"We know too much about him," Vishniak said. "He has no choice."

"Fair play demands I give you something in return," Hal said, smiling. "Some information. General Shtemenko is dead."

"Shtemenko is dead? While you were holding him?"

"They sent a killer. From Moscow. As soon as they knew Shtemenko had defected."

Vishniak smiled slowly. "I see. You want me to pass it on: the killer carried out his task successfully. General Shtemenko is dead. I assume it doesn't matter that I don't believe a word of it."

"You don't have to," Hal said, getting up. "Just as long as the MGB believes *you*."

It had stopped snowing. Through the windshield, Hal watched the other car approach. Only when he was certain that Jack O'Sullivan was driving it did he get out and stand on the sidewalk.

O'Sullivan brought the car to a skidding halt beside him. The back door flew open, and Jennifer Hunter seemed to rise up in front of him in a flurry of fox fur and perfume. He enclosed her in his arms and held her tight. "Poor Sarah," she said. "She was a spoiled, self-indulgent brat. But she didn't deserve to be a part of all this."

He released her slowly. "We're all part of it," he said. "We'd all prefer not to be. We'd all prefer to leave it to the professionals and pretend it just doesn't happen. But it's not possible, Jennifer."

She nodded slowly, not far from tears. "Jack O'Sullivan says you thought it was me for an hour or so."

"For an eternity or so," he said.

She squeezed his hand. "Behind you," she said. "My husband is standing on the steps of the house watching us."

"It's his house."

She nodded. "But he's unlikely to have missed the fact that you have one hand inside my fur coat caressing parts of me that he would probably think of as distinctly off limits."

"I decided when I heard you were alive that I don't plan to be Mr. Nice Guy," he said.

"Good."

"I must go now." He released her.

She didn't move away. "When Jack O'Sullivan told me that when he phoned you, you had no special message for me, I was very disappointed," she said.

"I've a message for everybody." The gesture over his shoulder included Hunter, standing on the house steps. "I love you," he said. "And I want you to be mine. Always."

In Hal Jones's Georgetown apartment, there was no sound but the slow ticking of the clock. The two men faced each other, their expressions set.

Alexander Trenton said, "You have no right to ask me to take a risk like that."

"I'm not talking about rights tonight," Hal said. "I've laid it out for you. Joseph Stalin must be assassinated."

"I don't see that I am the only possible candidate," Trenton said, the tension drawing in his cheeks. "You must have people in Moscow."

"We have. The British have others in contact with Ukrainian nationalists in the army and government. The French too have a man there for whom assassination would not be a new experience. But *nobody* can get to Stalin's quarters without an invitation. He leaves the Kremlin only to go to his dacha at Kuntsevo. The route is lined by MGB guards. The convoy is escorted by more guards. He is obsessed with the knowledge that he is the most hated man in Russia. Without you, Alex, we cannot get through to him. Without you we certainly can't get through to him in time."

"And you believe that he will receive me?"

"I believe he will receive Shtemenko's killer."

"They think he's dead?"

"Yes. That part has already been arranged. You are a Soviet hero."

"Can you also guarantee that I won't go the way of General Peter Voronov?"

"Guarantee it, no. Nobody could do that."

Trenton paced the carpet while Hal watched him. "This much I can tell you, Alex. You can make any demands, any conditions, however impossible they seem. I give you my word I'll do my best to fulfill them. But you've got to be the one to do it, Alex. Because at the moment you're the only one who possibly can."

Trenton smiled briefly. "And if I still refuse?"

Hal shrugged.

"You would hand me back to the MGB?"

"One way, you have a slight chance of survival. If I hand you back to your ex-friends in the Lubyanka, you'll have no chance at all."

"So I go—or I'm handed back."

Hal nodded. "That's about the size of it," he said. "Either way, you'll be back in Moscow in twenty-four hours."

"What makes you think you have to kick me so hard?"

Hal looked at him. "You mean I don't?"

"I'm a Russian, Hal," Alex said vehemently. "I may sound to you like an American but I'm not. I fought at Stalingrad. I grew up with ordinary, uncomplaining Russian soldiers. I made love to Russian girls. I have come to believe that for Russia everything Joseph Stalin has touched has meant misery, labor camps and death." He paused. "I have other reasons, too, for going back."

"You're saying you'll go?"

"Do you mind if I pour us a drink?" Alex walked to the bar and poured two large whiskies. "When do you want me to leave?"

"Tonight."

He handed Hal a glass. "There's a lot we could drink to . . . but then again, maybe no—"

Hal shook his head. "Just drink," he said. "We've got two whole fifths to get through before you get on that plane."

CHAPTER
19

"A penny for your thoughts," Jennifer said.

"Not these thoughts." Hal got up and crossed to the table where the whisky was kept.

"You're drinking a lot tonight," Jennifer said. "Why is that, Hal?"

He looked back at her, the bottle half raised above the glass. She sat in the corner of his big English sofa as if she had been sitting there for years. "Have a drink with me," he said.

"Okay." She got up, crossed to stand behind him, kneading his shoulder muscles gently as he poured.

"That's good." He straightened up and handed her a drink. "What do we drink to?"

"I don't know." He smiled. "Us would maybe be a bit corny."

"Sarah," she said. "We could drink to her." They touched glasses. "And Alex. We could drink to him. Where is he now, Hal?"

He hesitated. "On his way to a debriefing center in the South. He'll be there awhile."

"Will they give him a hard time?"

"I don't see why." Hal moved across the room, put down his drink and began to select a record. "He's not going to hold back, I guess. He'll tell everything he knows."

"And his father is, after all, a distinguished Kremlinologist."

"He's a pompous bastard."

"That's what Alex told me. It's not a case of refound, long-loved father."

"I guess not. Or vice versa." He put on a record.

"What is it?" She nodded toward the record player. "Russian?"

He nodded. "Very popular number at the moment with the *Vlasti,* the Soviet bosses."

"What is it called?"

He sat down and lay back. "It's called 'Laugh with a Stranger.'"

"Pretty title." She sat at the other end of the long sofa.

"The story line's not so pretty," he said.

"How does it go?"

"Girl meets boy. Boy falls in love with girl. Girl falls in love with boy. Boy strangles girl."

"What?" She sat up.

He nodded.

"Why does he do it?"

"A poser, huh? Matter of fact, we set it as a question for our young trainee spooks. After they've listened to it three hundred times, they write a couple of volumes of analysis each."

"So what *does* it mean?"

"How the hell do I know?"

"Don't the trainees ask you?"

"Sometimes," he conceded. "Then I tell them it's not all neat role-reversal stuff. The analysis they've just written will prove to be a complete analysis of their *own* personality."

She laughed. "Is everybody crazy in your business?"

"Most are," he said. "All this fancy training in Moscow and Washington leads to constantly overrating the opposition. Everybody on the other side is assumed to be as slithery as a highly intellectual eel."

"They're not?"

"No." He said seriously. "Most agents are dim and flawed." He nodded. "Most *people* are dim and flawed. Except you. You're not dim, and"—he looked at her appraisingly—"you're certainly not flawed."

"Thank you."

"But that doesn't mean you might not be a spook."

"Oh, Christ," she said, throwing herself on him. "Come to bed."

The phone rang on the table beside the sofa.

"Leave it," she said, one hand on the receiver.

He shook his head.

"You don't want to come to bed with me?"

"No." He lifted her hand off the receiver. "For a lot of reasons—not tonight." He put the telephone to his ear. "Hal Jones," he said into the mouthpiece.

"Jones," a slightly slurred voice said, "don't think I don't know what you're up to. You've got my wife at your apartment, goddamn you . . ."

Hal covered the phone. "Your former husband," he said. "What shall I tell him?"

"Tell him all."

He uncovered the phone. "Yuh," he said. "Jennifer's here."

"I'm coming around to collect her," Hunter said.

"No," Hal said evenly. "There's no point, Mr. Hunter. She's staying. For good."

In Moscow, the night was coming to an end. From where he lay, propped up by cushions in the deep angle of a sofa, Joseph Stalin could see the first dawn light at the window. He would sleep soon.

He rarely rose before late afternoon anymore. He spent listless evenings in his room at the Pleshny Palace, moodily reading reports, signing directives, occasionally flipping through the pages of a book that had fleetingly caught his attention, but for the most part dozing, eyes half-closed, recalling the past. For several years now, it was only in the hours of darkness that his mind warmed to activity. It was then that the vast schemes, shaping the future of the country and the world, would form and crystallize in his brain.

Stalin moved a cushion behind his shoulders into a more comfortable position and settled back, allowing a host of memories to float up into his mind's eye: half-forgotten events, places and people, many from his childhood, all vague and ill-defined, gently passed before him, slipping away, leaving a pleasing sensation of tranquility which seemed to soothe and calm his spirits. A dusty village, a dog asleep on a step lifting its

head as a group of chattering children hurried by on their way
to the schoolhouse; a sparkling river with a crowd of smiling
people, their shoes tied around their necks, splashing along in
the sandy shallow water near the bank; a jostling throng,
cheering enthusiastically as they marched, waving their hats
and scarves in the air. Then one of the faces, separating and
drifting up from the rest, appeared to turn in on itself, slowly
coming into focus as it rotated again to draw near and con-
front him. As the features formed and became clear, the
mouth twisted into a leering grin. Stalin felt his body jolt as he
recognized the image, the arrogant eyes, the small, pointed
beard, the sneering, insolent intellectual look. It was the greatest traitor of them all, his deadliest rival, Trotsky. The mouth
was moving, miming unheard words of denunciation. How
could anyone ever have been deceived by his sly glibness? A
dark venom of utter hatred rose in Stalin as he remembered
how desperately close Trotsky had come to succeeding Lenin.
His rage boiled as he recalled the moment when Trotsky had
stood up before the Central Committee and accused him, Stalin, of poisoning Lenin. But Trotsky had paid dearly for that
and for all the other gibes and insults. Exiled to Siberia, de-
ported to Turkey, deprived of his citizenship, relentlessly
hounded out of Europe, the wretch had finally sought refuge
in the Americas. And an agent had been dispatched to kill him
there.

Stalin's heart was pounding in his chest in time with the incessant ticking of the clock. The two sounds merged, shaking
his body, filling the room. The synchronized, omnipotent, ticking bore down on him with a terrible pressure, squeezing, driving him ever deeper into a dark, bottomless void. As the
darkness was about to envelop him, Stalin broke the spell. With
a gasping lunge, he rolled off the sofa.

After a full minute, he got to his feet and shuffled to his
desk. Releasing the electronically operated bolts on the door,
he went out. Although it was barely dawn, the lights in the
hallway had been extinguished. Stalin moved to the top of the
grand staircase. At the foot of the wide flight of steps,
Poskrebyshev's bald head bobbed like a buoy in the gloom.

"Is that you, Marshal Stalin?"

The lights came on. Stalin blinked down at the upturned, startled face of his chief secretary.

"Marshal Stalin, are you all right?" the thin voice called.

Stalin came slowly down the stairs, leaning heavily on the bannister. "What time is it?" he barked as he reached the bottom.

Poskrebyshev glanced at the watch on his wrist. "Almost seven o'clock, comrade."

Stalin turned and began to stumble back up the stairs. Poskrebyshev followed a dutiful step or two behind him. "General Petrov is waiting to see you, if he may, for a few moments."

"Not now," mumbled Stalin.

"He has important news," ventured the secretary. "News you were awaiting."

At the top of the staircase, Stalin stopped and turned, heaving a sigh of annoyance. Poskrebyshev opened the door to a small, unheated waiting room and beckoned the MGB general out into the corridor. Petrov stopped and came to attention. Stalin gave him his grimmest stare. "Well? Well, Petrov?"

"You recall I dispatched my own stepson to America, Comrade Marshal."

Stalin's eyes narrowed, almost disappearing into the folds of flesh.

"His task has been successfully completed," Petrov said. "The traitor is dead."

For a moment Stalin stood swaying, his hand resting on the bannister. "After all these years." After pursuing him through Siberia, Turkey, Europe . . . Trotsky was at last dead. He looked at Petrov. "After all these years," he said.

"All these years . . . ?" Petrov felt the alarm rise in him.

Stalin's eyes closed. "After all these years!" His eyes flicked suddenly open. "There must be no mention of this fact. There must be no growth of the Trotsky myth." Stalin turned away and moved on.

Petrov stared at the broad, hunched back, desperately trying to suppress the idea that Stalin was now quite mad, terrified that by some strange telepathy his merciless master might detect the treasonous thought. He called after the receding figure, trying not to raise his voice too much. "I meant Shtemenko, Comrade Marshal, General Shtemenko is dead."

Without breaking his faltering step, Stalin went into his room and closed the door. Behind him, the electronic bolts clicked automatically home.

The door bell rang, and Hal got up. "I guess this is your husband," he said to Jennifer.

She nodded. "You're a big fellow. Tell him to go home."

Hal reached the front door and slipped the chain. Opening the door, he saw Harry Hunter, drunk, swaying a little, but with a confident grin on his face.

"I want to talk to you, Jones. I feel it's time we had a word together."

"Jennifer's here."

"That's okay with me."

Hal lifted his eyebrows.

"I've more important things to talk about," Hunter said, "than middle-aged ladies looking for a new bag of oats. I'm here to talk about Shtemenko."

Hal hesitated, then opened the door wide to allow Hunter to enter. He walked into the living room. "Jesus," he said to Jennifer, "this place *reeks* of body-contact sports."

"What is it you've got to say?" Hal came into the room behind him.

Hunter looked about him. His eyes passed over Jennifer and returned to Hal. "Aren't you going to offer me a drink?"

"No."

Hunter shrugged. "Okay, General, let's get down to business. I've just heard on the intelligence grapevine that Shtemenko is dead." He stabbed the air on each word. "That a senior Soviet general has been murdered while in your custody."

Jennifer sat forward in her seat.

"If you want to discuss this matter, you must discuss it with the proper authorities," Hal said.

"Is my information correct? Is Shtemenko dead?" Hunter's eyes glittered.

Hal glanced down at Jennifer's drawn face. "I have nothing to say, Hunter."

"You're his goddamn jailer, for Christ's sake, and I'm a United States congressman. I demand to know what's happened to General Shtemenko. Get it? I demand to know."

"Listen to me, Jones," he said more quietly. "I'm calling a TV press conference for tomorrow morning. Senator McCarthy will hold it himself. We're demanding that the body be examined by competent police specialists. I'm going to break your ass, General. In public."

"You cancel those arrangements, Hunter, or I'll have the White House thundering down on your head."

Hunter laughed. "I've already warned the senator of the chances of a cover-up."

"And what was his answer?"

Hunter paused. "You may be aware, General Jones, that the U.S. Army is not, at this moment, Senator McCarthy's favorite institution. The death of the most important Soviet defector *ever* while in custody of the military is exactly the sort of event the senator has been warning the president and the American people was bound to happen."

"Stop ranting, for Christ's sake," Hal said, "and get out."

"I'm not ranting, General. I'm telling you the senator will go ahead. You'd better be ready for an independent autopsy within one hour of the end of the broadcast."

Jennifer was silent for a long time after her husband had gone. Then she stood up.

"Is this Russian general the man Alex was sent to kill?"

"He told you a lot that night in Angleton."

"He told me about a girl, too, named Katya. Is the general really dead, Hal?"

For some moments, Hal hesitated. "No," he said at length. "Shtemenko is alive."

"But you want it believed he is dead."

"Right."

"And Harry is going to foul up the whole story?"

"Right."

"I think I can help," she said. "I've got something to show you."

They took her car and drove across Georgetown through snow which was already turning to drizzle. As they entered the house, Doonan, the butler, appeared from his basement apartment.

"Are you drunk again, Doonan?" Jennifer said without severity.

"I sure hope so, Mrs. Hunter. If not, I've spent a lot of good whisky on nothing tonight."

She nodded. "Let's go downstairs," she said. "General Jones and I have to talk to you."

Hal followed them both down the winding stairs into the basement. The apartment was in chaos. Empty beer bottles lay where they had been kicked beneath the furniture, ashtrays spilled over in a mass of snapped cigarette butts and gray ash. A half-empty whisky bottle stood beside a single glass on the carpet before the imitation log fireplace.

Doonan hooked his thumb toward Hal. "The general's a good guy," he said to Jennifer. "You should marry him."

"Doonan, tell General Jones exactly how you come to be working for me."

"You want me to do the old family-retainer routine," Doonan said as he found glasses and slopped whisky into them. "You want me to tell him I've been with the family, man and boy, since my pappy sold up in Georgia on account of his grief over my dear mother's demise. He won't believe a word of it."

"Just get on with it, Doonan. We don't have time to waste."

"Everything, ma'am?" Doonan shuffled uncomfortably.

"Yes. Everything."

"Well, General, when you first sent me to the stockade in the 82nd, you were about right." He turned to Jennifer. "Do I have to do this?"

"You do."

"Well, I don't like it, General, but here it is. I first met the good lady here when I snuck up to her outside the Library of Congress and flashed a single picture of her congressman husband about to do something very naughty to a young lady. And when I say a young lady I mean a very young lady."

"He means Sarah," she said briskly. "Aged fourteen to fifteen."

"Jesus."

Jennifer nodded. "Yes. Jesus. There were other pictures, too, which Mr. Fine Art Dealer Doonan had for sale."

"Now please, Mrs. Hunter, don't make me out worse than I was."

"Tell the general."

Doonan finished his whisky. "I asked eight hundred bucks. Nothing outrageous. I had five photographs taken through the mixer shower in a little hotel down by the river."

"The mixer shower?"

"Yeah, some guys specialize in this sort of shot. Through the shower nozzle, past the curtain onto the bed. Everything arranged to get the shot. Like I said, they specialize."

"Why didn't you take the pictures straight to Hunter himself?"

"I already had," Doonan acknowledged. "He put a marker on me, and I ended up with a few cracked bones in a back alley. After that, good business, not to mention good health, suggested I go straight to the lady."

"And?"

"Well, of course I didn't know what I was getting into yet. Respected political figure likes the young stuff, that's not good. Respected political figure is balling the girl whose moral welfare is entrusted to him, that's different."

"Stop moralizing, Doonan. You're not impressing the general."

"Okay. I showed the lady the pictures. I asked for the same eight hundred. I don't know what I expected, but it wasn't what I was offered. I was offered a job. As the butler. Me, a butler. The lady said I looked the part, the duties would not be onerous, an apartment would be supplied and the salary would be generous."

Hal turned to Jennifer. "Why the hell did you do that? Why didn't you kick out your so-called husband and put the police on Doonan?"

"When this happened," Jennifer said, "I'd been married a matter of six months." She paused. "Harry and I were joint guardians. We were trustees of Sarah's considerable fortune. To eject Harry from the trust would have created one of the biggest Washington scandals since the war, with Sarah the object of every prurient press photographer in the country."

"His political career would have been ruined. Wasn't that enough to make him step down?"

"No. Because he knew that the moment he stepped down two things would happen. First, he would lose all the prestige, the financial clout, that being chairman of this sort of trust confers. Second, he'd no longer have access to my money."

"So he refused to step down, and you decided to hang in for Sarah's sake."

"I decided to stay with Harry until Sarah came into the first stage of her inheritance at the age of twenty-one."

"And you hired Mr. Doonan here as a reminder."

"I hired Doonan to keep an eye on him. To keep an eye on *both* of them."

"What did Hunter think of that?"

"I told him openly what Doonan's job was in this house. I had no illusions about Sarah. I could easily imagine she'd encouraged Harry or at least played her part freely."

"So what happened?"

"My husband kept away from her. And Sarah developed an almost pathological hatred of him." She shrugged. "Better than screwing him, I suppose." She smiled bitterly. "My guardianship turned out to be less than a success for poor Sarah. So that's the story. I'm sure you can do something with it." She put down her untouched whisky and walked quickly from the room.

In the darkest corner of the Cascade Club, Harry D. Hunter sat watching the tall figure of Hal Jones thread his way through the tables. "I don't like to be seen in places like this, Jones," he said as Hal slid along the bench seat next to him.

"All the same, you decided to come at one o'clock in the morning."

"There was a message from my wife at home. It said you wanted to see me—something important."

"Who gave you the message, Hunter?"

"What difference does it make who actually gave it to me?"

"Doonan gave it to you."

"Yes, yes, as a matter of fact he did. He let me in. There's nothing unusual about him giving me a message."

"No," Hal paused. "There'd be nothing unusual about

him giving you a hint of what I wanted to see you about, either."

Hunter remained silent.

"The last floor show starts in a few minutes, Congressman. Do you like girls?"

"What is it you have to say, Jones?"

"I'm really here more to jog your memory. How about a small, discreet hotel, not exactly sleazy but then not exactly ritzy either. It's called the Ascherman-Keeble. Remember it?"

Hunter stared out toward the stage where preparatory noises were coming from behind the curtain.

"Remember the Ascherman, say four or five years back? Remember these?" Hal dealt onto the black polished tabletop five photographs, like a poker hand revealed.

Hunter slid them together and put them into his inside pocket. "I won't stay for a drink," he said, getting to his feet.

"No press conference," Hal said. "Tell the senator you were mistaken."

"Is that the deal?"

"That's it, Congressman. Don't even mention the name Shtemenko for the next twenty-four hours."

Hunter inclined his head. "The negatives and any copies that might have been made?"

"They've been buried five years, Hunter. Keep your fingers crossed they stay buried."

Harry D. Hunter walked toward the entrance. Sitting at the bar, Jennifer turned and nodded good night to him.

Hunter ignored her, Hal saw. He crossed to stand beside her.

"I've been thinking. The Russian general is alive—although he will now be thought by the Russians to be dead," she said.

"Yes."

"And Alex Trenton is safe. At least for the moment."

There was a hardness in her voice he had not heard before. "Yes," he said. "For the moment."

"The way I see it, that's for only one reason. You're preparing the ground for Alex to go back. In *triumph*."

He stood beside the bar stool, one hand resting on the leather bar. She turned slowly toward him. "How did you get Alex to go back to spy for you, Hal?"

He reached for his drink on the bar.

"He told me at the cottage he would never go back."

Hal shrugged. "They change their minds."

"Under any circumstances," she persisted.

"It's a dirty business, Jennifer. It does no good to know how dirty some of the answers are. I can only tell you that what he's doing is absolutely essential."

"You forced him somehow."

"In a way."

"You told him you'd hand him back to their security police if he didn't work for you."

"Something like that."

"Why?"

"It was important enough. Take my word."

"Nothing's important enough," she said. "What chance does he have in Moscow?"

"Not much," Hal said. "Not much at all."

"But you sent him all the same."

"Yes."

"Because it was important enough."

He moved to take the bar stool beside her, but she lifted a hand to stop him. "Fuck off, Hal," she said, then paused, considering. "I've never used words like that before. It's remarkable how satisfying they are."

"Jennifer—"

"Fuck off, Hal," she said sadly. "Fuck off out of my life."

CHAPTER
20

Among the very senior army officers and the political members of the *nomenklatura*, the move to leave Moscow built quickly in the last days before *Gopak*.

Bulganin had already pleaded an inspection tour of the Soviet reserve army forming in the Ukraine. His military advisors had long suggested the southern Ukraine might be the safest area in the western Soviet Union in the first weeks of nuclear war. Of course Kiev would be targeted, and in the Russian Republic, Leningrad and Moscow, but the general military belief was that the balance of U.S. atomic power would be used to destroy Soviet front-line concentrations and Russia's few atomic weapons based in Poland and East Germany.

Other members of the Politburo found themselves desperately calculating the moment they could safely leave the capital. A call from Stalin to an empty office could mean their death warrant. Voroshilov had already slipped away. Molotov stayed on. Visiting Nikita Khrushchev's apartment on Saturday, *Gopak* minus 3, Georgy Malenkov had found servants packing stores of food and even rolling up carpets. Alarm communicated itself rapidly. "You're leaving Moscow?"

"Of course we are." Khrushchev pulled Malenkov into a room and slammed the door. "Within three days Moscow will be in ruins."

"The Soviet government can continue from the Kremlin bunker. In the event of war, members of the Presidium are expected to make their way there."

Khrushchev cut him short with a quick gesture. "Haven't we heard enough about bunkers run by madmen? There was one in Berlin a few years ago, remember?"

Malenkov flinched in shock. No member of the Presidium had been that outspoken about Stalin before. "There's a message from Eisenhower. It demands the abandonment of *Gopak*. Have you seen it?"

"Of course I've seen it." Khrushchev shook with fear and anger. "Every member of the Presidium has seen it. But Stalin refuses even to *read* it."

"What will happen?" Malenkov asked. "You're close to the military. What do they say?"

"They say we will smash through a line—Trier, Saarbrücken—in six days."

"Paris in twenty-one days?"

"No. By then our military infrastructure will be totally destroyed. Not to mention Moscow, Leningrad and Kiev. We will never make Paris."

General Osklupov was almost eighty, one of the last surviving members of the Bolshevik Old Guard. With close-cropped, fine white hair and twinkling blue eyes, he looked like a wrinkled cherub as he sat on one of the carved wooden chairs in the Pleshny Palace waiting room. He had survived the great purges of the thirties, when over almost half of all Red Army officers above the rank of captain had been eliminated, and fought the war against Fascism from the undistinguished safety of various supply and training commands far behind the front line. Now he was one of the select group of old generals, many close to senility, whom Stalin chose to trust, or rather chose not to openly mistrust.

Along the corridor from the waiting room, behind the fourth oak-paneled door on the left, Joseph Stalin sat at his desk, writing and smoking a favorite pipe. His mood was tense, excited. He wrote quickly, map opened in front of him, the operational orders for divisions, armies. In the last days, the burden he had had to shoulder alone had become almost intol-

erable. He had acted as both Generalissimo and his own chief
of staff at the same time, checking ammunition supply, fuel,
mechanical replacements.

Gopak minus 3. He thought back to the last war, but for a
moment a hundred battles merged into one. Paris in twenty-
one days! The Soviet flag over the Arc de Triomphe as it had
been raised in Berlin over the Brandenburger Tor.

Stalin sat back in his chair and relit his pipe. The specially
installed air-purification system hummed like a trapped bee in
the ceiling. Lifting his head at the sound of his secretary's voice
from the door microphone, he pressed a button on the desk
and released the locks.

"General Osklupov is waiting," Poskrebyshev said, standing
in the open doorway.

Stalin frowned. His mind now moved slowly, ponderously
from one subject to the next. "Osklupov," he repeated vaguely.

"It is time to choose tonight's guard, Comrade Marshal."

"Of course." He was in charge again.

"Shall I send him in?"

Stalin stroked his mustache. "Send him in," he said.

"There is one other matter, Comrade Marshal."

Stalin lifted his heavy eyebrows.

"The young hero who liquidated the traitor Shtemenko in
Washington . . ."

"Ah, yes."

"I assume you wish to see him."

Stalin nodded. "Yes. Yes, if I have time."

"Tonight, Comrade Marshal?"

"Tonight?" Stalin frowned. "Perhaps, perhaps . . ."

"I will arrange it," Poskrebyshev said. "And now General Osklupov."

With a deep sigh, Stalin eased himself up from the chair. He
could never relax, never delegate; he was forced to do everything himself. Collecting a small canvas bag, tied at the top,
from a drawer, he moved stiffly to a game board supported by
a pile of books at each corner. It was a bagatelle, with a series
of numbered holes guarded by lines and half circles of nails.
Stalin had long ago discovered the game, as he wandered
through the great chambers of the Pleshny, among the piles of
objects from the time of the tsars. Despite a concerted search

by half his staff, the original balls used to play had never come to light. The nails were rusted and the varnished surface of the wood cracked and peeling, but it served his purpose.

Stalin untied the string around the top of the canvas bag, delved in and pulled out a handful of shiny ball bearings. Ignoring the chute at the side meant to launch the balls, he threw them down. They scattered haphazardly, bouncing off the nails, running in all directions and rolling into the numbered holes.

He patted the breast pocket of his tunic, feeling for a pen. Where was that writing pad? He had decided some weeks ago to banish the cleaning women, who had moved everything out of place as they dusted. But he still seemed to mislay things the very moment he needed them. General Osklupov's voice at the door microphone made him turn and release the bolts.

Osklupov stood panting like a puppy. He had rushed from the waiting room carrying a sheaf of papers with the name and rank of every man allocated to mount the Kremlin guard that month. "I'm ready, Comrade Marshal," he puffed.

Stalin shambled over to the bagatelle. "We'll start with the outer gate." He rolled the ball bearings in. As they bounced against the nails and dropped into the holes, he called the numbers. "Guards number eight, three, seven and four. Got that?"

"Yes, comrade." Struggling to keep up, Osklupov ticked off the corresponding names on the lists.

Stalin had devised this method of random selection to ensure that the sentries never knew when they would be on duty or at what particular post they would stand guard until the very last moment.

"Inner guardroom," Stalin continued. "Guard commander, twenty-one." Traitors lurked on every side, schemes and plots were in the air. He must be constantly ready to stamp them out. He could never give up. There was no one else. "Mobile picket. Number seventeen, forty, twenty-six . . ."

The long line of dark-clad figures descended the steps of the Finnair C-47 and made their way toward the wooden huts which carried the inscription MOSCOW-TUSHINO AIRPORT swagged in grimy red flags.

Alexander Trenton felt the fear churning in his stomach as he and his flight companions walked in line, like an ill-trained squad of conscripts, toward the lighted windows of the reception hut. Entering the planked reception hall, they were hustled into three lines in front of three separate doors through which one man was allowed at a time. To the right of each door was an enormous crudely colored head-and-shoulders portrait of Joseph Stalin. As Alex's line shuffled forward, he nervously examined Stalin's eyes in the picture, creased and turned down at the corners, below thick, dark eyebrows; they were eyes immensely crafty and indifferently cruel.

A young American in front of him pointed to the portrait. "Should we salute?" His laugh came out as a strange braying sound, so artificial it sounded as if he had been practicing.

"The achievements of Comrade Stalin are well known," Alex said gruffly. He immediately regretted that he had revealed he spoke English.

"They're pretty well known in the United States, too," the young man retorted.

The door in front of them opened, and the American passed through. For a few moments, Alex stood waiting, his eyes no more than a foot or two from those of the man he had been sent to kill.

Finally, the door opened. Alex picked up his bag and walked through.

At the desk, the MGB man took Alex's passport and scowled. Canadian passports were always trouble. He struggled to read the name in the unfamiliar script. "Mr. . . . Blaakborne . . ."

"Blackburn." Trenton automatically corrected the pronunciation. "I speak Russian."

"Ah . . ." The man grunted. "Your luggage, Mr. Blackburn."

"Just this suitcase," Trenton said. As he glanced up, he was aware of the American with the braying laugh watching him from the other side of the hut.

"Ah . . ." The MGB man was now more wary than before. Canadians seldom spoke Russian. Not Russian like this man's. "You will have to wait," he snapped, "while I make inquiries."

"Put through a call to Dzerzhinsky Square," Alex said coldly. "General Petrov's assistant will vouch for me."

The man's manner changed immediately. As Alex noted the suddenly too-eager smile and the bobbing and ducking head, he realized that there was still as much of the old Russian fear of authority as ever.

CHAPTER
21

Along the Leningrad Prospekt, the great holes for the new trees looked like bomb craters, and the half-completed official buildings added to the sense of a devastated city. On Stalin's personal orders, this end of the Old Imperial Highway between Moscow and Leningrad was being refurbished as a great boulevard to impress foreign visitors. Riding in the back of the limousine, Alex Trenton reflected bitterly that there were many more effective ways of impressing foreign visitors to Stalin's Russia than this new version of a Potemkin village. But the Georgian autocrat was incapable of seeing. Would his successors see more clearly? Alex wondered.

The car turned off the prospekt into the courtyard of the newly refurbished Sovietskaya Hotel, an old building, the site of the famous Yar Restaurant of tsarist days, now again the haunt of the privileged in Russian society.

In the columned lobby, Vanessa was waiting.

"My dear boy," she said, throwing her arms around Trenton, pulling his head down to plant kisses on his cheek. "My dear boy," she said happily, "you're a hero!"

In her expensive fur coat, her Paris silk dress and West Berlin shoes, she might have been standing in the Waldorf-Astoria in New York.

"These are heroic times, Alex. Of course you cannot understand exactly what your contribution has been. But it is vast. Pavel Semyonovich was briefed last night by Comrade Beria himself. We are on the brink of great changes in the world."

Alex looked bleakly at his mother. After more than thirty years, she still drove herself forward as a true believer. Perhaps she felt she had no choice.

Vanessa slipped her hand through her son's arm and walked him toward the restaurant. "You know, Alex," she said gaily, "what you need now is a woman."

"A woman?" he asked almost automatically.

"Not a mistress in some scruffy apartment you've arranged for her. I mean a real woman. A wife. Your position in Party matters from now onward demands it."

He watched her ringed fingers gesture across the room to where a group of Soviet officers and their wives were being introduced to each other. "You're too much of a solitary, Alex. It makes people uneasy, uncertain of what you're thinking. Last night when the news came through of your success in Washington, we were with Comrade Beria. He said some very kind things about you. But he did say that he'd always been, up to now anyway, just a little uncertain about you. He even hinted that a wife . . . children . . ."

"I don't have to remind *you* I already have a wife," he said shortly. "I don't imagine you've forgotten."

Only when she pursed her lips did the lines show at her throat. "Of course one forgets, Sacha darling. We *all* forget. Poor Xenia probably doesn't remember herself. She gets worse every month, Alex. You'll have to have her put away somewhere, you know." She squeezed his arm confidentially. "Pavel Semyonovich would raise no objections."

"You want me to shut her away?" Alex stopped in the doorway into the restaurant.

"It'd be a sort of hospital," Vanessa said coaxingly. "Comfortable enough."

"You know what it'd be." He unhooked his arm. "You know what you're suggesting. Or rather, what Beria is suggesting."

"Have it your own way. All I'm saying is that she's becoming a severe embarrassment to your career. I would have thought you'd be happy to take the opportunity of a way out."

"What a bitch you can be," he said, as the headwaiter approached.

She tightened her lips but pretended to have heard nothing. "General Petrov's table," she said to the waiter.

Alex strode beside his mother as they both followed the headwaiter.

"For God's sake." Vanessa surrendered her coat and waited while a second waiter pulled back her chair. "You are lunching at the Restaurant Yar, where every table is reserved for men or women who have contributed to all we believe in. You are honored because, like all these others"—she waved her hand toward the red-tabbed officers who sat with their companions at the other tables—"you have *gained* honor. Of course, the world can't be informed of exactly *what* you've done. But because you are here, lunching at the Yar, they'll know you're a man of achievement. Now stop nagging about Xenia. You might as well know that Pavel has already made up his mind. She is to go to a special hospital for alcoholics."

"And she'll never be seen again."

"She won't return to Moscow, no. But she'll be well looked after."

"They'll give her all the lemon vodka she wants, you mean."

"Semyon has offered to be a witness in your favor when you apply for a divorce."

The waiter brought champagne in a silver bucket sparkling with icy drops of water.

"Poor Xenia," Alex said.

"It's for the best." Vanessa nodded for the waiter to open the bottle. "Please, don't you play the boring romantic with me, Alex." She leaned forward confidentially although she was still speaking in English. "You can't kid me that a man who's done what you've done this week is subject to an attack of bourgeois morality." She lifted her glass, her lips twisted in a knowing smile.

Petrov bustled across the restaurant toward Vanessa and his stepson, rubbing his hands together with the satisfaction of a man on a cold day who is at last approaching a blazing log fire.

Alex got to his feet, and Petrov hugged him. "So, Alex." Petrov pushed him to arm's length. "You're home. Home and drinking champagne, as you deserve."

Alex Trenton, watching him, realized that Petrov was genuinely trying to control an emotion. The older man snuffled and turned to give a quick smile to Vanessa. He pulled out a

large blue handkerchief, wiped it across his nose and looked at
Alex, his eyes brimming.

"This morning," he said, "early, I saw the comrade marshal."

"Does he never sleep?" Vanessa said, shaking her head.

"He was awake enough when I told him the news," Petrov
said. "Comrade Beria insisted I take the news to Comrade Stalin in person."

"Did he say anything about Alex?" Vanessa asked.

Petrov paused. "Yes," he said. "The marshal gave me his famous, distant look. 'Convey my own deep gratitude and that of
the whole Soviet people for what he has done.' It has been
arranged that he will see you in person, Alex."

Alex nodded slowly. "I'm honored, Pavel Semyonovich," he
said.

"I'm dying to ask questions," Vanessa said, with savage enthusiasm. "Was it night or day, for instance?"

"Vanessa, silence," Petrov laughed. "No more talk of it. Alex
will write his report. It will be studied, and he will be debriefed. Only then may he perhaps answer a question or two
from his mother." Petrov's eyes twinkled. "But first, lunch."

He turned to wave to the waiters at the long table loaded
with dishes of salmon and caviar and crabs' claws. Trenton followed his glance, as a frown crossed the general's forehead.
Captain Roy Morosov was making his way through the tables
toward them.

Petrov slewed around, his knees dragging at the tablecloth.
With the instinct of a survivor, he knew that only a very serious
matter would allow a uniformed captain to disturb his lunch at
the Yar.

Petrov and Morosov spoke privately together, Petrov's bald
head nodding vigorously. Alex could hear nothing. Then Petrov turned back to the table, no longer smiling. A hovering
waiter was waved violently aside.

"What is it?" Vanessa asked anxiously.

Petrov sat down without replying. "You landed this morning
at Tushino," he said to Alex after a moment's silence.

"Yes."

"Do you know the history of Tushino?" Petrov asked. There
was menace in the softness of his voice.

"No. To me, Pavel Semyonovich," Alex said, "Tushino is
what it is. An airport, the center for the Moscow Air Show."

"You've never heard of Tushino Vor, the 'Scoundrel of Tushino'?"

"No," Trenton said, holding Petrov's gaze. "Who was he? A traitor to the Revolution?"

"No," Petrov said. "He was known many centuries ago as the 'False Dimitry.' The man who tried to pass himself off as a true friend of the Russian people."

Vanessa's eyes moved from Petrov's face to her son's.

"The 'False Dimitry' was uncovered, there at Tushino," Petrov spoke slowly. "Thus he became known to history as the 'Scoundrel of Tushino.'"

"Pavel Semyonovich," Vanessa said, "I don't like it when you speak like that." She reached for Petrov's arm, but he shrugged her hand off, keeping his gaze on Alex's face. "We have just received news from Washington," he said slowly. "You know what I'm saying."

A nerve began to throb violently above Alex's right eye. He raised his hand and stroked his eyebrow.

"News from Washington." Trenton struggled to keep his voice even. "What news, Pavel Semyonovich?"

"What news?" Vanessa said desperately.

"General Shtemenko is not dead."

"That's not true," Alex said, calling on every mental reserve to display his anger. "I shot him three times. At least one bullet entered the head."

"No," Petrov said, shaking his head.

"You mean Shtemenko survived the wounds?" Vanessa said.

"No. There was no wound to survive. Because there was no attempt made on his life." Petrov leaned across the table, his face barely more than a foot away.

"What's your source?" Alex said, backing down before Petrov's glare.

Petrov got to his feet. "We know it," he said slowly, "for a fact. Our source, in this case, is infallible."

Vanessa's face was contorted with fury. "You fool," she said to her son. "What in God's name do you think you're playing at?"

As Captain Morosov stepped forward toward Alex in response to Petrov's nod, Alex ducked under his outstretched arm. For a moment, he had no idea what he was going to do. As Morosov came around the table toward him, Trenton had a momentary glimpse of the shocked faces of the people at the surrounding tables. A second MGB officer ran to cut off his escape through the door. Every movement seemed that of a jerky silent film. Then the noise of breaking crockery brought him back to his senses, and he charged forward between the closely placed tables and threw himself at the swinging doors to the kitchen. Scenes hurtled past him as if he were the driver of an express train. Red faces and white smocks. Stainless-steel ovens and wooden work surfaces piled with meat. Steam and stacks of plates.

A heavily built man in a chef's jacket blocked his path between the stainless-steel ovens. Alex saw the man's mouth open, the blade of a cleaver glinting as it came forward, low, like the thrust of a Roman sword. He twisted sideways, rolling across the countertop, scattering pans of boiling liquid, as the blade of the cleaver cut into his thigh. As he landed, crouched between garbage cans overflowing with kitchen refuse, others ran toward him.

Shouts mingled with the clatter of boots on the tiled floor. Through the glass of the door at the far end of the kitchen, Trenton could see the parking lot and the long line of Leningrad Prospekt. Running forward, he wrenched the door open and felt the cold air smack his face.

When the black car pulled up in the street below, Katya, standing at the window of her room, watched as four men in civilian clothes got out.

She was looking directly down on their wide-brimmed gray felt hats. Two of the men detached themselves from the group and made their way to the rear of the building. Katya, forehead close to the glass, felt a cramping fear in her stomach. She reached out and took her coat from the hook beside the window. She knew she must not make a blunder. There were a dozen or more people living in the building, all illegally. The MGB men could be after any of them.

The remaining two men crossed the sidewalk toward the ruined front entrance. She turned quickly and moved to the door, easing it open an inch or two. If she could get past them on the stairs, the bicycle offered the best chance of escape. A car couldn't follow along the narrow canal path, and she knew she could outstrip a man on foot. She grinned nervously to herself. Provided that it was she they were after, she forced herself to remember.

She heard the voices of the police agents rising in the stairwell now. "Try there," one of them said. "There's someone in. I can smell stew cooking."

The thumping on the door below was thunderous. It brought, not surprisingly, an immediate response. Katya recognized her friend Anna's voice raised in theatrical protest.

"We're looking for a blond girl," a man's voice said. "A Perlinka whore. Young, pretty . . ."

"You must mean me, darling," Anna screeched with laughter.

"I'd throw up first," the man said. "Where does she live?"

"Try the very top floor," Anna said. "I see her go up every day."

"Well done, mother."

"The very top floor," Anna bawled up the stairs after the men. "Her name's Katya. She's the one."

Blessing Anna under her breath, Katya eased closed her door. The men's footsteps approached and passed as they moved up to the top floor. She counted the moments until they would have turned the corner of the stairs. Above her, she heard the pounding on the door. Taking a deep breath, she carefully turned the handle and pulled her own door toward her. The noise and shouting from above covered the faint creak. She stepped forward silently onto the landing and was immediately grasped around the waist and hurled violently to the floor. The noise above stopped. A man's head appeared over the stairwell, looking down at Katya. She stared up at him, watching his face split with an evil grin.

"Oldest trick in the world in a thieves' den like this. Shout and scream and give the wrong directions." He straightened up and came clattering down the stairs. "As we go down, give the old gray-haired bag a clump on the side of the head for her help," the policeman said to his companion as they dragged the trembling Katya to her feet.

For two hours, Alex lay beneath a tarpaulin in one of the craters along the boulevard, listening to Roy Morosov's men searching the parking lot and the building sites beyond. Not daring to raise his head, he had no idea how narrowly he had missed discovery. Once, as he lay trembling with cold, someone had dragged up the edge of the frozen tarpaulin, but the weight of the canvas had pulled it from the man's hand before he had been able to make out Alex's form beneath. From time to time he thought he heard Morosov shouting instructions, and once he picked out his mother's voice—even she was involved in the hunt.

He had no way of knowing whether the men were still there. He knew the search would not be abandoned, but his experience told him that now it would be continued at checkpoints such as the metro stations and bus depots. It was rare for the MGB to fail to find its quarry. The impossibility of registering at a hotel without ration tickets and an identity book meant that most wanted men were forced onto the streets at night, where they were quickly picked up by the militia.

The tarpaulin crackled with breaking ice as he lifted the edge. The parking lot was now almost empty of automobiles. A single pair of uniformed men, militia rather than MGB, were pacing the perimeter. He wriggled forward. His left hand, scalded by the boiling water in the kitchen, seemed to be encased in flames. In his leg, he registered no more than a deep, numbing ache.

CHAPTER
22

Alex made his way down to the Byelorussian Station on the back of a builder's truck. He could now see that the meat cleaver had cut deeper into his leg than he had thought, but the cloth of his blood-soaked trousers, now frozen, was acting as a crude dressing.

Dropping off the back of the truck in the station square, he started down toward the Red Presnya district. He knew he was in imminent danger of being stopped by the militia. A man without a topcoat and a fur hat in Moscow winter temperatures invited attention. At the Barrikadnaya metro station, the officials were checking identity books, and a long line of shivering people stretched back toward the militia statue outside Krasnopresnenskaya. He knew that in all probability it was a simple permit check, a regular Moscow feature to prevent unauthorized residence in the capital. But equally he knew that if he had traveled by metro it could have drawn him into the net.

The cold now seemed to concentrate the pain in his leg into a menacing, throbbing agony. He turned into the street where Katya lived. Moving from doorway to doorway, he looked back toward the end of the street, at any moment expecting a vehicle or armed men to emerge. But there was none. At last he was there. The street door swung open as he pressed. Alex entered and limped toward the crumbling staircase. Shafts of

light from the street outside shone through broken fanlights.
He climbed the stairs to Katya's floor and knocked on the
door.

There were no sounds from within, and he was struck suddenly by the certainty that she was not there. He turned the
handle and the door gave. He entered, closing the door, leaning back on it. The room had been ransacked. The mattress
had been torn from the bed and ripped open. The contents of
the pine chest of drawers had been dumped on the floor. The
wall rug had been wrenched down. It was as if the room had
been wrecked by a clumsy and vengeful burglar. But Trenton
recognized it immediately as the work of MGB men, not seeking evidence, but simply on the make.

He stood listening in the late afternoon shadow. Crossing to
the door, he held it ajar and strained his ears for a sound on
the staircase. He had no doubt what had happened to Katya.
He stood on the landing, consumed with guilt. Perhaps somewhere below there was a sound in the stairwell. As likely a rat
or a blast of wind as an MGB squad. He closed the door behind him and began to descend the staircase. At that moment,
he heard the woman's voice calling his name.

For a moment there was the wild hope that it was Katya behind the slowly opening door. Then the old, seamed face of
Anna emerged from the shadow. "She's been arrested," she
said. "They came for her this afternoon." She pulled him into
her room. "It's your fault," she said bitterly. "I warned her she
couldn't expect to go with a policeman without trouble coming
from it."

He stood just inside the door. "Listen, Anna," he said carefully. "Did any of them say anything?"

"One of them came down and gave me his hand on the side
of my head," she said. "He said about you being a general's son
or something. And about the general not approving of your
running round with a Perlinka whore. I warned her," she said.
"I warned her no good could come of it."

She turned back to watch a piece of pork frying in an iron
skillet on the wood stove. "I warned her," she repeated. Taking
up a fork, she prodded at the piece of meat.

"I've got friends, Anna," Alex said to her hunched back. "Influential friends."

"Friends who are willing to countermand a general's order?"

"Perhaps. Today's Friday. They'll be entraining the week's prisoners at Yaroslavl Station. Tonight they'll leave for camps in the north and east. If the train can be stopped before she gets too far—"

Anna laid her hand on his arm. "What are you talking about, man?" she said. "Nobody ever comes back."

The clock of St. Stefan the Indomitable sounded the hour. The church on the corner was no longer used, the door locked and barred with heavy timbers nailed across the face, although an old man used the side entrance to the tower to maintain the clock in working order and wind it once a week. He performed this simple, self-imposed task without official permission, but the authorities had made no move to prevent him. Alex approached the white-haired, wizened figure as the old man crossed himself before the tower door.

"I've been sent by old Anna, comrade," Alex said. "She says you can help me."

The old man stopped, his hand on the catch that opened the church door. "It's not the weather to be out without an overcoat, comrade," he said. "This old Anna you speak of, how do you know her?"

"From the Kalpretta. She trades there."

The old man allowed himself a faint nod. "And how is it I can help?" he asked. His eyes were already traveling down to Trenton's torn trouser leg and the black, frozen blood from thigh to ankle.

"She tells me you know of a doctor, comrade. Someone I can trust."

"You can trust no one in Moscow today," the man said, with a sudden bitter ferocity in his voice.

"I have no choice," Alex said. "I must see a doctor."

The old man nodded gravely. "In that case go to 7 Ulitza Glem. You have money?"

"Yes."

"Doctor Zinoviev will see you. She's a good enough woman, comrade."

"But . . . ?"

The old man shrugged. "In Godless Russia we are all of us

only as good as we dare be." He stood nodding to himself. Then he pushed open the tower door and was lost in the darkness beyond.

The walls of the basement surgery were painted in a drab, cheerless green. There was a large, framed photograph of Stalin hanging opposite the one small window, which faced north and was blinded by the high building across the street next to the market. The light barely penetrated the dark, grime-smeared windowpane.

Doctor Zinoviev was a tall, lean woman in her mid forties, with a sallow complexion and a shock of frizzy hair, graying at the front and temples. She sat at a large, rosewood rolltop desk, in a swivel chair turned to face Alex Trenton, who was seated beside her. Working by the light from an angled brass lamp, with deft movements she dressed his burned hand, threading the roll of bandage around and between the knuckles, leaving the fingers uncovered.

"How did you do this?" she asked, the ash from the end of a cigarette perched between her thin lips falling to the threadbare carpet as she spoke.

"An accident at work," Alex said.

The dressing was so skillfully applied that it looked like a neat white mitten. "Accidents at work are treated by factory doctors," she said.

"I'm up for a production bonus," Alex said calmly. "I can't afford a black mark against me just now."

"Show me the leg," Zinoviev said brusquely.

As Alex stood to pull down his trouser leg, the doctor lit another Belomors from the stub of the first. Then she pulled the leg around to the light and leaned forward, cleaning the wound, pushing at the swelling with her thumbs.

"When did this happen?"

"An hour or so ago," Trenton said, wincing as the prodding continued.

"And you've been outside in the cold ever since."

"Yes."

"You're a lucky man." Doctor Zinoviev smiled grimly. "The cold cauterized the wound. In midsummer you would have already died of loss of blood."

Taking a medical probe from a kidney-shaped enamel dish, she held it for a few seconds in the flame of a alcohol lamp burning on the corner of the desk, then used it to again explore the gash.

"Did you fall onto some glass?"

"I was carrying a bottle. It smashed."

"Vodka?"

"A Russian worker can't get through the day anymore without a half liter of vodka in his pocket."

The doctor leaned back in the chair and took the cigarette from her mouth. "But you didn't get that wound from a bottle. It's a cut. Were you in a fight?"

Alex shrugged. "I was drunk. Who knows what happened?"

"I need to know for my report." She wrapped the wound with a thick dressing.

"Is a report necessary?" Alex asked.

"For the hospital," she said. "I am only allowed to treat certain categories of injuries. Technically, this would be classified as surgery. I can do nothing more."

"I have an urgent appointment. I would rather you dealt with it now."

The doctor shook her head. "No. If I treat you here the wound will bleed again and you will require a transfusion. It would be better to go to a hospital."

"Better to pay than to lose my bonus," Alex said. "I'm sure you can do it."

For three long, desperate years she had served as an army surgeon in field hospitals, sometimes little more than a kilometer behind the front line. She had removed bullets and shrapnel of every kind, patched up broken bodies, amputated limbs, operated in flapping, wind-swept tents under a single oil lamp, seen the liquid freeze in hypodermic syringes, walked a thousand miles in retreat, starved, been wounded twice and almost died of frostbite and hypothermia. Could she do it? "A private arrangement will cost you twenty rubles," she said.

"I can pay."

"No anesthetic. Only the hospitals carry anesthetic."

He nodded. "I understand."

As she treated the wound, she talked with him. Between gasps of pain he had told her that he had been in a rifle regiment at Stalingrad and afterward in Konev's army on the Ukrainian front. She worked on the leg until she was satisfied, but she had been unable to resolve for herself the main complication. She knew she was outside the law. Not only did she not believe he was a Stakhanovite factory worker—his suit and shoes were far too good—but his whole manner pointed to something different. Could she take the risk of not reporting him? Much worse, could she take the loss? Her husband had been in a camp since his arrest, without trial, two years ago. Each time she reported a piece of significant information to Dzerzhinsky Square she was allowed to receive from him one single-page letter. If her information led to an arrest, she was granted the right to send a small food parcel. She detested herself for trading a man's liberty against these privileges, jealously granted by the MGB officers at the Lubyanka, but she knew she could not herself exist without the reassurance, once every month or two, that her husband still survived out in the snow wastes of Siberia.

When the treatment was finished, she had refused money. Watching him leave, watching him cross the road and limp toward the market, she fought her longest, hardest battle yet with her conscience. Then, as the memory of his face faded, she had lifted the receiver of the telephone beside the crammed bookcase and dialed the familiar number. The call was answered almost at once, and she heard the faint click of one of the recording machines as it started to tape the conversation.

"What number are you calling?" said the anonymous voice.

"Central 0132."

"Give your full name and the section or person you require to contact."

"Doctor Irena Zinoviev. I want to talk to someone in section fourteen."

There was the usual pause. She always imagined her name was being checked on some enormous list. She waited, fumbling to light another cigarette, the receiver still held to her ear. Finally, another voice came on the line. Moments later, two MGB trucks drove off to pick up Alex Trenton.

CHAPTER
23

He knew the green-painted corridors, the bowl-shaped lamps, the ornate old stone staircases intimately, as well as the new wooden ones where boots clattered and sounds carried. Although he had never been in an Interrogation Section during his time in the MGB, Alexander Trenton knew too well the way down to the cells below.

He walked briskly, Roy Morosov slightly behind him and another interrogation officer to his right. At the corner of a long corridor, an old friend would turn to greet him before he was stopped in midsentence by the realization that Trenton's arms were chained behind his back. Natasha, for years his secretary, had gasped in horror, her hand flying to her mouth as she watched, the papers she was carrying fluttering to the floor.

They turned left and passed through the cream-painted stone archway that led to the old Lubyanka. The corridor stank of stale cooking and echoed to occasional cries of pain from the rooms below.

They descended the stone stairs. The cells here were large, with a dense array of names and dates and initials carved on the walls. The hinged, iron-grilled window was just large enough to pass a coffin directly out into the courtyard beyond.

The reek of disinfectant hit him as he entered the cell. It meant, he knew, that a "vigorous" interrogation had recently

taken place. The blood and vomit on the stone floor would
have been newly swept away into the channel along the wall
which led to the drains. Some disinfectant remained in the
shallow, concrete channel. Its milky whiteness was tinged pink
with blood.

"Are you going to take these off, Roy?" Alex rattled the
chains that secured his arms.

Morosov nodded, feeling for the key. "What got into you,
Alex?" he said, unlocking the chains. "If you didn't want to do
the job, why take it on?"

"It's too complicated," Alex said. "Have you got the interrogation list yet?"

"Give us a chance." Roy Morosov shook his head. "The general's working on it now, though if you ask me there is only
one question."

"What's that?"

"What made you come back from Washington?"

"Who's to be I.O.?" Alex breathed in deeply, trying to adjust
to the sickly smell of blood and disinfectant.

"Petrov put me in charge," Morosov said, looking at him
steadily.

Alex Trenton leaned his back against the wall. "When do
you start?" His mouth was dry.

"Right away," Morosov said. "As soon as I get the list."

In Washington, it was already getting dark. Sitting opposite
General Bolsover in the White House military briefing room,
Hal thought the stark little white room looked like nothing so
much as a prison cell. "Bad news, I'm afraid, General," Hal
said slowly.

"Okay, give it to me, Hal."

"We had a man at Tushino Airport when Trenton landed."

"Tushino in Moscow?"

Hal nodded. "He was met by his mother at the Yar. Kisses,
hugs, smiles, a hero's welcome."

"The Yar?"

"The sort of restaurant where only the elite eat. The place
generals take their favorite girls . . ."

"What happened in the restaurant?"

"An MGB officer arrived and spoke to Petrov. Then all hell
broke loose."

"You mean he was arrested?"

"He took off through a back door. Our man stayed around as long as he could. They had an entire MGB unit search the area."

"Did they get him?"

"That's the hell of it, General. We don't know."

"Is there any way we can find out?"

"Not for certain."

"So what do we do?"

"I think we assume the worst."

"You think that somehow they discovered that he had *not* killed Shtemenko?"

"Yes, sir."

Bolsover lifted his heavy body from the chair. "Then I've no alternative but to inform the Joint Chiefs that the assassination option no longer exists. You know what this means, Hal?"

Hal nodded. "It means the United States is less than twelve hours from a preemptive atomic strike."

"I was right about the interrogation list," Roy Morosov said, handing Alex a cigarette. "Question one: What was Trenton's objective in returning to the Soviet Union?" Morosov lit Alex's cigarette. "There are no other questions."

Trenton sat on the chair that had been placed in the middle of the room. He inhaled the cigarette.

"Scared?" Morosov asked.

"Of course."

"I've always wondered about all the teams that play the Moscow Dynamos," Morosov said. "They all know it's an MGB-owned team. They must know all the profits come to us. Do you think they lose on purpose?"

"Sometimes, I suppose."

"You never were much interested in soccer, were you?" He paused. "So what's this all about? You going to be a good lad?"

"I'll do my best."

"Question one." Morosov took his blackjack from his pocket.

"I came back because I thought I'd done the job assigned to me. I left the target for dead."

Roy Morosov swung the blackjack, and it slapped heavily against the side of Alex's neck. Then with incredible speed Morosov flicked his wrist, and the weighted rubber tube thudded against the other side of Alex's head, high up on the temple. Alex felt a whiplash shock and a hot rush of blood from his nose. "For God's sake, Roy," he spluttered through the blood, "why *else* would I come back?"

The next blow left him crouching on the floor, on all fours like a dog. The rough flagstones had become a carpet of thick green mist, spotted with his own blood. When the chair crashed down on his kidneys, he began to lose consciousness. The kicking seemed to come from men ranged in a circle around him. The green mist now swirled around his head. Blows struck him quite painlessly, as a pressure on the head or chest only.

The trouble with giving someone a good beating, Roy Morosov observed to himself as he waited for Alex to regain consciousness, is that the plain physical stuff is always counterproductive. Within a few minutes, the prisoner hardly knows where he is. Within ten minutes, he's unconscious. Morosov lit a cigarette. He had been moving in a different direction lately and with some success. The way he saw it now, a few minutes' terror was as effective as a full hour's beating. Of course, most prisoners were already softened up by that first walk from the main gates to the cells. They knew they were in the Lubyanka.

But Alex Trenton was different. You wouldn't be afraid of a place you'd worked in for years. Or at least you wouldn't be as afraid. Morosov resolved to give him another beating and see what he had to say. If he still didn't break, Morosov would introduce the theatricals. He'd had very good success lately with the theatricals.

The phone rang shrilly.

"Mr. and Mrs. Harry Hunter's residence," Doonan growled.

"Doonan, it's General Jones. Is Mrs. Hunter there?"

"Not for you, she isn't, General. You been a naughty boy."

"You can cut out the Irish, Doonan. Get her to the phone for me somehow, will you?"

"I can only ask. Hold the line."

Doonan crossed the hall, knocked and entered Jennifer Hunter's small sitting room. She sat at a desk, writing letters.

"Who is it, Doonan?"

"I guess you know already, Mrs. Hunter. It's the general."

"Okay." She turned back to her writing. "You know what to do."

"Hanging up on him seemed kind of strong stuff. He's a nice guy."

"Mind your own business, Doonan," she intoned, still writing.

"You're not going to find another general like that one," Doonan said.

She turned toward him with a faint smile. "In the role of butler, Doonan, you're impossible. But as Cupid, you're crazy."

"He's still waiting on the line, ma'am."

"Put him through."

Doonan ducked out and closed the door after him. "I persuaded her to talk to you, General," Doonan said a moment later, "though in my judgment it's not going to do you a lot of good. I only wish I could listen in and see how you make out."

Jennifer's clear voice came over the line, and Hal listened for the click as Doonan hung up.

"Jennifer?"

"I asked you not to call, Hal. I meant it."

"I know," Hal said. "But I've something to tell you."

"Okay."

"I called to tell you about our friend."

"The foreign one?" she asked cautiously.

"Yes. Since you and I are probably the only people in Washington even remotely concerned about him, I thought maybe we could share it. I could tell you over a drink."

"What's the news, Hal?"

"Our friend has been arrested."

"Oh, God. Were you planning that?"

"No. We believe that somehow others found out that he had not carried out his assignment here in Washington."

"You think Harry's somehow responsible?"

"I'll break his back if he is." He paused. "Will you meet me, Jennifer? Have dinner with me?"

"I don't think you understand, Hal. I hate what I see, whether it's in politics or in your work. I'm divorcing Harry because I want no part of the whole duplicitous business. So please . . . don't call, don't ask me to dinner. Just . . . fuck off, Hal. Please, darling . . ."

He could hear her crying as she put down the phone.

CHAPTER
24

"**A** wild animal you want," the dwarf said.

Sitting at his desk in the outer interrogation office, Captain Morosov nodded vigorously. "You can do it, Dimitry," he said. "Absolute darkness. The middle of the night. He's fast asleep in his cell. You rush like a mad animal. You *savage* him, right? And you get out before he even knows for sure what it is that got him."

The dwarf, his face torn and scarred from years of dogfighting, grinned to show his gapped teeth.

"He should think—" Roy Morosov considered carefully. "He should think that he's just been attacked by a giant sewer rat."

In the private theater of his dacha at Zuchoe, a few miles outside Moscow, Lavrenty Pavlovich Beria, the Minister of State Security, commander of the secret police and of the militia forces throughout the Soviet Union, was watching his favorite musical, *Singing in the Rain,* when an aide came to tell him that General Petrov was on the telephone. The film was stopped. Beria exchanged his spectacles for the familiar pince-nez the world saw him wearing in portraits when he stood, symbolically, by Joseph Stalin's side. He walked into his private office and sat at his desk. "Pavel Semyonovich, how are you, my dear man? No bad news for me, I hope. I was just watching my favorite American film . . ."

"Lavrenty Pavlovich," Petrov said uncertainly, "I would not telephone you for trivial reasons."

"No. What is it then?"

"I have just received information from Washington of the greatest possible significance."

"I'm listening," Beria said coldly.

"It appears that the report I was able to give you yesterday was incorrect."

Beria frowned, his skull wrinkling from just above the eyebrows far back across his bald head. "The report on General Shtemenko?"

"Yes, Comrade Minister. A subsequent report from Washington, the most reliable possible source, claims that Shtemenko is not dead."

"Wounded but not dead? Is that what you mean?" Beria asked quietly.

"No, comrade. The report makes clear that there was no attempt upon Shtemenko's life."

"Yet when the officer returned, he continued to claim that Shtemenko was dead, that he had killed him."

"Yes, comrade."

Beria nodded. He was known for his slow, cautious appreciation of problems. "The officer was, of course, selected by you."

"Yes, comrade."

"He is in fact your stepson."

"Yes, comrade."

"You have him under arrest?"

"He is being interrogated now."

"With what results so far?"

"The interrogation has only just begun," Petrov said desperately.

"Why should this officer risk his life by returning, bringing with him a false report of Shtemenko's death?"

"In an hour or so we shall know."

"Yes . . ." Beria held the phone away from him and squinted at it through his pince-nez.

"Comrade Minister . . ." Petrov's voice emerged faint but

urgent from the phone as Beria grimaced and replaced the receiver.

Very slowly, Lavrenty Beria got up from his desk. He placed his hand on the back of his chair. Three of his predecessors as chief of secret police, Menzhinsky, Yagoda and Yeshov, had been poisoned or shot in the Lubyanka basement. Plots and counterplots, some real, some imaginary, had been part of Beria's rise to power since he had joined the Cheka under its founder, Dzerzhinsky, the man whose statue stood in the square in front of the Lubyanka. Plots and counterplots—of course Pavel Semyonovich Petrov was ambitious. But until today Beria had also believed he was loyal. Lavrenty Beria slowly circled his office. Why had Shtemenko not been killed? Why had someone tried to pretend that he had been successfully assassinated? Why had Petrov's stepson been chosen? Beria's head began to ache. He could sense a plot developing, smell it even. But he could still not discern its shape. Shtemenko, obviously, was at the center of it. And Shtemenko meant the Soviet army. And Petrov—where did he stand? Somewhere in alliance with Shtemenko? Beria's stomach lurched in fear. Could he contact Khrushchev? Perhaps dangerous. Or Molotov? Unless he too was in the plot. Or, most terrifying thought of all, was the man who was plotting Lavrenty Beria's downfall Joseph Stalin himself, there in the Pleshny Palace, senile, paranoid, infinitely dangerous?

Beria rang the bell for his chief of staff, Colonel Merkolovsky. In control of his fears now, he issued orders. He required first that Merkolovsky should draft 20,000 MGB troops into Moscow to reinforce all militia stations. And that a squad should be sent to the Lubyanka to escort General Petrov and his lady out here to Zuchoe.

Alex Trenton rolled onto his side. It was dark outside in the Lubyanka courtyard, and the normal activities of the day, the delivery of wagon loads of cabbage or beetroot, as well as the less ordinary removal of a coffin in the unmarked hearse, had ceased to cause the huge wooden gates to be opened. He had no understanding of the passage of time. As if in a fever, he had drifted back and forth through various layers of consciousness. His neck was locked in one position, painfully swollen. His jaw, along the line of his back teeth, was almost impossible to open. His nose felt less badly damaged than he had feared. He heaved himself into a sitting position on the sleeping mat on which he was stretched. His back ached intolerably, but he could stand up. Then, somewhere under the door, he heard a sniffing and scratching, as if an animal were trying to get in.

In his office three floors above the basement cells, Pavel Petrov could not disguise his fear. "Colonel Merkolovsky, Beria's man, has invited us to go out to Zuchoe," he said.

Vanessa sat back, her heavy fur coat wrapped around her. "Why should he do that?"

"Beria's afraid," Petrov said vehemently. "I know how these things work. He fears some sort of plot or coup against him. But he'll fight back. There'll be arrests, shootings. Do you know how many men, senior officers, are disposed of every day in the Soviet Union?" He leaned toward her. "Two days ago I personally ordered Peter Voronov to be shot beside his car. Peter Voronov, an outstanding officer, newly promoted to general."

She looked at him, puzzlement clouding her hazel eyes. "Why should you or anyone else order the death of General Voronov?"

"Because Voronov was a suspect. As I am now."

"What was he suspected of?"

"Everybody's mad with fear, Vanessa. Don't you understand? Stalin sees plots in his dreams. The night we intercepted Peter Voronov's car on the highway, he had an interview with Stalin. That alone was enough."

She raised her hand peremptorily. "That alone was not enough. Voronov was Shtemenko's man."

Petrov shrugged. "Yes."

Her eyes were glittering. "You tell me many generals believe *Gopak* will fail. Shtemenko believed this. No doubt many of his staff agree."

"Perhaps. What are you getting at?"

"You need me, Pavel," she said. "God, you need me. To do your thinking for you, you great oaf."

"What in God's name are you talking about?"

"I'm talking about Voronov. Do you still not see why he was appointed general?"

"All right, I'm an ignorant Russian oaf. No, I don't see."

"Because," she said quietly, "Comrade Stalin, sick and old and suspicious, receives almost nobody these days. Except the Politburo—sometimes. But he still loves to be the Generalissimo. He personally presents new generals with their badge of rank. Always." She stood up, as tall as he was, her French perfume wafting. "If you wanted to introduce an assassin into the Kremlin, an appointment to general would be *almost* the only way."

He swallowed hard. "An assassin?" he repeated.

"In the last twenty-four hours," she said, "all those who fear *Gopak* have been seeking a new way to introduce the hunter to the prey."

"Someone with a pretext," he said, "to meet with Stalin."

"Yes."

"Like a hero," he said slowly, "newly returned from the West."

"After the successful assassination of the Soviet Union's most dangerous defector."

Petrov nodded. "Yes, even now that guarantees an interview. Even now when Stalin shuts himself up in the Pleshny Palace with his guards around him."

"And now you have the answer to your question—why did Alex come back. He defected in the United States, or he was turned. We thought he came back as a hero. But he came back to murder Joseph Stalin."

A long silence hung between them.

"Colonel Merkolovsky will be here in less than an hour," Petrov spoke into the silence. He turned toward the window and looked out to where Dzerzhinsky's statue stood in the square below.

"We must save ourselves, Pavel."

"How? We have barely one hour."

She took his arm and turned him to face her. "If Stalin falls, Beria will fall with him."

"It seems certain."

"And the politicals will take over—Khrushchev, Bulganin. Those who fear *Gopak* could destroy us all."

"What are you getting at, Vanessa?"

"In an hour we will be under arrest."

"Escape from Moscow is out of the question, Vanessa. We would be hunted down."

"I'm not talking about escape."

"What are you saying?"

"I'm saying that we have it in our power to ensure that tonight Russia has new rulers. Rulers who will thank us for what we have done."

"Are you mad?"

"I'm fighting for my life," she said harshly. "Joseph Stalin's meeting with Alex is still scheduled. It's in your power, Pavel, to allow it to go ahead."

In his cell in the lower basement, Alex lay on the floor, fighting to control his terror. He had fought for his life as the huge, unknown animal had charged him, clawing and tearing. He had believed it at first to be some sort of ape. Then, suddenly, light had flooded the room. Outside the window, a truck was entering the courtyard, and its headlights illuminated the short, powerful figure of his attacker.

They crouched in opposite corners of the cell. Just as Alex had believed the dwarf would again attack, Roy Morosov's voice came from the corridor outside. "Back in your kennel, Dimitry," he shouted cheerfully. "The old man wants you upstairs right away, Alex."

CHAPTER
25

2–3 March 1953

At 11:00 P.M., Moscow lay silent in the winter's final fall of snow. Red Square, the snow as yet unmarked by the track of vehicles, stretched virgin white from the candy-striped onion domes of St. Basil's Cathedral to the tiny, strutting figures of the guards below the swallowtail crenellations of the great Kremlin wall.

A bell began to ring the hour, and another and another, until from every clock tower and belfry within the Kremlin, bells were pealing in a confused cacophony of notes. Then one after another ceased, and only the Great Tsar Nicholas continued with two, three, four more hollow, ethereal reverberations until Moscow fell silent again.

Petrov sat at the wheel of a car parked in deep shadow at the point where the Ulitza Kuybysheva touches Red Square. His gloved hand played nervously with the star set in the center of his astrakhan *shapka*. Beside him, Alex Trenton sat dazed with fatigue. He wore a fresh MGB captain's uniform, as well as a high *shapka* with a red star like Petrov's. "How can I be sure you will bring back Katya Filanova?" Trenton said to Petrov, glancing out at the falling snow.

"Your Perlinka whore," Vanessa said contemptuously from the backseat.

"I've already sent orders. You will have to trust me," Petrov said, touching Trenton's arm reassuringly.

"I've no choice." Alex opened the car door. "We're all in this together now."

"Of course."

He nodded. "I still can't bring myself to hope that both of you end up shot against some vomit-stained Lubyanka wall," he said, "with your boss Beria. But I do wish that you could just quietly disappear from the face of the earth forever." He turned to Vanessa. "How dare you, after the life you've lived, call anyone a whore?"

She threw her head up angrily.

He turned and pushed his way out through the car door. The wind cut across his face. Behind Petrov's car stood an open jeep, with Roy Morosov at the wheel. Alex walked slowly through the soft snow. Stopping beside the jeep, he gestured with his gloved hand for Morosov to get out.

The motor was running. Alex climbed into the driver's seat.

"No hard feelings." Morosov extended his hand.

Alex ignored him, looking out across Red Square. He put the jeep in gear and drew out past Petrov's car. In front of him, across the great square, across the virgin expanse of snow, he headed the jeep toward the strutting guards at the Kremlin gate, the tires leaving a pair of stark, dark lines on the sheet of whiteness behind him.

The book, bound in red leather, was a source of strength and inspiration to Stalin, and never far from his side. Even the title had a solid, reassuring ring: *Joseph Vissarionovich Stalin—A Short Biography,* boldly embossed in gold across the front.

Sunk into an armchair, his stockinged feet resting on a hassock, Stalin pulled the cashmere shawl across the front of his white peasant blouse and opened the book's cover. Millions of copies had already been sold across the length and breadth of the country, and yet another edition was about to go to press. Near the front was a photograph of the young Joseph Dzhugashvili outside the church school he had attended as a boy, his oiled hair severely parted down the middle and allowed to grow long as a sign of one destined for the priesthood. The Orthodox Church was disestablished and all Church property nationalized immediately after the Revolution, but Stalin had insisted the photograph be included. The justification was in the text: "Even at this tender age he had read Darwin and decided to become an atheist. Already there began to grow in his young mind an awareness of the social and national inequalities that were to make him the rebel and revolutionary of later years."

Stirring words and all very true. Stalin nodded in self-satisfaction, none. could argue with that. He turned the pages slowly. Most of these opening pages he knew by heart. As he read odd snatches of the text, his lips, etched with a film of dried saliva, twitched into a smile. The greatest chapter was about to be written.

Most visitors to the Kremlin were awestruck at the prospect of entering the hallowed gates. Last week the chairman of a collective farm in the Ukraine had fainted when he stepped inside the walls. But the major commanding the Alexander Gate guardhouse noted at once that the captain before him was different. "Trenton. What sort of name is that, comrade?"

"Just a name," said Alex evenly.

The major went back to the identification documents, studying them minutely. Alex glanced out of the window at two guards in their long green overcoats slowly circling the jeep. He had been ordered to park just inside the gates while they checked his papers. One guard kicked a mudguard with his boot, dislodging a frozen lump of discolored snow.

"Purpose of visit?" The major examined the documentation at his desk. His head pulled back in surprise. "Private audience with Comrade Stalin?"

Alex watched him without speaking.

"Even so, comrade," the major said respectfully, "you will be subjected to the normal search procedure."

"Of course."

"If you will just follow my sergeant, Comrade Captain, I will telephone Secretary Poskrebyshev to confirm your appointment."

"Please hurry, Comrade Major, my appointment is for three o'clock."

Both men looked up at the carved wooden clock on the guardroom wall. It showed twelve minutes to three.

"The Revolution's strategist of genius and its greatest military leader found a situation of confusion and panic when he arrived at the front," Stalin read. Yes, he remembered it all so clearly; they were exciting times. "Stalin quickly devised a brilliant new operational plan." Let anyone try to deny it. In some of the early histories, Frunze had received the credit. Frunze had died under the surgical knife during an operation ordered by the Politburo. But the record had been put right. It had been his own, Stalin's, will, his unflagging determination that had saved the day.

Feeling a sudden stab of pain at the center of his brow, Stalin looked up from the page, but the extra-large print was retained in his vision, dancing before his eyes. The pain passed as suddenly as it had struck, but for some reason the wall lights seemed to have grown very dim.

Scowling with the effort, Stalin strained to read the words, which seemed to grow smaller, merging together into an indistinct mass. "From 1918 onward Joseph Vissarionovich was undoubtedly Lenin's deputy."

"Well, wasn't I?" Stalin called aloud, as if to an objector. "If it wasn't me, who was it? Tell me that."

Stalin riffled through the pages and settled on another photograph. The photo showed him in an official pose, a portrait taken during the Great Patriotic War. Ah yes, he recalled the dark days of '41. He had ordered the nation to stand and fight to the death. But the people had retreated to the gates of Moscow.

"It was the nation's great good fortune that in the traumatic years of war, the Motherland was led by a wise and trusted leader, the Great Stalin."

Excellent, and so obviously true. Truth had never failed to calm and soothe his spirits.

Twenty feet away, Poskrebyshev paced the floor of the adjoining office, nervous tension racing through him like a series of electric shocks. Moments before, he thought he had heard the voice of his awesome master through the heavy, locked door, but now all was silent. He glanced at his watch for the

fifth time in as many minutes. The fateful, terrifying moment
when he must start to act was inexorably approaching. His future depended on it. It was now a minute or two before 3 A.M.

The search had taken ten minutes. As Alex followed the
armed sentry past the bell tower toward the steps leading to
the main entrance of the Pleshny Palace, he realized he was
now behind the carefully scheduled timetable of the plan. At
any moment, Stalin might choose to cancel the appointment.

Inside the tall, elaborately carved doors, the magnificent entrance hall was ablaze with the light from a huge chandelier
suspended from the domed ceiling high overhead. The sentry
took Trenton's papers and knocked on a door marked GUARD
COMMANDER.

"Come in," a voice answered immediately.

The sentry entered the room, leaving the door ajar. Alex
noted the Chekist guards, armed with semiautomatic Ka-
lashnikov assault rifles, standing at attention at each corner of
the hall. One, swiveling his eyes without moving his head, returned Alex's look.

"Come in, Comrade Trenton," the guard commander called
through the half-open door. The colonel examined Alex's papers with little interest.

Alex glanced at the fine ormolu clock on the mantel. "Comrade Colonel, I'm sorry, but I have to point out that it is three
o'clock now."

"You've had a wasted journey, comrade."

"I don't understand," Alex said.

"Marshal Stalin is seeing no one. Someone should have told
you."

Alex tried to think. Something had obviously gone badly
wrong. "I have a specific invitation, as you can see from my
papers."

The colonel moved closer and lowered his voice. "Listen,
comrade. He's flatly refused to see anyone for the past three
days. Don't ask me why."

Alex felt stunned. The colonel held out his documentation.
"Here," his voice was normal again. "I'll get someone to escort
you back to the gate."

As he turned to leave, the telephone on the side table rang.
The colonel picked up the receiver. "Guard commander. Yes,

he's here with me now." The colonel listened a moment. "I see. Yes, immediately."

Alex waited as the colonel replaced the receiver with deliberate care. "That was Marshal Stalin's secretary, Comrade Poskrebyshev," he said. "It seems you have a very specific invitation."

Wiping his sweating palms on a white handkerchief, Poskrebyshev went to the corner of the office and crouched low against the box on the wall. Slowly he undid the small screw, his hands trembling. Swinging open the metal cover, he counted along the line of fuses and stopped at number four. This one act could cost him his life. If Stalin noticed, Poskrebyshev knew, he would not see another dawn. Closing his eyes, he pulled the fuse from its socket and held his breath.

With a series of clicks the electronic bolts on the two doors to the sitting room slid open, and the incessant low hum of the fans in the ceiling slowly died. Enervated by sitting too long, Stalin noticed nothing. He grunted in irritation: to his failing eyesight, the wall lights behind his shoulder had become so dim it was impossible to continue to read.

Clutching the book, he pulled himself up from the armchair and shuffled heavily toward his desk. The floor seemed to sink and sway beneath his bootless feet. He stopped, but the strange, undulating motion continued. Then the whole room tilted, swimming in and out of focus. Tiny yellow stars flashed and sparked briefly before his eyes, then changed into black globules spreading quickly, like ink across a polished surface. What was happening? The book slipped from his grasp. He staggered to the desk and slumped down in the padded leather chair, gasping for breath. His whole body began to tremble in great, shuddering convulsions. His groping hand pushed frantically at the buzzer on the desktop, but the circuit was dead. He wanted to cry out for help, to call a friend, but he knew outside in the cold darkness there were only enemies. He believed in nothing, trusted no one. Even his daughter, once his favorite, had been rejected. He was utterly alone. Fear moved over him like a paralysis.

Flanked by two MGB lieutenants, Alex marched along the Pleshny's central corridor. At ten-yard intervals, armed sentries stood by the marble pillars on either side. Turning left at the end of the corridor, he followed the guards up a short flight of steps. The door at the top opened into a huge, darkened chamber.

A thin voice spoke from the shadows. "I'll take care of this man. Return to your posts."

"Yes, comrade." The guards went back through the door.

Poskrebyshev blinked. "You're late," he hissed.

Alex could see his face was ashen. From under his jacket, Poskrebyshev took something wrapped in a green cloth and held it out to Alex on his upturned palm. "No mistakes, comrade," he said quietly.

Alex took it and folded back the cloth. He recognized the gun as a Colt A1 automatic. "Comrade Poskrebyshev," Alex said, marveling, "the loyalest of the loyal."

Poskrebyshev pointed to a door to the right. "You go through there, down the staircase. Turn right at the bottom. Fourth door on the left."

Alex weighed the gun in his hand, then checked the clip of seven rounds. "What about the lock?"

"Done. Done," Poskrebyshev whispered, starting to edge away, staring at the Colt as Alex snapped the clip back into the butt. "When it is over, leave by that door." The secretary indicated a smaller door in the corner to the left.

Alex noted his escape route.

"The steps lead to a courtyard. Go across the courtyard and into the Alexandrovski Gardens."

"Where is the key to the door in the wall?" Alex asked.

"It won't be locked," Poskrebyshev said. Then he turned and hurried off into the dark depths of the vaulted chamber.

Alone at the foot of the grand staircase, Alex listened intently: nothing broke the silence. Moving on, he peered down a short passageway that opened out into the central corridor. The marble pillars stood as silent sentinels.

With a surge of excitement, he went on, the gun clasped in his right hand, the arm held stiffly, close to his side. He noticed the air was warmer. He stalked slowly and silently forward over the last few yards.

The fourth door was made of polished oak. He pressed gently against it, his body tightening as the door gave a fraction. Slipping off the Colt's safety catch, he steadied himself, then placed his hand flat against the woodwork and threw open the door. The room was empty; he could see no one. Filthy stacks of glasses and empty wine bottles lay scattered on every surface; the floor was littered with books, screwed up balls of paper, open files, old pieces of clothing and trays of cold, untouched meals. The air had a thick stench of stale tobacco and body odor.

Then he saw him, sitting in semidarkness at the desk. A hunched old man with wizened folds of skin hanging from his neck and jowls, his matted hair still thick, the famous mustache shaggy and drooping, the withered left hand perched like a talon on the desktop, the mouth gaping open, bubbling with saliva.

Stunned, appalled, Alex moved closer. Could this really be the man who had pervaded his life? He had seen his image in ten thousand pictures and photographs, on posters, flags, banners and placards of every kind. The strong, implacable face had stared back at him, unflinching, awesome. As a child and young man, Alex had looked up in fear and wonder at a hundred towering statues in sandstone and concrete, marble and bronze. Was this the same colossus?

Stalin lifted his rheumy yellow eyes and seemed to beckon with a clawlike hand. Alex aimed the gun. With a supreme effort of will, Stalin forced his dripping lips to move. He was begging for mercy.

Alex fired into the grotesque head. The body fell sideways, collapsing as if someone had cut the strings of a marionette.

CHAPTER
26

He was dead: it was over, done. Stalin's pallid yellow eyes had held him for a moment before the slobbering head had fallen below the level of the desk. It was difficult to forget those eyes, staring, showing neither fear nor surprise, expressionless, yet not completely drained of life. Running now, stumbling, intoxicated by a heady mixture of euphoria and fear, Alex retraced his steps. When he reached the great hall, he realized he no longer held the Colt in his hand. But he had no recollection of how or where it had fallen from his grasp. Perhaps he had dropped it in the long, uncarpeted corridor, or in the shadows on the wide staircase. Perhaps he had pulled the trigger and flung the gun down into the darkness beside his victim. What did it matter? It was done.

Alex was sweating heavily, although the chamber he was crossing, a vast room housing tsarist relics, was cold with the dank smell of neglect. He hurried forward, the sound of his footsteps accentuated by the high, vaulted ceiling. The huge carved-ivory throne of Ivan the Terrible shimmered dully in the half-light from a line of tall, fretted windows. As he ran, his eye caught a dusty glass-fronted display cabinet he had not noticed before. It contained a number of priceless jewel-encrusted imperial crowns. One, covered in diamonds, was split down the middle like a melon. His thoughts, racing wildly, were carried back to his apartment at the old Moscow Variety Theater, to the split figure of Queen Victoria.

He reached the corner where Chief Secretary Poskrebyshev had been waiting. There was the door he had entered. He wrenched it open. The narrow spiral steps descended steeply into the gloom. Alex started down, the stone damp and slippery underfoot. He felt calmer now, his breath steadied. He must be resolute: the worst was over. Then, as he took the last turn before the door, a sudden blaze of light streamed in through a long, recessed window. Flattening himself against the curve of the outer wall, he leaned his head and shoulders into the recess and peered cautiously out. A searchlight had been set up. Its beam flooded the courtyard below. The glass was etched with frost, but Alex was able to make out a group of men silhouetted against the brightness. Their dark, cutout forms wore greatcoats and calf-high boots, and as they began to move, he caught the glint of the light on rifles. They could only be waiting for him, their guns trained on the door at the foot of the spiral steps, ready to unleash a deadly volley the moment he stepped out into the courtyard.

Now the stark reality of his situation was clear. He had been allowed to enter the Kremlin, but they could never permit the man who had murdered Joseph Stalin to escape alive. Alex turned and raced back up the steps, possessed by the knowledge that he was running for his life.

As he ran, his footsteps echoing the length of the great hall, another searchlight flooded in at an angle through the windows, illuminating the ceiling with splashes of light. Through the door at the end, down the wide staircase he raced, his pulse pounding in his ears as he took the steps two and three at a time. To the left lay the corridor leading to Stalin's office; to the right, a darkened passageway disappeared into pitch blackness after a few feet. He hurried into the passage on the right, but was forced to slow and feel his way forward, running one hand along the wall as a guide. He discovered a door in the wall, but found it was locked. Alex continued on. The passage seemed to twist and turn, and soon he had lost all sense of direction. He tried to quicken his pace, only to collide with something hanging on the wall, sending it crashing to the floor. The sound echoed in the narrow corridor. Listening, he fancied he heard a distant shout. This was madness, he thought; the darkness was impenetrable, and he had no idea of where he was.

A glimmer of light ahead showed him that the passageway went down three steps and then widened out. The light came from a small window set high in the wall. As Alex approached, he saw that the passage ended abruptly a few yards farther on. He managed to jump, gain a handhold on the ledge below the window and haul himself up. The window was not more than a foot above ground level. The glass was cracked and broken in one corner but protected by heavy steel bars set deep in the stonework.

He was trapped.

"Take some men to the main entrance. He must still be inside." Two guards ran past outside the windows. Alex dropped to the floor and crouched low, watching as more figures ran past the window above, the sound of their boots muffled by the snow.

As he was about to go back, Alex noticed a door, little more than a hatch, set low in the wall opposite the window. It took all his strength to force it open. When it gave, it swung inward with a grating creak. A rusting iron ladder, fixed to the wall, descended into a cellar. Alex lowered his legs through the opening and began to climb down, pushing the hatch shut as he went. As he reached the bottom, his hand closed over something hooked onto one of the rungs. It was a cheap tin candle holder with a distinctive handle, the type millions of Soviet peasants, still without the benefit of electricity, kept at their bedsides. There was a stub of a candle at the center.

"If Joseph Stalin knew what was going on right under his very nose," the young girl said to Katya, "I can promise you some heads would roll."

"You think so, comrade?" Katya leaned her head back against the slats of the swaying cattle car. From where she was sitting, her hands clasped round her knees, she could see the outline of the other women, perhaps twenty or thirty of them, their faces a whitish blur as a shaft of light slipped between the slats of the cattle car's wooden sides. Most of the women seemed cold and bewildered at the sudden turn of fate that had made them prisoners. Most had been, like Katya, arrested this morning while shopping or readying the children for school. There had been no trial, no accusations made against them. Some were Jews, some the wives of suspect officials or petty criminals. They made up yet another trainload of prisoners to join the ten million *zeks* already working and dying in Siberia.

"I myself," the young girl, Svetlana, said, "was arrested this morning on the way to the university, where I am studying diamat."

Katya pulled her coat tighter around her. "What's diamat?" she asked indifferently.

"Dialectical materialism, of course." Svetlana was shocked at her companion's ignorance. "Without diamat as a tool, we can't possibly expect to understand the dynamic processes of society at any given stage of its development."

The train rattled through a small town, and a shaft of light flicked across Svetlana's face. She was, Katya could see, younger, if anything, than Katya herself, her mouth thin, determined, compressed to a line.

"What did they pull you in for?" Katya asked her.

"A mistake," Svetlana said.

A woman laughed in the half-darkness.

"I was denounced by a fellow student for anti–Party activities."

"Is that what you were, dear?" an old woman's voice said, mock reprovingly. "Anti–Party!"

"I'm a member of the Komsomol and chairman of the university Victory to Socialism committee," Svetlana said desperately. "The girl who denounced me was my deputy chairman. Isn't it obvious why she did it?"

"Perhaps it should be," Katya said. "But the sadness is, that it doesn't make a damn bit of different whether you're anti–Party or not."

Svetlana instinctively moved away a few inches. "When we stop tonight, I'm going to make my protest. And I've noted what you've just said, comrade."

"We're going into another world, Svetlana," Katya said. "Don't make it harder for yourself. And don't believe you can buy yourself out of it at the expense of others. None of us are leaving this cattle car until we arrive at whatever camp they marked down for us."

On through the night, the long train rattled. The women slept, some crying, some coughing in their sleep. Katya slept fitfully, her arm around the young girl beside her. Already Svetlana had moved closer; from the darkness where she huddled came a relentless quiet sobbing.

The flickering yellow flame cast a thin light as Alex held the lighted candle high over his head. The cellar was vast, seeming to stretch under half the palace. The air was damp and stale, with a peculiar, acrid tang. Water dripped somewhere out in the shadows with a constant, steady splash. Moisture seeped between the masonry of the walls; blind fungi grew from the cracks between the stones in grotesque, hanging clumps. Above, massive cross beams, thick with tangles of filthy cobwebs, supported the heavy oak planks of the ground-floor rooms. The flagstones were wet and littered with broken chairs, old bottles, bundles of dank, rotting newspapers tied with string, the forgotten, discarded rubbish of many years. To one side stood a pile of coal, and in a corner an enormous, sodden, rolled-up carpet lay like a fallen tree trunk. Alex brought the light down close and recognized the faded imperial crest of the Romanovs woven into the fabric.

The crash of running feet shook the floorboards above his head, bringing down a shower of dust and grit. The soldiers were inside the palace, searching overhead. Doors banged as they hurried from room to room, raining down more cobwebs and grime. Alex moved as quickly as he could between the soaking piles of remnants, then came upon a flight of concrete steps leading up to the main entrance of the cellar. He froze as he reached the solid wooden door at the top. Someone on the other side was drawing back the heavy bolts. The handle turned.

"It's locked. Where is the key?"

"How should I know?"

The voices were clear and hard.

"You two," came a voice of command. "What's happening there?"

"There's no key, Comrade Commissar."

"Leave it. I'll get the key. Search upstairs."

The candle was sputtering, near the end of its life. Alex stared around in desperation. Then he saw it—a fine sprinkling of powdery snow on top of the pile of coal. It had been out of his line of vision from down on the level of the cellar floor. The candle fluttered briefly and then died.

As Alex clambered up the coal pile, each step sent a small, black avalanche of coal clattering down. Using hands and feet, he clawed his way to the top. Standing unsteadily, he reached out. A large trapdoor, used as a delivery chute, was cut into the floor above his head. He could see chinks of half-light through cracks in the planking and feel the faint draft of cold night air. He pushed up with the flat of his hand. The trap moved a couple of inches, then stopped as it met the resistance of a fastened latch. Bracing himself, he drove the back of his shoulders against the trapdoor, but his feet slipped under him sending a cascade of coal tumbling to the floor.

A key rattled in the lock. The cellar door at the top of the concrete steps was flung open, spilling in light.

A shout rang through the cellar. "There he is!"

The sharp report of a rifle reverberated through the vault. Alex strained against the door in a final effort. The latch gave way with a crack of splintering timber. He threw the trapdoor back and lunged the top half of his body out over the edge. Another shot exploded in the cellar as he pulled himself clear. Once on his feet, he stumbled blindly forward, vaulting a low wall in his path. Behind him, a soldier was already emerging from the door, yelling to the men manning the searchlight.

"Over here. He's over here."

The beam swung toward the voice.

Alex ducked blindly into the unkempt Alexandrovski Gardens, brushing past shrubs and crashing through an overgrown ornamental hedge. The probing flare of a searchlight was turning toward him. He flung himself down into a drift of snow. The beam floated over his flattened form like a silent specter. Glancing back, he could see a line of men fanning out as they moved forward, urged on by the shouts of their commander. Others were maneuvering a second searchlight around into position.

Suddenly, a shot, misdirected far to the right, caught the pursuers' attention.

"Did you see him?"

"I think so, Comrade Captain."

"Over here with the light, then."

Seizing the opportunity, Alex ran for the public road to his left.

CHAPTER
27

Through the clapboard main street of Surgansk, high up in the Demyansk Hills, the column of cavalry jingled toward the railway station on the edge of the town. The wind was lessened here by the close-set wooden buildings, but the early dawn temperature was still twenty-five below zero, and the riders in their rough khaki cloaks hunched themselves in the saddle and shrunk deeper into their cloth balaclava helmets to protect their eyes from the stinging cold. The leader of the cavalry detachment, a young Siberian major, knew there was no hurry. In the half-light, he watched the train winding back and forth below them like a great serpent trying to find a passage through the hills. Now the major could see the glow of the red-hot smokestack as the train slowly hauled its cars up the final steep slope toward Surgansk.

Led by the major, the detachment entered the station yard. Turning in his saddle, the officer gave a few laconic commands to his section sergeants, then urged his pony forward, up the two or three wooden steps, clattering along the planked platform beside the single-line track.

As other ponies negotiated the steps, the door opened in the station house, and a boy of about fifteen, wearing an official cap, emerged. He stood under the single string of electric bulbs, which was all the platform offered for light, and watched the cavalrymen assemble beside their officer.

The train was no great distance away now, snorting sparks as it reached the last crest, blowing a double blast on the whistle as the brakes were applied and it slowed to a halt in the station.

The boy came forward and with a quick, agile movement swung himself up onto the footplate. A single passenger car was attached to the locomotive. Behind that, a line of perhaps five or six cattle cars was visible within the canopy of light. The major nudged his horse forward and rapped his riding crop on one of the windows of the passenger car.

He was forced to rap a second time before eliciting an angry shout from within, and yet a third time in order to persuade someone to open the door. The MGB detachment commander, of the same rank as the cavalry officer but older by ten years, stood on the steel steps waving his arms in fury. "This is a police train," he snarled at the young major. "Prisoners. You understand me?"

The Siberian's almond eyes creased inside the slit of his balaclava. "I've orders to take off one of your consignment." He jerked his thumb toward the line of boarded cattle cars. He leaned from the saddle and handed the MGB major a fluttering piece of paper.

The other man looked at it and brought his head up level with the horseman. "You expect me to act on this? It's a telephone order, man."

"It's from General Petrov in Moscow. I received the message myself."

"I didn't," the man on the step growled. "To me, it's a telephone order. Nothing more."

The Siberian major turned to his sergeant. "Open up the cars. Get the prisoner out."

As the MGB major opened his mouth to object, the cavalryman leaned forward in his saddle, his machine pistol lifted beneath his cloak. "My orders are quite specific regarding anyone, MGB or otherwise, who refuses to cooperate."

The MGB major looked at the horsemen lining the platform. Behind them in the station courtyard, he could make out several others. In a less remote part of the country he could have called for MGB reinforcements from the Prison and

Camp Directorate, but in a godforsaken place like Surgansk he knew there would be only army men. He looked again at the horsemen. "Take whom you want," he said. "But just wait until *my* general hears about it."

Farther down the train, Katya, a sack of possessions over her shoulder, was being led toward the station by one of the cavalrymen.

"My orders," the major said to her, "are to keep you here, comrade, until a vehicle arrives to take you on to Okulovka."

"Comrade," Katya spat out. "Comrade, you call me." Her clothes were filthy, her face streaked with grime. "Do you know what the whip guards call us prisoners?" She glared at the MGB major.

"What do they call you, comrade?" the Siberian said.

Katya drew her finger across her neck. "Dog meat," she said. "It's their mark of Revolutionary respect."

The black Pobeda automobile cruised along Boulevard Tverskoi, waited for the militiaman in his booth at the intersection to change the traffic light to green, then turned right past the Marlinsky Hospital for the Poor, where Dostoevsky had been born. An official ZIS, with its three dour-faced occupants, followed, making no attempt to conceal the fact from the passenger in the first car.

The passenger in the leading car, Robert Haynes, was the youngest first secretary at the U.S. embassy. It was he who had kept an eye on Alexander Trenton at Tushino Airport.

"Would it be permissible to ask where you would like to go, Mr. Haynes?" the driver said in English. He was tired and irritable after driving all night through the streets of Moscow.

The car and its Russian driver were at the disposal of the embassy at a cost of 150 rubles a day. The arrangement was made through Burobin, the official Soviet agency that supplied chauffeurs and transport to the *corps diplomatique* and all accredited journalists. No American stationed in Moscow had yet managed to pass the severe Russian driving test, which included a searching physical by a panel of doctors and the ability to take apart and reassemble an engine. Burobin saw to it that no foreign diplomats were up to standard.

"Repeat the same route we drove just now." Haynes stared

uncomfortably at the small oriental rug on the floor. It was the fifth time they had toured around the city. The driver, obviously suspicious, shrugged. The secret police who were tailing them followed as the Pobeda turned again. Haynes leaned back in his seat, wishing he had the faintest notion of what his instructions were all about.

Alex climbed the last few narrow steps to the top of the derelict building where he had first set up the meeting between Vassily Nozenkov and General Jones.

As he reached the top of the stairs, his shoulder dislodged a huge, dripping icicle. It fell and splintered, sending a crash echoing through the crumbling shell. Alex waited, motionless. But the house was silent, except for the low, creaking draft of the wind through the boarded windows.

The door to the attic room was closed. Alex eased it open, pushing back a layer of broken plaster littering the floor. With a sudden flap of feathers, two roosting starlings flew up and out into the night through a gap in the tiles. He crossed the room and pushed his hand through the broken slats on the sloping attic wall. The leather wallet rested in the angle of a rafter as Hal Jones had promised it would. Alex took it, opened it and drew out the two stamped travel warrants and two tickets for the special Red Arrow train to Leningrad. Slipping the wallet into his pocket, he bent to pull aside the old tarpaulin in a corner. Underneath, he found the cans of kerosene. Emptying the first can over the walls and floor, he carried the other two onto the upper landing. He quickly soaked the area and the top of the stairs, then descended with the last can, splashing a trail on the rotten wood of the steps.

The first match went out in his cold, trembling fingers. The second flared bright in the gloom, and he threw it down, stepping back from the expected roar of flames. The match fluttered briefly and then went out. He tried another, and at last the kerosene flared violently. Fire ran quickly up the steps, engulfing the stairs and landing in an oily blaze.

Out on the street, it was getting light. Alex crossed to the opposite sidewalk and walked for fifty yards before stopping to look back. A plume of thick, black smoke billowed up against the lightening sky, and as he watched, long fingers of flame began to shoot out between the broken tiles of the roof.

Ten minutes later, Robert Haynes's chauffeured Pobeda, with its MGB shadow close behind, turned for the fifth time into the street and passed the now blazing house. The moment he saw the fire, Haynes realized that that was what he was to look for. He directed the driver back to the embassy.

The name of the cipher clerk on duty was Howard. Haynes liked him, they often worked out together in the well-equipped gymnasium in the embassy basement.

"Let's see," said Howard. He scratched his chin and read the handwritten sheet, torn from the message pad, that Haynes had just handed him. "'Can confirm at 2030 hours local time, number 107 Dudzinsky Street seen to be on fire.' That's it?"

"Right," said Haynes, leaning back on the closed door to the radio room on the second floor.

"What is it, Bob?"

"It's a signal," Haynes said.

"Yeah, right. One to you, pal. What does it mean?"

Haynes shrugged. "Beats the hell out of me. But it's the signal General Jones has been asking for in Washington for the last two hours."

CHAPTER
28

"General Bolsover," Hal said carefully, "we received the signal tonight. I don't know how, but Captain Trenton has managed to complete the mission."

"You've got a signal from your man? Fine, but I can't advise President Eisenhower to stand down the Strategic Air Command because of a bonfire in a Moscow street. I need proof."

"I think we'll be able to supply the proof you need, General. Within less than twelve hours, Soviet tank divisions will be pulling back. At the same time, I hope to see a major realignment of the air force."

"That's not good enough, Hal. On what basis do you expect these things to happen?"

"Shtemenko. I don't like him—but I believe him. I think we should allow him to return to Moscow." Bolsover got up from the table and began to pace the cell-like room. When the cigarette in his hand burned low, he stubbed it out and lit another.

"General." Hal waited until Bolsover stopped pacing. "You're wondering what happens if I'm wrong."

"Of course I am."

"If I'm wrong about Shtemenko, General, it won't make a damn bit of difference to anybody. In the middle of World War III, nobody's going to care about the fate of one Russian general, however eminent."

Bolsover sat down heavily. "Of course you're right. I'll talk with the president. But I'm sure he'll agree to let him go. When we do, take him over to Europe yourself. When do you think Moscow will announce the news?"

"As soon as the battle for the succession is over, General. As soon as the new man is clearly seen to be at the top."

When Hal left the White House, he took a taxi to the Hunter residence in Georgetown. At the door, Doonan watched him paying off the cabdriver. "You know, General," he said, "you get me into a world of hurt. To you, the lady is not in. Between us, she's in, alone and probably ready to throw her arms around your neck. She's been red-eyed and snappy all day. I been thinking of giving up my job."

"You going to let me in, or do I have to force it?"

"I'm going to let you in, General. Just to show how deeply concerned I am about the lady's happiness. Not to mention my own skin." He stood back and nodded toward the small sitting room which opened off the hall. "If it all works out for you two," he said, "I might even offer to take the job of butler in the new establishment."

Hal grunted dubiously, knocked on the door and opened it. Jennifer rose slowly from the armchair in the window alcove and put aside the magazine she had been reading.

"Joseph Stalin is dead," he said. "I received a signal from Alex Trenton an hour ago."

She stood still, her lemon-yellow dress bright against the tans and pale greens of the room's furnishings. "Is that why you sent Alex back?"

"Yes. Stalin was about to launch a massive all-out attack against Europe. He was mad. The only way to stop him—according to the Soviet Union's own army—was by assassination. But Stalin is so well protected that only a Soviet 'hero,' Alex, could get close enough to do the job. I'm sorry, but I had— and Alex had—no choice."

She walked toward him and reached out to touch his hand. "So arrogant I've been . . ." She looked at him. "Even so, I still don't like your world, Hal."

Hal took her into his arms. "I never said I liked it either."

Through the side window of the bar at the Yaroslavl Station, Alex could see the long, sleek passenger cars of the Red Arrow waiting at the main-line platform. The rolling stock itself and

much of the equipment aboard came from Hitler's personal
train, which the Soviet Union had seized as part of the repara-
tions program at the end of the war. Alex watched as a fur-
coated attendant climbed into one of the shining blue sleeping
cars, with the newly painted symbol—OK, for *oktyabr*—embla-
zoned on the side. There it was, the October line. Three hundred miles to Leningrad; he could be there by early evening.

He left the bar and walked toward the gate. He stopped before the ticket collector and lit a cigarette. The collector saw
only a tall MGB officer with the dismissive superior man-
nerisms of all other MGB passengers. He took his ticket and
stamped it without even looking at the attached *propiska*.

On the train, Alex sought out the fur-coated sleeping-car attendant. He pressed a single dollar bill into the man's hand.
The effect was immediate. "This way, comrade." The attendant knew exactly what an American dollar could buy in a foreigners' shop in Leningrad and he knew that the very best of
service might even earn him another when the captain left the
train. He showed Alex to his compartment and called a waiter.
The man bustled forward with a tray of vodka and a selection
of glasses.

"Do you want something, comrade?"

Alex nodded. "Vodka."

"Large or small?" the waiter asked, his free hand poised over
the two sizes of glasses. Vodka had been a state monopoly in
Russia since the time of Count Witte, long before the Revolution. It was sold in 50- and 100-gram measures.

"Large," Alex said.

The waiter took the appropriate glass and filled it with casual expertise.

Alex entered the large double compartment, the glass of
vodka in his hand. Throwing his fur *shapka* onto the leather
seat, he sat down and began to sip the vodka. Outside, he
could hear the shouts of porters loading the luggage of last-
minute passengers. He let his eyes wander around the compartment. It was richly furnished in deep blue material. The
leather seats were a matching blue, as was the carpet, and the
curtains were oversewn with a slightly darker motif. He smiled
to himself as the thin sunlight caught the tiny pattern of inter-
locking swastikas.

Whistles blew, doors slammed, and the Red Arrow, the Soviet Union's premier train, pulled away, the tiny swastikas in the slowly swaying curtains discreetly catching the light.

The names of the towns through which they passed had a ring that evoked for Alex those days in 1943–44 when he had been part of the vast Soviet army that had gradually pushed the German forces back toward East Prussia. Two hours out of Moscow, they passed through Novo Zavidovski and onto the long bridge across the lake where his regiment had advanced in a bitter struggle across ice shattered and made treacherous by artillery fire. For a few moments as the train clattered across the long bridge, he remembered the flaring crack of exploding shells, the tanks lurching and sliding below the ice, the crews screaming as they tried to leap free. He had no regrets. He found, in fact, that in recollection it was the only clean, straightforward episode in his life. Nazism had to be destroyed; for a young man there was no need or time to think. But he was sick with shame now at the moral labyrinths he had trod since the war. Prodded on by his mother, he had joined the security police as a translator. He had seen too much for his conscience to live with. He had seen men broken, families destroyed, evidence casually manufactured. Only in those seconds when he had stood over the wild-eyed tyrant in the room in the Pleshny Palace had he felt he had done anything to clean the record. The only thought that helped assuage his conscience was that if Russia had a future, he had contributed in some way to it.

Once past the city of Kalinin, he could no longer keep Katya from his thoughts. He believed he had taken every precaution possible in those last rushed minutes before he had left for the Kremlin. He had insisted on being alone in Petrov's office to give the orders to take Katya off the prison train at Surgansk. If Petrov had wanted to discover what happened to Katya after that, it would not take more than an hour or two. But Vanessa had made it clear they didn't have an hour or two. Lavrenty Beria was on their track, and they would surely take the sensible course of going into hiding until Beria himself was put up against a wall by Khrushchev and the new masters.

The train sped on: Kalinin, Likhoslavl, Vyshniy Volochek, Bologoye. Then the long hundred-mile stretch to Okulovka.

As they approached the small northern township, Alex sensed
the change in the rhythmic clatter of the train. He realized
they were approaching the outskirts. The change was now defi-
nite, a slowing of the rhythm, a lessening of the swaying motion.

He got up and went into the corridor. The attendant was
seated on the flap seat at the end of the compartment. Immediately he was on his feet, coming forward, his smile ingratiat-
ing. "Is there anything you want, Comrade Captain?"

Alex stood silently for a moment. "The train's slowing," he
said.

"It appears so, Comrade Captain, although there is no
scheduled stop at Okulovka, the red emergency signal was
showing at Samsorets. To warn the driver to stop at the next
station. An important government official due in Leningrad by
morning, no doubt."

Alex felt in his pocket and drew out a bundle of dollar bills.
"The stop," he said, "was arranged for me. There'll be no need
to talk unnecessarily to other passengers." He counted off five
dollar bills and handed them to the man. "Go into your
kitchen. Stay there."

"State security business, Captain. I understand."

With a hiss of brakes, the train slowed into a single-platform
station. The wooden roof structure, which had been almost entirely burned down during the war, had not yet been replaced.
The deep pockmarks of heavy machine-gun bullets patterned
the plaster walls. A small group of people stood on the platform. Two MGB officers sat in their car beside the wrecked
waiting room. As the train stopped, Katya stepped from the
middle of the group on the platform, her clothes stained, her
face streaked with dirt. Without looking back, she swung herself up onto the steel step of the sleeping car. She was exhausted and stunned with lack of sleep. The man in the
darkened entrance to the sleeper seemed crazily familiar. As in
a dream she had no wish to break, she let the man pull her
toward him and kick the door closed.

He watched her while she stripped off her clothes and
washed her body and her hair in the basin set in the corner of
the compartment. He knew from her silence and the frenetic
quality of her activity that she was suffering from shock. Even

as she took the larger of the towels and wrapped it around herself, tucking it in so that it was held up by the swelling of her breasts, he realized that she was struggling to control herself. "America," she said, her lips trembling.

He lit two cigarettes and gave her one. "I can get you coffee or tea."

"Vodka? And perhaps a sandwich?"

He pressed the bell for the attendant. "There are clothes in the bag," he said. "They won't fit too well, but for the moment they'll have to do."

She unclipped the canvas bag and took out a silk blouse and held it against her. It was clearly too large, the arms too short. "Your wife's? A bosomy lady, but not too tall." She pulled out a skirt. "And perhaps a little broad in the hips."

He nodded grimly. "I knew you would need clothes. I went back to the apartment just before I came to the Yaroslavl Station."

"You went back to see your wife?"

"To get the clothes for you and to say good-bye."

She nodded. "Was she sad?"

"No—she was asleep in an armchair. Poor Xenia. She was too drunk for me to waken her."

Katya rubbed at her wet hair and deftly twisted the hand towel into a head scarf. "You know that all this seems part fairy tale, part miracle to me," she said. "A few hours ago I was lying on the floor of a cattle car. There were thirty or so women there, huddled together. All sorts of women—the wives of high officials who had just been arrested; doctors' wives, lawyers' wives, army officers' wives. And suddenly, at some freezing shantytown in the Demyansk Hills, the train was stopped. Someone was to be taken off. Touched with some magic wand. But it was not the wife of some high official. Not even a doctor's wife. It was me. When the magic wand touched one of us on the shoulders it was me, Katya Filanova, the Perlinka whore."

The tears were streaming down her face. "Get dressed, Katya," he said softly. "We're not safe yet. We won't be safe until we've crossed the frontier into Finland."

Hurrying toward his tiny kitchen at the end of the car, the attendant could not believe his luck. He had just served one

cup of coffee to the strange foreign civilian in the number-
three compartment and he had been given a *ten-dollar* tip. The
world was going most pleasantly mad. And now, in compartment six, the tall MGB captain had just ordered vodka and
sandwiches. Was it possible that this would merit another tip?
Again in dollars? He reached the end of the swaying corridor.
It was early afternoon but already almost dark. Lights from a
building site flashed by the windows.

In their compartment, Alex and Katya felt the brakes applied. With a long, slow screech, the train came to a halt.

"Where are we now?" Katya asked, unalarmed.

Alex pressed his head against the window. There was no
scheduled stop, he knew, until they reached Leningrad. At
an angle, he could see a signboard that read ELEKTROSILA
STATION. They were a few miles south of central Leningrad,
still a mile or two from Moscow Station.

"Wait here," he said suddenly, communicating his anxiety.
She nodded, unconsciously passing her tongue across her bottom lip.

He opened the door and let himself into the corridor. At the
far end, he could see the attendant on the step. By some trick
of the reflection in the train window, he did not at first see that
the man was talking to three militiamen on the platform below
him. He had taken no more than half a dozen paces before the
attendant looked up. "Bad, bad news, Comrade Captain," he
said, his face creased with worry. "It appears that the radio has
just announced that Comrade Stalin, God save him, has been
taken sick. It's serious, Captain."

Unable to move away, Alex nodded. "No details were
given?"

"No more than the bare facts, it seems."

"Even so, it is strange to stop the train to announce that
Comrade Stalin is not in the best of health."

"The train was not stopped for that, comrade," one of the
militiamen said, swinging himself past the attendant and into
the corridor. "We're conducting a routine examination of papers."

"Routine?"

"Your papers please, Captain," the man said, adjusting his
tall *shapka* on his head as he waited.

Alex hesitated.

"I must see your papers please, Captain." The militiaman moved forward.

In the reflection in the glass beyond the man's shoulder, Alex could see people emerging from their sleeping compartments behind him. Some were in pajamas, others wore uniform jackets wide open at the neck. He caught for a moment a glimpse of Katya's worried face. Behind her stood the young man with the braying laugh from Tushino Airport. Then he saw the American take her arm and pull her back toward the far end of the car.

"I've my ticket here . . ." Alex felt in his inside pocket.

"Your *papers*, Captain." The militiaman's face was set. In the glass behind him, Alex saw Haynes and Katya leave the train.

For a long second, the two men looked uncertainly at each other. Then Alex hurled himself past the militiaman and the attendant. The young militiaman's two colleagues on the step rocked back as Alex twisted from their grasp and struggled with the door latch on the other side of the train. As the door swung open, he heard a carbine being cocked five feet behind him and he leaped into the darkness and down onto the track beneath. Scrambling under the train through the steam hissing from the pistons, suddenly he felt Katya beside him, pulling him by the hand back between the great steel wheels. Huddled together on the oil-stained track, the ex–Führer train shuddering above them, they watched the militiamen leap down and run forward into the darkness.

For nearly an hour, they crouched there while the guards hunted back and forth along the trains drawn up in Elektrosila Station. Then, with last shouts, the doors were slammed, the whistle blown. As the great piston arms began to move, Alex and Katya scrambled clear of the wheels and began to run for the jumble of dark wooden sheds across the crisscross of tracks.

CHAPTER
29

Through the early evening darkness, they made their way from Leningrad's Vitebsk Station toward the Fontanka Embankment. Turning just before the river, they plunged into an area of small streets and narrow alleys, the houses already crudely numbered for demolition in splashes of white paint on the brickwork.

"And you believe you can trust this American of yours?" Katya said, her head down, her shoulders hunched against the biting wind.

"We've no choice, Katya," Alex said, holding her tightly by the arm. "If we don't trust him we're lost." They stopped at the next street corner and lifted their faces to the wind as they tried to make out the street name on the battered tin plate that hung from the wall. They were near the address General Jones had given him, Alex was sure of that. But the district seemed so rundown, whole streets of houses standing empty, broken by the German shelling during the Great Siege, that a hotel for foreigners seemed unlikely to be located among the ruins.

It was Katya who heard the music, faint at first, brought to them on blasts of wind as they rounded the next corner. A building at the end of the seemingly deserted street had lights in the window. They hurried toward it and caught still-stronger sounds of a phonograph playing peasant dances from Russia's past.

There was a large front door in a once-handsome stone building with a hotel sign on a painted board across the porch. A narrow alley ran along the side of the building. With the instinct of the hunted, Alex and Katya turned into the alley and stopped uncertainly before a dark, half-glazed door.

"As you pointed out," Katya said, kissing him lightly on the mouth, "we've no choice."

He nodded and reached for the cast-iron knocker. It was in the shape of the once-proud symbol of the tsars, a double-headed eagle. For a moment, he held the cold iron in his ungloved hand, then he lifted it and rapped twice.

They waited, their eyes fixed on the darkened glass. The wind, whistling through the alley, carried the sound of the music away from them so that, for a moment, they felt themselves to be standing before the door of an empty dwelling. Then, as Alex knocked again, a light flicked on behind the patterned glazing and a wide figure, distorted by the frosted glass, began to undo the bolts. They could recognize their benefactor as a woman by the sound of her voice as she yelled to someone in the passage behind her.

The door opened. Before Alex could speak, the woman reached forward and drew Katya into the passageway. "Come in, come in," she said. "Not a word until I get this door shut tight." She bustled, pushing closed the door. "What a night to be out, the two of you." She straightened up, raising penciled eyebrows in a heavily made-up face. "So now, who was it that sent you to Madame Sophie?"

Katya looked toward Alex.

"Who sent us isn't important," Alex said carefully. "We're here to see Vikonnen the Finn."

The woman's wide red lips twisted in a not unfriendly smile. "Vikonnen," she said, "will get his throat cut by the MGB one of these days."

"Is he here?"

"He's here," the woman said. "And as drunk as he usually is. Come into the kitchen. I'll get you some coffee, then see if I can drag Vikonnen out of bed."

"Bed?" Alex frowned.

"He likes the girls as much as he likes the vodka," Madame Sophie said. She waddled forward on high heels and led them into the kitchen. When she had poured them good-smelling coffee, she left to find Vikonnen.

"What is this place?" Alex looked at Katya and was surprised to see she was laughing. He frowned for a second or two before the laughter gripped him too.

"Your American friend has no tact," Katya said. "His safe house in Leningrad turns out to be a brothel!"

He had clasped her to him when they heard the sound of footsteps coming down into the corridor. The man who stumbled into the kitchen was about fifty, blond bearded and red faced. He eyed them amiably as he stood tucking his plaid shirt into his trousers. Then he straightened up, bowed crisply and announced himself. "Vikonnen," he said. "Drunk, but nevertheless at your service."

On 4 March, some thirty-six hours after his actual death, radio and television networks throughout the United States broadcast the news that a second announcement from Moscow Radio had described Stalin's condition as worsening. Moscow Radio described in detail the usual modern drugs for the stroke from which he was supposed to be suffering. The announcement went on to say that Marshal Stalin's doctors had also prescribed an hourly application of leeches.

One hour later, the first report from NATO headquarters in Paris reached President Eisenhower. The Soviet military commander in East Berlin had sent a personal message, "as a matter of courtesy," to General Ridgway, the NATO commander. The message said that in recognition and deference to the serious condition of Marshal Stalin, the 1953 Winter Maneuvers, code-named *Gopak*, would be canceled.

Clouds of powdered snow, whipped up from the drifts by the crosswind, danced in the headlights. Alex shifted down a gear as the two battered trucks began to climb a hill. It was still dark. He had driven through much of the night, straining his eyes to make out the red-painted highway markers. The snow on the road surface was a thin, hard crust, rising to deep drifts on the curves. But the old trucks with their heavy snow tires had struggled slowly but successfully on, and the road signs now showed them well north of Vyborg, less than twenty miles from the Finnish border.

They had started out at just before midnight, the first truck driven by a man named Lasser, the second by a now more sober Vikonnen. Beside him in the passenger seat, Alex and Katya had watched the darkened northern suburbs of Leningrad pass by. Once across the Neva and past the fateful Finland Station, they rattled onto the North Highway to Vyborg. It was a journey, Vikonnen told them, of about a hundred miles, but made more dangerous in the last part by the fact that the border police, controlled by a certain Yuri Andropov in this area, were more efficient than most. "Nevertheless"—he shrugged—"it is the only way across."

It was during the first minutes too that they had learned what Finnish farmers like Vikonnen and Lasser and perhaps a dozen others still at Madame Sophie's were doing in Leningrad.

"The answer," Vikonnen said, "is that we are here because we're useful."

"Useful!" Katya exclaimed. "When we arrived you were too drunk to be of use to anyone, comrade."

"Ah," Vikonnen laughed ruefully. "We take our pleasures in return."

"In return for what?" Katya persisted.

"We are farmers," Vikonnen said. "We produce food of the best quality. Here in the Soviet Union, there are also farmers, but it seems, mysteriously, that they are unable to produce food of the same quality. So, by private arrangement with Leningrad police headquarters, we deliver hams, cheeses, sides of beef to the MGB stores. Afterward we spend a few hours' relaxation at Madame Sophie's, a place off limits to your ordinary Leningrader."

"How do they pay you?" Alex asked. "Rubles are no good to you."

"No." Vikonnen shook his head. "They pay in trinkets, a gold ring, a necklace perhaps, pretty little things from the tsarist past looted from the museum so that the *Vlasti* can live like kings."

"One day," Alex said, "the Russian people will give the leaders what they deserve."

"Perhaps someone like this man Andropov," Vikonnen said. "He doesn't approve of our little commerce in Leningrad. The rumor is that you can't even force a bribe on him." Vikonnen roared with laughter. "A man like that will probably be shot before he's forty. But if he isn't, then he'll go a long way in your poor benighted Russia, mark my words."

After Vyborg, Alex had taken the wheel from Vikonnen. The Finn was sleeping soundly in the back of the truck. Ahead, Alex could just discern the dim taillights of Lasser's vehicle as it lurched and slid forward.

Lasser had led them off the main highway onto a side road which deteriorated into a winding track, almost merging into a dark snowscape on either side.

Katya, napping fitfully beside Alex, had been jolted awake as the wheels bumped over a ridge of ice across the track. She stared out into the frigid darkness. "Where are we?" she asked huskily.

"A few miles from the border," he said. "Just a few more miles."

"Will the American be waiting?"

"He'll be waiting," Alex said. "We have to believe that."

She smiled. "Where would we be, you and I, Alex, without your belief in this American? What sort of man is he?"

Alex thought for a moment. "Perhaps I'm wrong," he said. "We shall see. But he seemed to me a man very much like myself. A man who will at least *try* to keep a promise."

The trucks trundled to the top of the hill. Alex slowed as the brake lights ahead flashed dully in the white fog of swirling, snow-filled wind, then pulled to a halt. Vikonnen came awake as the rocking, swaying motion of the truck was broken. Grunting and coughing, he sat up rubbing his eyes, then pulled himself into a kneeling position and stared forward through the windshield. In the yellow beam of the headlights, Lasser was coming back from the other vehicle. He stopped and waved as a signal that Vikonnen should join him.

The truck radio, which had been playing music from a Finnish station, crackled violently as an announcer began to read the news. Vikonnen listened intently for a few moments, then reached out and switched it off.

"Bad news?" Katya asked.

Vikonnen grimaced. "For us, just at the moment, not good. A further announcement on Stalin's condition. He's fading fast, it seems. In any sort of crisis, the Soviets have one reaction: call out the militia, double the border guards."

"Is that what they've done?"

"They've increased guards all along the frontier. Mounted patrols. Don't worry—they won't have time to do anything about the guards on the bridge."

Katya opened the cab door on her side, and Vikonnen clambered over the back of the seat. He paused, his flat, peasant's face close to hers. "What about a good-bye kiss?" he said cheerfully, as the wind cut into the cab.

Katya smiled and pecked him on the cheek.

"Remember," the Finn said gravely, turning to Alex, "when you get to the bridge, just trundle on across. The MGB guards there know my truck well. It's too cold a night for them to come out and inspect it. Watch Lasser and me go through first. Leave it a few minutes and follow. And on the Finland side, your American friend will fix things there."

"Thanks for all you've done, Vikonnen," Alex said, holding out his hand.

The Finn shrugged. "I've been paid well. All the same . . ." He grinned. "I'm only a farmer, but it's a pleasure to be able to do something."

Great undulating snowdrifts patched with trees stretched to the horizon. Within minutes they were passing through a stand of conifers, their dark branches sagging with the weight of layered, frozen snow. As they emerged from the blue-black shadow of the trees, Alex braked to a sliding halt. Below them they could just make out the long curve of the frozen river. There was the wooden bridge. A faint grayish-yellow glow shone from a window in what must be a small guardhouse. Alex studied the Russian map Vikonnen had given him. "Across the river is Finland," he said quietly.

Katya covered his hand. "What would happen," she asked, "if your American is not there?"

"He'll be there," Alex said crisply. "He hasn't failed us so far."

"But if he's not there?"

"If he's not there, Katya, it doesn't make any difference if we get past the Russian side of the bridge. The Finnish border guards will have to turn us back. Only if General Jones is there with a senior Finnish officer will we be allowed into Finland."

Below them, Lasser's truck emerged from a dark patch of fir forest and headed for the bridge. They heard clearly in the night air the double note of Lasser's horn and watched the truck, hardly slowing, trundle on its way across the bridge to Finland.

Alex turned on the engine and put the vehicle into gear. As the truck moved forward, it slewed violently, slithering across the track. Alex fought the wheel to regain control, but the truck skidded helplessly off to the right, embedding itself in a drift.

Katya was shouting over the roar of the racing engine. "What is it?" For the first time, there was panic in her voice.

He shook his head desperately. As he tried to reverse, the back wheels spun hopelessly on the packed ice. He opened the door and jumped down from the listing cab. The wind had dropped, but it was still bitterly cold. A glistening, razor-sharp shard of ice had ripped a three-inch tear in the front tire.

The sound behind him, which he could hear now that the engine was still, was a muffled, rhythmic thud. Alex stared beyond the truck, trying to locate the source. The dark silhouette of a horse and rider closed, looming in, tall and dark. The animal seemed to float through the deep, clinging snow, using a strange, high-stepping prance to cover the ground. Its legs were covered by leather gaiters against the numbing cold, and its hooves carefully bound with strips of flannel. The rider wore a helmet and an enveloping cloak. A lantern attached to the pommel of the saddle glowed orange in the gloom.

The horse swung to a halt facing Alex. The rider took up the lantern, playing the light over the damaged wheel, then settling it on Alex's face. His other hand pulled the high collar of his cloak away from his mouth. Beneath the skirts of the cloak, Alex could glimpse the high, black boots and dark green uniform of a border patrol guard. The man's eyes roamed across the Finnish truck and settled on Katya in the cab. He still had not spoken.

"Are you Russians?" The guard's hand went under his cloak to the holstered pistol on his belt. "Soviet citizens?"

Alex jumped forward and seized a booted leg. The guard swung the lantern at Alex's head but he twisted aside and took the blow on the shoulder. Holding on desperately, he dragged the man toward him. The horse reared in panic, almost yanking him off his feet. As the girth snapped, the two men were thrown sprawling in a tangled heap. The guard clawed and punched as they rolled, locked together, over the frozen snow. With one arm trapped in the folds of the cloak, Alex struck out with the other until, with a sudden slumping movement, the man rolled facedown in the snow.

"Look the other way, my prince," Katya said, slowly descending from the cab. "I'll cut his throat."

"All Chekists are not the same, Katya. Who knows what sort of a man he is?" Alex unbuckled the trooper's leather belt and strapped his hands behind his back. As the man regained consciousness, Alex dragged him to his feet and pushed him up into the back of the truck.

Plunging through the drifts, Katya had grasped the horse's bridle. Swinging herself into the saddle, she brought the animal to the truck so that Alex could mount behind her. As the border guard began to shout, impotently, in the back of Vikonnen's truck, Katya kicked her heels into the horse's flanks, and it began to canter forward in its strange high-stepping gait along the road toward the frozen river.

At the bottom of the hill, the road turned sharply right to run a matter of about a mile to the bridge. Their plan, now that it was impossible to pass with Vikonnen's truck, was to rush the bridge, passing the MGB post before the guards emerged from the warmth of the guardroom. To take the bridge at a gallop, they were forced to leave the road and plunge through snowdrifts toward a copse of fir trees. Lasser's truck, they realized, must by now be trundling along deep into Finland.

Through the swirling snow, they spurred the horse on. Beneath the unaccustomed weight, it plowed forward, never quite losing its footing, even when up to its girth in a drift or slithering across icy, exposed rock.

The coppice itself masked them from the bridge and provided some respite from the teeth of the wind. Dismounting, they tied the horse and together crept forward through the wood.

They could hear the distant voices and jingle of a bridle before they saw the lights of the guardhouse against the paler sky. A mounted officer was questioning the shivering guard sergeant.

"One truck came through, Comrade Lieutenant. I checked it myself. A farm truck, one of the regular run."

"You checked it—or you stayed by your stove and let it through with a wave of the hand?"

"I checked it, comrade."

The officer snorted his disbelief. "Get your idle cardplayers out of that hut. Let down the barrier. I want everybody who tries to cross tonight detained until I've checked them myself. You understand me?"

"I'll get the barrier down right away, comrade," the sergeant said. "Nobody will pass tonight."

"And what about the river?" The officer turned to the immense breadth of flat ice, more lake than river at this part of the border, which stretched to the Finnish bank.

"The bridge is the only way across, comrade," the sergeant said, with a touch of surly pride. "The icebreaker passes every morning." He gestured downriver toward the Gulf of Finland. "She's not big, but she's got a good steel nose. She cracks open a channel at least twenty feet wide."

The lieutenant pointed. "It's frozen hard enough now," he said.

"Next to the bank, it's four or five feet thick," the sergeant agreed. "Enough to carry a tank. But in the middle, the channel was dredged only yesterday. There the ice could be no more than an inch or two. Would you like to try it out, comrade?" he said, recovering some of his confidence.

The lieutenant scowled. "What time this morning is the icebreaker due?"

"At dawn, comrade. Always at dawn."

The lieutenant turned away, nodding.

*   *   *

Twenty minutes later, a deep rim of light had appeared on the eastern horizon, painting the sky's pallor with long fingers of pink. Beneath a canopy of bare alder branches rimed with frost, Alex and Katya looked out across the river toward the village lights glittering on the Finnish bank. The distance across the ice was almost three hundred yards where the river opened to fill the coastal flatlands. To their right, the lake narrowed to the point where the bridge crossed the river which fed it. To the left, the hills closed down, forcing the river to narrow and twist on its way to the Gulf of Finland. "Are you ready to try?" Alex crouched on one knee, his arm around the girl next to him.

She looked briefly across his shoulder to where the guards stood, tiny figures on the bridge. "If we wait any longer," she said, "they must certainly see us. I think we must go now."

He leaned toward her and kissed her warm mouth. For a moment or two, they held each other, giving comfort and confidence.

They stood pushing the thick-rimed alder branches from their faces. He stretched out and took her hand. "We stay together," he said. "Whatever happens on the ice."

She nodded, and they stepped forward out of the cover of the overhanging trees.

They were not more than fifty or sixty yards out when they heard the cataclysmic sounds of the icebreaker as it cleared the bend between the hills and began to churn its way across the lake.

For a moment, they stopped in horror to watch the steel-bowed tug shatter the ice and push it up and aside like great sheets of plate glass. The boat's searchlight, wavering before it, had not yet reached them. They stood, momentarily transfixed, as the monstrous apparition crushed and chewed its way through the ice toward them. Then, together, still holding hands, they began the impossible dash beneath the bows of the icebreaker for the far bank.

On the Finnish side, General Hal Jones at the wheel of a four-wheel-drive Land Rover flicked his lights once and then again and accelerated down the bank and onto the ice. He

knew from his Finnish colleague waiting in the customs house
on the Finland end of the bridge the risk of driving across the
ice in the central channel. Years later, he would suffer night-
mares of cracking ice under spinning snow tires, but now,
caught up in the excitement of the moment, his mind was
blank as he gunned the Land Rover forward toward the two
struggling figures.

Picked up now by the boat's searchlight, Katya and Alex
were running forward through a haze of white. The shouts of
guards, the crashing of the ice plates and the crackle of gunfire
barely penetrated the glare of the searchlight exploding upon
them. As the Land Rover skidded violently to a stop beside
them, they reached automatically for the darkness of the can-
vas-covered rear seats, scrambling for a handhold while Hal
Jones spun the machine around to send it hurtling back toward Finland.

CHAPTER
30

In his college rooms, Charles Trenton poured sherry. "If she's downstairs in the car, you should bring her up, my boy," he said, turning toward his son, decanter in hand.

"I think it's better she doesn't meet you," Alex said.

"Really?" His father turned back to the task of pouring sherry. "Embarrassed, is she? Perlinka Lane. All that sort of thing naturally makes her reluctant—"

"No." Alex waved aside the proferred glass.

"No sherry?"

"You know why I'm here," Alex said savagely.

Charles Trenton carefully replaced the glasses on the table. "Yes," he said. "Yes, no doubt I do."

For a moment he stood in the middle of the room, his eyes on his son, his lips pursed into something between a bitter smile and a grimace. "You must believe that I never for a moment realized that you'd gone back to Moscow. Jones kept that from me. When I informed them Shtemenko was still alive, I had no idea I was endangering you."

"Would it have made any difference?"

"You mustn't say such things. We're the same, you and I, Alex. Both idealists at heart. Both men who have painfully decided that it was right in the end to change sides. We follow our consciences, we Trentons. Always have. It's a most uncomfortable thing to inherit, of course."

"Iron Cross. That was your code name. What a ragbag of hypocrisy you are," Alex said quietly. "Even after eight years of spying on your own country. Even after God knows how many betrayals and denunciations! It was you who betrayed Nozenkov and Voronov, wasn't it? I think you should know what happened to one of your victims. Vassily Nozenkov was beaten and kicked and deprived of sleep and submitted to unspeakable acts. But that's usual at the Lubyanka. That's happened down there in the basements to every single man you've ever denounced. But Nozenkov was different. Senior officers decided he must become an example to all of us. Nozenkov, or rather the still-living husk of Vassily Nozenkov, was thrown before my eyes into the Lubyanka furnaces."

Charles Trenton watched him in silence.

"He leaves two children and a wife, now at a hard-labor camp in eastern Siberia."

"I'm not responsible for the casual inhumanities of the system."

"The casual inhumanities of Stalin's system engulfed millions of people."

"It is never easy, Alex, to choose the right road. Did your mother ever tell you how I came to make my choice?"

"She told me that during the war you headed an Anglo-American mission in Moscow. That you were there for some months. And that you began sleeping together."

"We resumed marital relations, yes," Charles Trenton said stiffly. "By early 1944, Alex, there were many people, loyal, patriotic Englishmen and Americans, who felt they could no longer understand Churchill and Roosevelt's attitude. You were a soldier. You know how, in war, everybody becomes an armchair general."

"What does this have to do with what you did?"

"I was one of those who believed that Churchill was *deliberately* delaying the invasion of Europe in order to allow Russia to burn out her strength against the German army. At first, I approved. You must understand, Alex, that I had no reason to love Russia, or the Soviet system which had won your mother's affections, so to speak. Taken her—and you—away from me."

"Before you returned to Moscow, you had no love for the Soviet system."

"On the contrary. I deeply resented it. If Winston Churchill was forcing Russia to continue to endure alone, or virtually alone, then I applauded. You might say," he added, "that I looked on Soviet Russia, and perhaps, if I'm at all honest, I looked on Stalin personally, with intense jealousy. As if Russia, almost as if Joseph Stalin himself, had been your mother's lover, had taken her from me."

"Then you went to Moscow."

"Yes. And remet Vanessa. You know her as a mother. You can't know her as a woman. I doubt if I had ever in all those years escaped her spell. Certainly when we met again I was as deeply attracted to her as ever. I was deeply moved too by the plight of the Russian people. By their sufferings. You see, like so many Westerners for over a century, I had always separated Russia from the Russian people, hating the one, feeling fondness for the other."

"So when Vanessa asked for your help, you gave it?"

"Vanessa was in trouble with the Cheka. The secret police suspected her renewed relationship with me. Petrov himself was the investigating officer."

"And Vanessa asked you for something, some kind of information to hand to Petrov as proof that her loyalty was still to Russia."

"Yes. I did it willingly. For her. But also because by this time I'd seen enough to change my mind. As I said, I was deeply moved by the sufferings of the Russian people."

"Except Vanessa didn't show you *all* their sufferings."

Charles Trenton waved his hand dismissively. "You're talking about the rumors of prison camps and deportations on a vast, improbable scale."

"I'm not here to argue the merits of Stalin's Russia, least of all with someone like you," Alex said. "What you can't understand is what you were doing beyond betraying your own people with your grubby little practices. You were betraying the *Russian* people too. You were making it easy for the Stalins and

Yeshovs and the Berias to imprison and torture and starve and deport."

"You forget, I was protecting your mother. I still considered her my wife."

"And Vanessa? What did she think?"

"We agreed, both of us, to think of ourselves as married once more. Even though of course she is not able to leave the Soviet Union."

Alex Trenton looked at his father. "Throughout the war," he said coldly, "and certainly at the time you were in Moscow, Vanessa was Petrov's mistress." He turned toward the door, unwilling now to look at the shocked, crumpled face opposite him. "Petrov *knew* she had seduced you. He approved the strategy."

Slowly, his back half turned to his father, he took out a cigarette and lit it. "You were an easy mark. Full of self-pride and certainty. Never imagining that a woman could double-cross you twice."

Charles Trenton stood, one hand resting on the back of an armchair. "You've told Jones about me."

"It was he who told me. He put everybody involved with the Shtemenko defection under surveillance when I left for Moscow. You, it appears, tried to send a birthday message through your Zurich contacts to Vanessa."

Charles Trenton watched him silently.

"A birthday message!" he repeated as he opened the door.

"Alex . . ." His father's face was twisted in pain. "Is it true that she was Petrov's mistress all the time? Is it really true?"

"It's true." Alex closed the door behind him and walked slowly down the oak staircase. Outside, Katya was waiting. She took his arm as they walked without speaking along the gravel path.

On a harsh, squally afternoon, Hal Jones stood, Jennifer in black beside him, and watched as the coffin was lowered into the grave. The men among the many mourners removed their hats but, though he was in uniform, Hal Jones did not salute.

"We are here," the dean said, "to mourn the passing of a remarkable man. His death by his own hand last week has been a most shattering blow to all those who knew him. Why a man of his gifts chose to end his life we shall never know. He was recognized throughout the academic world as a leading commentator on Russian culture and politics. For thirty years he interpreted for us the strange and sometimes apparently menacing activities of the Soviets. Many students who had the privilege of being taught by him will also testify to the depth of his humanity. Morally and intellectually, he was a quite outstanding American, a genuinely superior spirit. We, his oldest friends, know how deeply Charles Trenton believed in a better world."

Nobody lingered by the graveside. When the ceremony was over, most of the mourners marched briskly toward their waiting cars.

"I think," Hal said as they walked toward the cemetery gates, "the guy got off too easy." He shook his head angrily. "Bottle of sleeping pills, fifth of whisky and a long eulogy from the dean of the university. Some of his victims didn't have it so good."

"Excuse me, General . . ." The voice from behind was that of the dean. "I feel I must ask you . . . something that puzzled me. I was watching you as the coffin was lowered. You didn't salute."

"I didn't salute, sir, because—"

Jennifer took his hand and squeezed tightly. "Because his mind was on other things."

"Other things, General?"

Hal put his arm around Jennifer. "Yes, on other things, sir," he said as they walked on toward their car.

EPILOGUE

The funeral of Joseph Stalin took place on 9 March 1953. The embalmed body of the most terrifying despot of all time lay in state in the Kremlin, while members of the Soviet government, foreign diplomats and visitors and thousands upon thousands of ordinary Russians filed by the catafalque. Green-uniformed members of the MGB kept the long line moving. Only Per Lundstrom, a visiting Swedish doctor, managed to observe what he thought was the sign of entry damage by a bullet just above the dark hairline.

Within six weeks of the death of Stalin another death occurred in the Soviet leadership. After a rapid and secret trial, Lavrenty Beria, Chief of the Soviet Secret Police Forces, suffered the same fate as his predecessors Menzhinsky, Yagoda and Yeshov. He was executed in the same Lubyanka he had done so much to make ever more fearful, shot in an interior courtyard on or about 15 April 1953.

Secretary Poskrebyshev, the regime's great survivor, disappeared on the night of Stalin's death. Persistent rumors that he was alive in the West and planned a volume of memoirs caused the Brezhnev government to shudder with alarm throughout the late sixties and early seventies.

General Shtemenko reappeared in the Soviet Union shortly after the death of Stalin and continued his military career under Khrushchev. It may well have been the independence and unorthodoxy he had shown during the final Stalin crisis that prevented him attaining the rank of field marshal or the position of Commander of the Soviet Armed Forces he is known to have coveted.

General Pavel Semyonovich Petrov was commended by Khrushchev for his part in the Stalin plot. On Lavrenty Beria's execution, however, Petrov was disappointed in his ambition to become head of the newly created KGB. His marriage to Vanessa Trenton was attended, as a sign of approval, by the new head of the Committee for State Security, Politburo member Ivan Alexandrovich Serov.

Hal and Jennifer Jones, following her divorce, were married, though they never moved to Hal's home state of Colorado. Offered a number of sensitive overseas commissions by President Eisenhower, he and Jennifer spent the next two decades in the Middle East and Southeast Asia. In 1971 they retired to Grasse, in the south of France.

In California, Alexander Trenton married Katya upon learning of the death of his wife, Xenia, in a Moscow asylum for alcoholics. During the remaining years of the 1950s, Trenton worked under an assumed name as a teacher in a number of Western universities. In 1963 he was offered and declined the Markham Professorship of Russian at the University of Virginia once held by his father.

Congressman Harry D. Hunter, for the sake of his career, was persuaded to grant his wife a quiet divorce; but he lost his bid for reelection anyhow, brought down with his leader, Senator Joseph R. McCarthy.

On 5 July 1985, a Russian-speaking visitor called at the home of Alexander and Katya Trenton. He carried with him an invitation to visit Moscow, to be present as a guest at the opening of a small English-language school on the Prospekt Marksa. The invitation was signed by the principal of the new school, but a codicil to the message, delivered verbally by the Russian visitor, indicated that the real originator of the invitation was the new General Secretary of the Communist Party, Mikhail Gorbachev.